Dirty PROMISES

Karina Halle

headline
ETERNAL

The right of Karina Halle to be identified as the Author of
the Work has been asserted by her in accordance with the
Copyright, Designs and Patents Act 1988.

First published as an Ebook in Great Britain in 2015
by HEADLINE ETERNAL
An imprint of HEADLINE PUBLISHING GROUP

First published in paperback in Great Britain in 2015
by HEADLINE ETERNAL
An imprint of HEADLINE PUBLISHING GROUP

1

Cataloguing in Publication Data is available from the British Library

ISBN 978 1 4722 2888 8

Typeset in Electra by Palimpsest Book Production Limited,
Falkirk, Stirlingshire

Printed and bound in Great Britain by
CPI Group (UK) Ltd, Croydon, CR0 4YY

Headline's policy is to use papers that are natural, renewable
and recyclable products and made from wood grown in well-managed
forests and other controlled sources. The logging and manufacturing
processes are expected to conform to the environmental regulations of the
country of origin.

HEADLINE PUBLISHING GROUP
An Hachette UK Company
Carmelite House
50 Victoria Embankment
London EC4Y 0DZ

www.headlineeternal.com
www.headline.co.uk
www.hachette.co.uk

Dedicated to the ones with the black hearts and dirty souls.

A NOTE FROM THE AUTHOR

Check your morals at the door – this isn't your typical romance. These are bad people. They do bad things. They are immoral. Depraved. Ruthless and brutal. They seem to lack scruples at times. Please keep this in mind when you read this book or you're going to have a very rude awakening. But if you like rude . . . go right ahead.

PROLOGUE

Javier

My wife was a liar.

Then again, I was a liar too. Perhaps the greatest liar of them all.

And because of this, I can't blame her for anything that happened. I lied and pretended everything was normal, that there wasn't a problem. Our lives ebbed and flowed in this state of organized chaos, but within that chaos, under the guise of mundane brutality and usual depravity, something was wrong. Yes, the violence kept my teeth sharp and my mind sharper. The two of us sat on our thrones, king and queen, with the kind of ease you'd find from an old married couple on a broken down porch, mosquitos buzzing hungrily at their ears.

But the mosquitos drew more blood each time. One drop here, one suck there. Eventually you'd be hollowed out. It didn't matter how content you were, how little they took. Bloodsuckers never rest until they're full.

I made two mistakes. I pretended everything was fine, that *I*, Javier Bernal, was fine.

I also let the mosquitos get too close.

I let them rob me of everything that mattered most.

Two mistakes cost me all that I'd worked for, all that I'd ever loved.

But I was not done yet. There was enough blood in me to keep me alive. And that blood boiled hot, red, rank with revenge.

Rage.

It fueled me.

It whipped me.

It *begged* me.

I would not stop until everything was mine again.

Until the heads rolled on the dusty floor.

CHAPTER ONE

Luisa

The heat made the blood smell worse, like you could sense it thickening in the air. It brought out the sharp tang of copper, mixed with heavy dust.

Blood these days reminded me of my mother. Not that she wasn't alive and relatively well, living with my father in an assisted living center in the quiet suburbs of San Diego. She was fine. She was safe. But I guess it made me aware of how disappointed she would be in me. In the person I had become. The smell of blood did nothing to me anymore. It didn't make me sick. It didn't make me feel anything. I was used to something I never thought I'd get used to.

And more than that, sometimes I liked the smell. Sometimes it meant an enemy was finished and we had lived to survive another day at the top. It was this constant climb and a never-ending struggle to keep our footing, and blood, blood meant victory. Security.

Power.

But I never wanted her to see me now, like this.

The wife of a drug king. The queen of corruption.

She knew all of this, of course. Knew what I did to

survive and provide a good life for her, my father, myself. She knew that I fell in love.

But I'm not sure if she knows that I am falling out of love. That I didn't realize the cost of trying to keep it. She didn't know that I had become a monster, that the ways of this life – my new life – were slowly sinking into my soul and turning it putrid and black.

Everything costs something now. In the past, when I was just a lowly waitress in Cabo San Lucas, working for a slimeball boss, I had to pay for the right to make money by putting up with his advances. When I married Salvador Reyes, the most powerful madman in the country, I paid for that choice with my virginity, my dignity, and nearly my life. Now, in order to sit on the throne of the country, on top of money and drugs and guns and blood that paved my way, the cost was my soul.

Sometimes I thought it was the only thing I had left.

The screams in the distance died off. Funny, I actually hadn't noticed them until they stopped. The smell of blood still hung in the air, like invisible smoke that would eventually seep its way into your skin.

I grasped my bottle of wine tightly, as if it were filled with precious gems, and got off the bench at the koi pond. This used to be where Javier and I would sometimes talk, when he was feeling particularly romantic or even philosophical. He hadn't been in any of those moods lately. It was like I barely existed.

Well, there were some things. But I didn't want to think about those, even though I knew where he was going after the torture was over and the last drop of blood was spilled.

I carefully made my way past the lotuses, pausing to

admire the elegance they granted such a brutal place, and headed toward the back of the pond where the reeds and palms grew thick. Behind them I was pretty much unnoticeable to the entire compound, a place that was nothing short of a palace, a place that had become my home for the last year and a half. But sometimes I still thought of it as less than a castle and more like a prison. After all, I was brought here as a captive and some memories were hard to forget, no matter how badly I tried to find my footing and rise above it.

A few weeks ago I took a bucket from the gardener's shed and brought it over, flipping it upside down to make a seat. I knew it was silly – I could have had custom made chairs or an outdoor sofa if I wanted. I could have had anything. But I wanted something that was mine and mine alone. A secret. I liked sitting here in the evenings, feeling totally protected from the watchful eyes of my husband, of his right-hand man Esteban, of the lackey Juanito, of anyone who worked for our cartel. By the time I finished a bottle of California pinot noir, I felt like another person in another land. These were the little things in my life that I clung to now.

I sat down on the bucket and took a long swig of wine. Javier got cases of it imported just for me, after I once remarked that I liked it. That was a few months ago, before his sister died and everything changed. Back then, I was Javier's queen. Now I didn't even know who I was. But I knew I didn't like her.

I was scared of myself.

I stayed hidden in my spot until the wine was almost gone and the sun was sinking below the hills to the west.

The air was still hot, muggy, like breathing in through a wet cloth. Though I'd gotten used to the smell of blood, I hadn't gotten used to the humidity around Sinaloa. Especially where our compound was, nestled deep in a valley along the Devil's Backbone. Javier liked the cover our location provided – the landscaping blended the house seamlessly into the jungle, but it also trapped the heat and added to the feeling of being closed in. Sometimes I woke up thinking I couldn't breathe, nightmares of suffocation bleeding into reality.

During those times, I'd sit up in bed, breathing hard and covered in sweat. Javier would reach for me, seemingly half asleep, and just hold my hand for a moment. Then he would pull me toward him and I'd be lulled to sleep in his arms. Sometimes he would brush the hair off my face and those burning eyes of his would light me on fire. We'd make love and make promises.

It had been like that for a while – his comfort, his presence . . . he never denied me anything. I knew I wouldn't be accepted into his life so quickly, not by the members of his cartel. I'd gone from captor to lover in a short amount of time, and then from lover to wife soon after that. But he stood by me, ever so proud. He wouldn't change his mind about me and my place in his life, and he'd slaughter anyone who dared to throw an unkind word my way.

For all his cunning ambition and ruthless ways, Javier Bernal really did love me. He was devoted and as much mine as I was his.

All those promises.

"Luisa." A voice drifted over the brush, causing me to freeze.

Esteban came around the corner and gave me a lopsided smile.

"Here you are," he said lazily.

I took my hand away from my chest, my heart beating like a drum, and looked down at the empty bottle in my hands. I felt utterly stupid, which was probably silly in itself considering this was my property and I could do whatever the damn well I wanted.

I also felt acutely disappointed that there really was no safe place left.

I cleared my throat and sat up straighter, even though looking regal was impossible when you were sitting on top of a damn bucket.

"You found me," I said.

He folded his arms and peered down at me. "Dipping into the pinot again?"

I glared at him. "What's your point?"

He shrugged. "No point. I was looking for you though."

"Why?"

"Do I need a reason?"

Esteban and I didn't always see eye to eye, though it pained me to say that lately it felt like he was the only friend I had. There was always Juanito, who was in his early twenties and an eager *narco*, but I think the boy was scared of me, which I found funny considering we both had to be around the same age. And Javier's chief of security, a big brute of a man named Diego, was as quiet as they came. This was a shame because he was a smart man with a colorful past, and I was certain he had a million stories to tell.

Esteban, however, wasn't quiet and wasn't scared, and

was there for me more often than not. Usually I found it annoying, how closely he tried to emulate Javier, how badly he wanted to be him. He'd tell you otherwise, of course, but Esteban was power hungry, bloodthirsty, and jealous beyond comprehension. He wasn't very smart, though. His lackadaisical surfer approach to life wasn't just an act, and no matter how badly he wanted to be in Javier's shoes, he could never, ever become him.

Naturally, I also knew I shouldn't underestimate people, and so with him I practiced more of a keep your friends close, enemies closer sort of relationship. While he could never become the *patron*, the ruler, the king, that didn't mean he wouldn't at some point try.

"I worry about you," he said, crouching down to my level.

I rolled my eyes. "Please."

He looked at the wine bottle. "I know things aren't . . . well, I know how things are."

I tucked the bottle on the other side of the bucket and gave him a pointed look. His green eyes were observing me a little too carefully, something I found off-putting.

"And what could you know?"

He rubbed his hand across his chin, seeming to think. "Well, I know Javier is uh . . . well, occupied most nights. I know where he goes and what he does."

A knife sliced right into my heart. I tried to keep a blank face, a mask. *Don't let the mask slip*, I told myself, and took in a quiet breath.

"Oh, is that right?" I asked, and winced once I heard the tremor in my voice.

His gaze softened and I hated the fucking sympathy I

could see. Of all people, I didn't want it from him. I didn't want him to feel that he was any better than Javier or any better than me. Yes, I knew, damn it I fucking knew what Javier was doing with those girls, and I knew what happened to the girls after, too. I knew everything, but I wasn't about to let him feel that made him better than us. Javier, for everything that had happened, for the person he'd become, was still my husband.

God, even the word husband pinched deep inside.

"Javier isn't well," I told him before he could say anything else.

He actually laughed. "Not well? That's the understatement of the year."

"It isn't funny," I said quietly.

"No?" He placed one hand on my thigh, peering at me closely. I sucked in my breath. "Then let's not skirt around it. Javier has been compromised. He's damaged in a way that is only going to hurt the business. It's only going to hurt you."

I tried to shrug away from him but his grip on my leg tightened.

"Don't pretend anymore, Luisa," he said in a hush. "You know the truth. Alana's death . . . he couldn't handle it. That was the straw that broke the camel's back. He's lost nearly all his sisters. His whole family. A man can look strong, but that doesn't make him strong. Perhaps some might find it sentimental that he cares so much about his family after all, but powerful people can't afford to be sentimental. He can't afford to lose himself like this." He shook his head. "No, it's been long enough."

Now I felt I had to come to his defense, something I

was used to doing, even in my own head, even against myself. "It's been five months since Alana died," I told him. "People need time to grieve. He's grieving in his own way. He will move on."

"Luisa . . ."

I suddenly got up, feeling emboldened by the wine, and shoved Este away. "No!" I yelled. "He will move on. I won't give up on him, no matter what he's doing. He'll find his way back to me."

"Will he find his way back to this?" Esteban spread out his arms, gesturing to the property. In the distance a few white parrots flew from the trees.

"He's doing fine," I told him, bringing my voice down. I jerked my head toward the place I liked to call the "torture hut." "What was going on in there? Did he not just weed out an informant? Last week, did he not order that safe house to be blown up? Lado's shipment to be destroyed? He's doing everything he needs to do to protect us, everything. We've never been stronger."

"He's being careless," he said imploringly, taking a step toward me.

"How so?"

He paused, eyes bright. "I guess he didn't tell you."

I swallowed thickly. "What?"

"We might have to move, temporarily."

I blinked at him, not comprehending a word of this. "What the hell are you talking about?"

Esteban licked his lips before taking in a deep breath. "I think Javier should be the one to tell you. It's not my place."

Since when did Esteban ever care if it was his place

or not? He was constantly handing out his unwanted opinion.

I reached out and grabbed his arm. His eyes met mine briefly and I saw something in them I didn't want to see right then. Anger . . . or something smokier than that. Almost sultry.

Quickly I let go and placed my hands on my hips instead. "Cut the bullshit and just tell me. That's why you were looking for me, weren't you? You just love being the bearer of bad news."

He sighed. "You know all about Angel Hernandez?"

Did I ever. Though our cartel, the Sinaloa, was arguably the biggest in Mexico, and Javier had been working on getting the other cartels united, or at least on "friendly" terms under one blanket organization, Angel Ochoa Hernandez remained cagey. He reigned over the Tijuana cartel, and with all of that, he controlled the Tijuana and San Diego border. Which meant he controlled all of the drugs going up in the trucks into America on the I-5. Currently we had to pay him a tariff to let our heroin through – five percent – which doesn't sound like a lot, but when you're dealing with millions of dollars, it is.

With our cartel getting more successful, that tax becomes a lot of money that is better spent on ourselves. Javier controlled Ciudad Juarez port for cocaine shipments and we had a free pass for Nuevo Laredo because he was close with Jose Fuentes who lorded over that. But Angel was determined to hold on to Tijuana with all that he had, and unless he was taken out of the picture, we'd never have control.

For months, Javier had talked about making it happen,

hiring a *sicario* to do the job. The only thing that prevented him was timing, and I guess that strange code of honor he carried with him like a reluctant badge. He would never inform on another cartel, and killing a king of one was nearly as bad. But we knew it was something that would eventually have to be done.

Then Alana was killed and it was forgotten. Though Esteban thought he was giving me bad news, the mere fact that he had mentioned Angel's name meant Javier hadn't let his ambitions go completely.

"What about him? Is he dead?" I asked hopefully.

He shook his head. "No, but Javier thinks he has a plan to ensure it happens."

"And what's so bad about that? You've both talked about this, how it would become necessary at some point."

"What's bad, Luisa, is that he wants to kidnap a PFM agent to do so."

"And how does that help?"

He gave me a look that said it didn't. "Anyway, once we get him, whoever the poor fucker is, we'll be off to one of our ranches in Chihuahua for the usual interrogation tactics. I think it's a fucking terrible idea."

"You'd rather him torture a federal agent here?" I didn't know – and didn't want to know – half the shit that went down on the compound, but I knew we never brought anyone here that was of much importance. A federal agent on our soil would be asking for a lot of trouble, especially since Javier had zero control over the PFM. Police and local military, yes. They were all bribed handsomely to look the other way. Hell, they protected Javier. But the government was something else entirely, and they could raise a lot of hell if they wanted to.

"I'd rather he not do this at all. There are other ways to gather intelligence. He could leave it up to me."

I raised a brow. Esteban was our intelligence man and the techie, but I knew that Javier was having problems putting trust in him as well. "I'm sure Javier knows what he's doing."

He shook his head slightly, his shaggy, blonde-streaked hair falling over his forehead. "But that's the thing. He doesn't. And we both know it."

He looked back at the house. "Come on, it's getting dark. You should go back inside."

But I didn't want to. I planted my feet firmly. I wanted to stay in the dark. I wanted to stay away from the house. The house that had a room Javier used to fuck whichever whore it was for the night.

My heart clenched at the thought of going inside, crawling into bed, and trying to survive another night of a marriage that was crumbling at the seams. But I knew, eventually, when the stars came out and the mosquitos became too much, I would go inside, as I always did.

"You deserve better, you know," Esteban said so quietly it was almost a whisper, before turning around and heading to the house, his tall form disappearing from sight. It was as if he read my mind, or maybe he was just good at reading me. Maybe I was an open book for the world to see. Everyone except my husband.

CHAPTER TWO

Javier

I was already awake when Luisa woke up gasping for breath. I kept my eyes closed as I felt her sit up, knowing she was panicking because of some nightmare, or maybe because of her cruel reality. I feigned sleep, sleep that never came for me anymore. I had always excelled at deception, at pretending, so this fit me like an old glove.

I kept my breath even and hoped she'd go right back to sleep. That she wouldn't want anything from me. How sick is that? The thought of her touching me filled me with revulsion. Not because I didn't desire her, because I did, now more than ever. I *needed* her. And not because I didn't love her, because I loved her to the best of my ability. Whether that equaled what she deserved or not, I didn't know.

Her touch, however, would spur me on. It would undo me more than I'd already been undone. I was a black, rolling pit of rage and exquisitely honed violence. The last thing I wanted was to unleash that on her. Maybe it was the most selfless thing I'd ever done, giving up sex with my wife out of fear of hurting her.

Or maybe I was just deceiving myself this time. Because it was more than just sex. It was everything.

I wondered how long this could go on before she'd had enough. When she found out about the other women. Could she possibly understand that it was better them than her? Could she forgive me for sparing her the brutality, the depravity?

I had my doubts.

I didn't want to be forgiven.

Her fingers trailed along my arm and I did everything I could to lie still, to not swallow the knot in my throat. It was easier to play dead.

"Javier?" she whispered, voice soft and disembodied in the dark behind my eyes. Just her voice had the power to shake me loose, even after a year of marriage, but I remained in control. As always.

She said my name again, her fingers clenching my arm. I was a light sleeper and she knew this. If I didn't wake up for her, she'd know I was faking it. What was the difference? Either way she'd be hurt.

I swallowed hard. "What?" I asked, voice hoarse. I still didn't open my eyes. I could see her in my head, the mussed up hair, the want in her dark eyes, an open, full mouth just begging to be put to use.

God, don't fucking tempt me.

I heard her lick her lips, those incredible lips. "I can't sleep," she said.

I can never sleep, I wanted to tell her. *You don't see me trying to wake you up.*

"I *know*, you know," she said quietly.

I sucked in my breath. "Know what?" I asked flatly.

She paused before she said, "About your plans for Angel Hernandez."

Esteban. That asshole. He was like a little fucking girl, always having to tell someone the latest gossip.

"Let me guess, Este told you." I finally opened my eyes and tilted my head to look at her. As I thought, she looked absolutely ravishing in the dim, grainy light, that beautiful combination of aching vulnerability and seething contempt. Her long dark hair flowed over her shoulders in waves, her silky black camisole hugging her curves. It amazed me that after everything, she still went to bed looking like a goddess for me.

I was a lucky son of a bitch in this respect. But currently, that luck wasn't enough. Luck is only valuable when it's across the board. One piece of luck is enough to trick a fool into thinking everything's going to be okay.

I wasn't sure if everything could be okay again. How could it, with Alana gone? How could it, when I was punished for loving someone? Family first. What was next? My wife? Best to cut those ties before it all went to hell.

Luisa was watching me, inspecting me. I didn't know what she saw. I hoped she saw nothing at all, just a blank space where I used to be.

"Yes, he told me," she eventually said, brows drawn together, entirely dissatisfied with what she saw.

"I was going to tell you," I said, not really caring to make excuses. "When it was all said and done. No need to involve you."

She went rigid as I knew she would. "No need to tell me? Javier, I'm your fucking wife. Your partner. I'm in this as much as you are." She let out a heavy breath. "At least I used to be. Am I not still your queen?"

I didn't say anything. I couldn't.

Her fingers dug into my arm. "Javi . . . please. I know things have been hard. I know you're sad, angry. I know you're suffering, I—"

"I am not suffering!" I roared, my vision flashing as rage forced me up. I pinned Luisa to the bed. She didn't fight beneath me, but I held her wrists nearly tight enough to break them. "Do you understand?" I seethed, glaring down at her as the adrenaline flooded through me. I shook her once. "Do you?"

She stared back at me, and I recognized the mask she slipped onto her face. We both wore them. "I understand," she said, her voice dull.

I didn't want to let go of her, but I knew I had to or this would turn into something else.

But something in her eyes changed. The mask slipped. She seemed to melt under my grasp.

"Fuck me," she said. It was a command. Her tone was languid, her gaze lush as she stared at me.

I wasn't used to her being so direct and I couldn't pretend that I didn't have an erection already. I slept naked, after all.

"Luisa . . ." I said, shutting my eyes and trying to compose myself.

"Fuck me hard," she said throatily. "Now." I felt my balls tighten, the blood pulsing in my cock.

I looked at her with intensity. "I will hurt you."

She wasn't deterred. "You've already hurt me, Javier."

"Not in this way."

"Then I want it this way." She squirmed beneath me. "Please. Be rough. Hurt me. Make me bleed. Give me *something*."

There was such breathtaking sorrow in her last words that it nearly shamed me to be as turned on as I was.

"You don't want this," I whispered, feeling myself slowly succumb to her wishes.

"I want everything." She bit her lip then closed her eyes. "Just fuck me. Fuck me up. Give me everything you've got."

She didn't want everything I had. I had given that to the whore earlier. As I fucked her raw, against the wall, tied with barbed wire, I took that same wire and brought it around her neck as she climaxed. She was still coming as the blood ran down her neck. She came until her windpipe was severed in two.

I'd be lying if I said I hadn't meant to kill her. But rage is a funny thing. I guess she had it coming though, no pun intended. Anyone who would willingly let themselves be choked with barbed wire wouldn't get very far in life, anyway.

"Please," Luisa pleaded.

I didn't let her beg anymore. I reached down and grabbed her by the hair, my fingers scraping along her scalp, and I yanked her up and over, like she weighed nothing at all. She let out a little yelp and I tightened my grip, pushing her face into the pillow.

I lowered my lips to her ear. "Is this what you want? Tell me now if it's not and I'll leave you alone."

She moved her cheek to the side and said, mumbling against the fabric, "Don't leave me alone."

I took in a deep breath. "I won't leave you."

But my voice was shaking.

So I straddled her, and with one hand fisted in her

hair, I pulled her camisole up with the other. She slid her arms out of the straps, obedient, wanting it, and I gathered the delicate fabric around her neck, wrapping it and twisting it around my hand until it was tight. Luisa was no stranger to this kind of bed play, but I knew I was squeezing her throat with enough power to shut it off completely. Luckily, the camisole had a touch of stretch to it.

"You say you want me," I told her gruffly, pulling her head back by the hair, by the throat, until her torso was lifted off the bed, like a mermaid at the bow of a ship. "You say you want to fuck me. But I don't think I am who you're looking for. He hasn't been around for some time."

She sputtered under my grasp, unable to talk. I could hear the breath wheezing out of her and none going back in. For one horrifying, startling moment I had a thought of her wanting to die. That this was her plan. That I'd made her life so miserable lately that this was the only way she thought she had a way out.

But even though I was no longer the man she knew, she was the Luisa that I knew. That I fell in love with. That I married. And that I pushed away.

With surprising strength she reached behind her and wrapped her fingers around my cock. She stroked my length and I felt like a balloon ready to burst. But not this way, not yet.

I let go of the camisole and her hair, shoving her back to the bed, her grip on me becoming free. I quickly reached under the mattress and brought out the large steak knife I kept there. Even though I had guards in the house, military patrolling out of the house, I'd be foolish not to have my own form of protection. I could reach the knife or the gun hooked under the bottom of my bedside table in a second flat.

Quickly placing the knife handle between my teeth, I brought Luisa's hands behind her back and knotted the camisole around them. If she handled me anymore, I'd be coming all over her in seconds. And while I had no problems covering her from head to toe, I hadn't been with my wife for a long time. I wanted to at least have her come first, before I made my mark.

There was something so carnal about having her lie on her stomach beneath me, her face unseen, her hands bound. Helpless. Even in the faint light I could still see the scars on her back where I had carved my name into her flesh, back when she was just a captive, before she was mine. In some ways it felt like yesterday.

I took the knife out of my mouth and held it in one hand while I let my fingertip trail down her spine. She shivered beneath me.

"Do you still want me to make you bleed?" I asked in a hush. My fingers twitched and ached, cycling between wanting to hold back and wanting to make it hurt.

She nodded.

"You need to say it."

"Make me bleed."

I slid my fingers between her soft ass cheeks, ripe like peaches and just as easy to bruise, and stroked around her hole before I dipped down into her cunt. It was already dripping wet, drenched for me. Such a good girl. Such a beautiful queen.

And somehow still my queen. I didn't know for how much longer.

With one swift motion I drew the blade of the knife down one side of her spine.

She cried out, a half scream. It reminded me of so many screams lately, but coming from her it made me pause. My heart thudded in my chest.

I wanted to ask if she was okay, but there was too much energy coursing through me. I quickly slashed another line to match down the other side, feeling that strange relief flow through me. She screamed again, breathing heavily as the blood ran down the sides of her back, pooling on the sheets. Such a shame to ruin such an expensive set but that was a minor price to pay.

"Do you want me to stop?" I murmured as I thrust my wet fingers into her ass and she tightened around me like a vise. "Or should I keep going?"

She took a shaky breath in and out. "Keep going." Despite the obvious pain she was in, she was determined. Stubborn.

I took the knife to her ass cheeks and slowly drew the blade across her skin until it sank in with a satisfying give. It took a second for the blood to rise, and then it was flowing hot and fast down the hills. I lowered my head and licked the blood off of her, the sharp taste of copper and salt satisfying some sort of vampire-ish thirst. When I had lapped up as much as I could, her body tensing now from desire, I moved my tongue inward, where it was sweeter, where it was all her.

A moan rippled through her body and she pushed

herself back into me, wanting more. I would give her more. I always did.

I devoured her, every inch, my mouth filling with her desire. I swallowed it deep, wanting to drown in it, remembering how much I missed this, missed her. Her taste was incomparable, the feel of her cunt and her ass beneath my tongue, between my lips, was a drug like no other. In that moment, I could have spent the rest of my life with my face between her folds, just taking in everything that was left of her.

I ended up nipping her clit, hard, between my teeth.

She cried out in surprise, in pain, then in pleasure as I licked the hurt away and she relaxed back into me.

Her breathing became shallow, her skin hotter. She was swelling beneath my touch. She was about to come. I pulled back, gasping for breath and quickly positioned myself. I hadn't meant to go inside her. Being inside Luisa was something I thought of as too much of a risk. The feelings she would bring me.

But at that moment I didn't care.

And when she called out my name, almost panting, "Javier, please," then I *really* didn't care.

I thrust into her, holding her hips in place, relishing how she felt, tight fucking silk. I moaned, my eyes rolling back into my head, a torrent of emotion beginning to swirl in my chest, something more than anger this time.

I swallowed it down and let out a hot breath as I slowly, agonizingly pulled back out of her.

"Is that what you wanted?" I asked her.

She nodded, breathless. "Yes, please."

"You're being very polite, my dear. I have a feeling

you're not asking for what you really want. You're not quite . . . full enough, are you?"

Her head shook once.

I bit my lip until I tasted blood, anticipating what I was about to do. Then I picked up the knife and turned it around. I held the blade with my hands, delicately at first, and slid the plastic handle into her ass. She tensed up, and as I pushed it in deeper, my grip on the blade tightened and blood began to seep from my hands. I barely felt the cut, I only felt her around my cock, that soft, wet sanctuary.

I thrust into her, the knife handle and my equally hard dick, moving in unison as she welcomed it more and more. My movements became faster, I went deeper. I could barely hold on to her hips with one hand, too much blood was spilling from the other, making everything red and wet and hot. It looked like a massacre, and I felt I was losing much more than blood.

I came inside her, hard and long, and I only needed to flick her clit to get her to do the same. She moaned loud, beautiful music to my ears, threatening to undo me. She quaked and shuddered as the orgasm rocked through her, and for a wonderful second I imagined my seed sinking into her, finding purchase. The chance at a child.

But when desire and lust lost their footing and my heartbeat slowed and I was spent, my mind could think clearly again. I could dispose of those feelings that had the power to hurt me in the end.

Family was everything.

Family got you killed.

There would be no child.

There was barely a wife.

I looked down at Luisa, my blood spilled all over her back and mixing with her own. I pulled the knife out of her and shook the remaining drops on her rising back as she caught her breath. I ran my hand down her spine, smooth, blending our blood together. It was the best that I could do, it was the most of me that I could give.

I didn't say anything to her as I got off the bed and went to the en suite bathroom. I washed my hands in the sink, the cut across my inner fingers not too deep, watching the water swirl down the drain, our blood together. Blood of family. Blood of marriage.

Then I looked at myself in the mirror and was glad to see a man I didn't recognize staring back at me. You couldn't take anything from this man. He had dead eyes.

When I emerged, she was standing naked, vulnerable, beautiful, the sheets and blankets piled at the foot of the bed, white splashed with feathering red. Our eyes met and I saw that need in them. She wanted me to come back to her. Maybe just to put her in the bathtub and wash the horror from her back, take care of her, like I always used to do.

I could only stare back at her, wishing she could see that this was all I had. That we were lucky it hadn't taken a turn for the worse. That her wounds on her back would heal.

Even if the wounds in her heart would not.

She nodded once, reading the futility of it all. She was so good at that, seeing the truth. It made me wonder what she'd seen in me all along.

Did she hate herself for losing her heart to a monster?

"I'll get clean sheets," she said, her voice small. She started for the door, seeming to forget that she was naked and bleeding.

I quickly walked over to her and put my good hand on her shoulder. She looked at it in surprise, the generosity of my touch. "No, you go clean yourself up," I told her. "I'll deal with the bed."

She blinked, then gave me a timid, grateful look.

"Thank you," she said, then walked to the bathroom. I watched her go, her back bloodied, yet she wore it like a cape.

And I knew she was thanking me for more than that. She was thanking me for being intimate with her. She was thanking me for waking up, even if just for a few minutes. Even if I brought her a lot of pain with some of the pleasure.

I hoped I had the strength to never let it happen again.

CHAPTER THREE

Javier

I dreamed about Alana again.

It's always the same fucking dream.

It was the last time I saw her. Wal-Mart of all damn places, just outside of Durango. Figures it would be in a fluorescent-lit hell. She'd met me and Luisa there, looking frightened and vulnerable. Lost. A cast on her leg. She thought her brother could save her. She'd survived an assassination attempt. Two, actually, if you counted her getting hit by a car. And the third attempt, the one that blew her and my boat up, that's the one that got her in the end.

I could have done more for her. Maybe that's why the dream didn't stop. Why I kept seeing her crumpled face, why I kept hearing myself say the last thing I said to her.

"I will take care of you, you got that? The only way I know how."

I would hear those words of mine when I was awake, too. They mocked me.

Because I failed. Because I didn't take her seriously enough. But I never did, did I? The only person I ever took seriously was me.

What I thought at the time was that Alana was a trail

straight to me, my compound, my cartel. I assumed that the reason she "survived" so many attempts on her life was because they never meant to kill her, whoever they were. They just wanted to scare her, right into my arms.

And it worked. I brushed her off. Of course I didn't turn her out to the wolves, but I certainly didn't trust the situation, nor her so-called Canadian boyfriend. I needed to get away from her, for my sake, for Luisa's sake. And yes, for her sake, too. Because when I was caught, when I was killed, what would happen to her? As long as I was unattainable – safe – she, in a sense, would be too.

But I was wrong. About everything.

I hadn't heard from her for a week. I thought she was going to call the number I gave her. I thought she would have trusted me to take care of her. But she didn't. And now I couldn't blame her.

I got a phone call at five in the morning from the chief of police in Mazatlán, someone who was already on my payroll. He said there had been an explosion in the Sea of Cortez, and the crew who went out to investigate found wreckage of my mega-ketch, blown to smithereens. Ironically I had named the boat Beatriz, after one of my other deceased sisters.

I had no idea what was happening, and it wasn't until they reviewed security footage from the marina, which showed a group of men, presumably dressed like old sailors, pushing a few wheelbarrows down the docks. One of the men stopped and pulled back a blanket that was lying across the wheelbarrow.

It was Alana's face. She was curled inside, unconscious or already dead.

The man kept his back to the camera, fuzzy grey hair sticking out of his sailor's cap that could have been real, could have been fake, but Alana was kept in full view. The man wanted us to see her.

He wanted me to see her.

The next thing they found was footage of Beatriz sailing out to sea.

Alana was on it.

Two horrible days later, while Luisa and I had hunkered down in Mazatlán, I was approached by the coroner. He had bad news. Alana's remains were found among the wreckage. They ran her through DNA testing and it was a match. They were one hundred percent certain that my sister was dead. And the police had no idea who was behind it. Even when they were paid handsomely by me, they still couldn't come up with any leads, and the police down in Jalisco, where Alana had lived, were worthless as well.

I didn't feel anything at first.

I remembered Luisa gripping my hand.

The breath being knocked out of me.

But it was all rather fitting. I recall thinking, *this figures*. Because it did. Violence, the cartel way of life, had taken my parents from me. My sister Beatriz. My sister Violetta, who I saw explode in a car bomb before my very eyes. Now Alana. The only Bernal left was her twin, Marguerite, who chose to stay as far away from me as possible, who wanted to forget that I was her brother. She lived in New York and had cut all ties with me, not only for her own safety, but because she wanted to pretend I didn't exist. My only family left hated me.

I hated me. Because this had all been my fault. Each death was on my head. From the years as the right-hand man to Travis Raines and his cartel, to overthrowing him, to starting my own, and then to overtaking Salvador Reyes, up, up, up to the top. They all died because I kept climbing.

Family is everything. That is the creed in this country. But that creed gets others killed. And it slowly kills you. Your family is the first thing you'll lose. Your soul will be the last.

Luckily, I didn't have much of either anymore.

I had Luisa, of course. She had become my family, my confidante, my lover, my friend. She had become everything to me, in bed and outside of it. But she was a weakness, my weakness. She was what they would go after next, the last thing I could possibly lose.

Unless I lost her first.

I was keeping her safe, as safe as I could, as safe as anyone could. I had all of Sinaloa under my finger, which meant the police and the military. Guards were outside my door, my compound was patrolled, the hills were watched . . . I had eyes everywhere. Radios, cell phones, everything was monitored with what the local military had. If anyone was coming, we knew about it.

In reality there were few to fear. America wouldn't touch me, not after I had informed on Salvador to the DEA. I had the Juarez plaza and unity with Nuevo Laredo. After I seized Tijuana, which was still my plan, I would control everything except the Gulf. They were not true Sinaloans, not like me, not like the real *narco* royalty. They were who I had to watch, my only real threat in the end. And they had tried before, only to be thwarted in the process.

But keeping Luisa safe from others also meant keeping her away from me. I couldn't let what happened last night happen again. She couldn't be my own victim. I knew I was hurting her by pushing her away, by keeping her at a distance. But it was for her own good, and mine.

I didn't feel like myself anymore. I knew I wasn't myself. I woke up with this deep-seated need to maim and hurt. To fuck. To make others suffer, as I suffered.

And I knew I had to use this anger, sharpen it like a knife. It would be greater than any weapon.

The only way through was up. To the top. Until I had all of Mexico. Until I was unstoppable.

Until there was nothing left to fear.

There was a knock at my office door. I didn't have to ask who it was. It was always Este. Luisa never bothered to knock anymore. She never bothered at all.

"Come in," I said, my voice sounding more tired than I'd like. I didn't want Este to think I wasn't on top of the game. He didn't need to know about my dreams, the sleepless nights. It had been a long day, though, and I supposed I was allowed to look like I'd been working at my desk from dawn until dusk.

The door opened and he stepped in. As usual he looked like a fucking moron in his board shorts and wife-beater. Flip-flops on his feet, like a damn Californian cartoon.

"Lose a bet?" I asked as I briefly looked him over.

"You used that line last week," he said, sitting down

across from me on the other side of the desk. He kicked off his flip-flops and crossed his legs at the ankles. My lip curled in disgust, the thought of his dirty feet on my sheepskin rug.

"I'll try to be more original next time," I said dryly, putting my agenda away. I folded my hands in front of me and gave him a pointed look. "Have we found him yet?"

A slow, crooked smile spread across his face. It told me everything I needed to know.

I opened my desk drawer and took out a file folder. Call me old-fashioned but I needed to have most of my intel in my hands as well as on the computer. My brain handled it better that way.

Flipping it open, I took out a picture of Evaristo Martinez Sanchez. He was young, twenty-four, a light-skinned, blue-eyed Mexican. Probably made the ladies go crazy. For a moment I realized he was about Luisa's age and that they would make a good-looking couple. I'm not sure if I was relieved or not when I found my stomach curling with jealousy over the thought.

It was a serious photo, like a mugshot, and in color, probably taken for his government ID. Evaristo was part of the task force for the Policía Federal Ministerial, or PFM, those lovely people our government hired to fight organized crime and people like me. This organization, unlike the AFI before them, were hard to bribe and did things by the book like many of the Americans liked to think themselves did. In other words, they were a pain in my ass and could do serious damage to any cartel, if given the chance. The *federales*, we called them.

Evaristo was ranked up there on the team that watched Angel Hernandez and the Tijuana plaza. He wasn't in charge of the unit – kidnapping the boss would be too risky for me and *federale* bosses would never talk. Stubborn little bastards. That stark loyalty and honor would be useful for my side, if only their morals weren't so fucked up.

But being second in command, Evaristo would know enough, and the more I read up about him, the more I liked him. He came from the barrios of Matamoros, dropping out of school when he was thirteen to become a petty criminal. He screwed up once and made enemies with the wrong people (are there any right people?) which put him in a precarious position at a very young age. Like most youth, he joined the Mexican army because there was nowhere else for him to go. He liked the discipline there and had the willingness to do jobs others wouldn't. He was a quick learner and more than eager. As soon as he was out, the PFM swooped in and recruited him.

The PFM wear masks when they do raids so that people like me don't recognize them. But the internet is a funny thing, and Este knew how to get information. I felt like I knew Evaristo well. Already he reminded me of our Juanito, who was essentially Este's guy Friday now, following him around like a puppy.

I was looking forward to kidnapping him. Torturing him, just a bit, at first anyway. I'm not an animal. Just to see how he handled it. To see if he was as good as the reports from his supervisors said he was.

Naturally, I wanted him to fail. When he failed, he

would give me the information I needed to take Angel out. When I took Angel out, I'd take over the plaza. Evaristo would be spared because of my graciousness, and hopefully I wouldn't have inflicted too much damage to his pretty boy face. Or maybe I'd be doing him a favor. Too much pussy can be tiring at times.

I was surprised that Este came through with everything. He opposed my plan at first. Said it was too risky and that our cartel was too good for this. Too elegant. That we didn't need to fall into stereotypical violence that besieged the country, that hiring *sicarios* to take out a lord was beneath us.

I don't think Este knew who I'd become.

But Este leaned over and tapped Evaristo's photo. "He's a sitting duck. Two days. I set up the staged bust and they've got the message. They're on it."

"Just as I asked," I reminded him. He had a habit of trying to take over my ideas, even if he didn't agree with them. Always trying to one-up me when he should have known there was no one-upping the *patron*, not when you were a barefoot fool.

"Yes," he said, rather reluctantly. "Should I go and make sure it all goes through?"

What was in motion now was that Este had tipped off someone at the PFM about a safe house location and an impossible amount of cocaine and meth looking to make its way up on a big rig to San Diego. But the safe house was a ruse. We would be there waiting for them. And we'd take out Evaristo as soon as we had the chance. It's hard to hide those blue eyes behind a mask, and at six foot two, he'd stand out among the men like a sore thumb. Of course with something like this, I wasn't involved. Other people did my dirty work for me. I had a growing team of ex-soldiers and cops who could go into any situation and come out alive with the target.

"No," I told him. "Let them do it. You'd just get in the way, tripping over your own sandals, your hair in your eyes like a little girl."

My insults didn't seem to work on Esteban anymore. He jerked his chin at my forehead. "Is your hair thinning a little bit? Must be the stress."

I raised my brow. "So is that all you came to tell me?"

"Is that all?" he repeated incredulously. "I come here to tell you that I orchestrated your plan exactly as *you* wanted, the bait has been taken, and you wonder if that's all?"

"I'm sorry, did you need me to pat you on the back, maybe make you burp a little?"

Este made a disgruntled noise and got out of his chair. "You know what, Javier? You may be the *patron* and this may be *your* cartel, and you may think that you earned it, but there is something other *narcos* do that you don't, and that's treat their brothers with respect."

I blinked at him, actually caught off-guard for once. "This isn't a preschool, Este. I will give you respect if you deserve it."

"And what about your wife?"

A block of ice froze in my chest and my eyes became cold as I glared at him. "What business is it of yours to even mention her?"

I could practically watch him think. He knew the wrong thing would get him in a lot of trouble. And he knew what I'd been up to lately, more than once. Sometimes he helped.

"No business at all," he said after some time. He started for the door, then paused. "Though I should tell you that your *appointment* is here. Should I show her in?"

After his comment, I should have said no. But while it made me think twice about what I was doing, it also made me mad. Still, maybe this one wouldn't piss me off tonight. It didn't always end in blood.

I nodded at him, and in that moment, I wondered if it made me seem weak. I knew Este was no better when it came to women. Maybe I only thought that because *I* used to be better.

He disappeared down the hall and I quickly checked the clock on the wall. It was already ten p.m. Luisa would be settling down for bed herself.

I was about to call after Este and tell him I'd changed my mind when he appeared at the door with a tall, striking woman. She didn't look like any of the other whores. Though all of them were beautiful, this woman had her nose right in the air, as if she were better than me, better than her whole profession.

I immediately disliked her. Perhaps there would be blood after all.

"This is Judia," Este said.

Judia? Named after a bean?

Este turned to leave but I called out after him. "Actually, Este, you can have her."

He stopped and gave me a funny look. I knew he didn't need my charity in this regard but I thought I'd offer it anyway. Even with the scar down the side of his face and his teenage clothes, Este was a ladykiller.

Then again, so was I.

"No offense, Judia," he said to her before eyeing me, "but I don't need anything you think I can have."

Judia smirked at him. "Am I supposed to be flattered, two men *not* fighting over me? What, are you both gay?"

I had to laugh. I hadn't laughed in a long time and the sound was jarring to my own ears.

"Yes, completely gay," I said, getting out of my chair and walking over to her. "Gayest *patron* that ever was."

She shrugged with one shoulder and looked down at me. "That will make things easier. I don't get off with men who are shorter than me anyway."

Este sucked in his breath. My mouth gaped open slightly. Did this *puta* just have the nerve to make fun of my height?

I nodded at her, unable to keep the smile from stretching across my face, and walked back to the desk. "You're very honest, *Judia*. And daring, really. But I don't think it's a very good career decision to be so choosy, especially with *patrons.*"

My fingers slipped under the desk and closed around a wide, wooden handle, the cut on my hand stinging from last night. I wore my smile well.

"You know, I am five foot nine, which is fairly average for a man," I told her, keeping my movements quiet. I may have added an inch. "How tall are you?"

She swallowed hard, seeming nervous for the first time. I've been told my smile can be unnerving if I use it long enough.

"Five foot eleven," she said.

I licked my lips, feeling my blood run hot and wild. "So I only need to take off about three inches or so."

Her eyes widened in a mix of confusion and then horror as I brought the machete out from underneath my desk. I'd been trained for this, to maximize force in a small space. It's all in the legs, in the way you spring. In one smooth motion I swung the machete better than any golf club, swiping across her legs mid-calf.

She screamed as she became an amputee in an instant, blood spilling to the ground as she fell to one side and her severed legs fell to the other. I guess I took off more than three inches, but it was better to overachieve than under.

"There," I said as I peered down at her face, an arc of blood spurting from her legs in time with her fading heartbeat. "Now you are shorter than me. Think you can come now?"

Judia screamed again, but her voice was fading, choked in her throat as shock overtook her. I sighed and stared at the sheepskin rug. First dirty with Este's feet, now this.

"You keep a machete under your desk?" Este asked, looking over my shoulder at it, the long bloody blade still in my hands.

I gave him a look. "Why wouldn't I keep a machete under my desk?" I handed it to him. "Here, put it back and get Juanito to clean this up." I gestured to the soon to be corpse and the bloody mess of an office. "I'm going to bed."

Este tried to take it from my hands but I found my grip tightening. "On second thought, I'll take it with me."

I didn't want Este to think he could go on about "respect" again, even though I knew he was thinking it with Juanito having to clean up my mess half the time. Everyone had to pay their dues, though.

I took the machete upstairs, my bodyguard Diego following me down the hall as he always did. I barely noticed him until I was about to go into my bedroom.

"Mrs. Bernal is sleeping in one of the guest bedrooms," he said in his low, baritone voice. He didn't speak much, one of the reasons I liked him. "The one at the end of the hall."

"Oh?" The one that used to be her prison cell. "Did she say why?"

"No sir," Diego said. "She just came up to me to let me know."

As if it would go unnoticed. "All right," I said, straightening up a bit, as if this arrangement was the new normal. "Can you make sure we have someone stationed outside her door as well? Artur?"

"Of course," he said before he strode off to gather Artur from one of the barracks on the property, probably interrupting his sleep. Artur was equally as trustworthy as Diego but usually worked in the early morning hours. Still, I wouldn't compromise her safety. The chances of someone getting into the house to get at her, or me, were practically nil, but sometimes you couldn't trust the people in your house either. I knew better than to underestimate those closest to me. I knew better but I never let on.

I closed the door behind me and got ready for bed. For all the troubles, this was the first time I'd gone to sleep without her. Perhaps she should have done this a long time ago. Perhaps she was tired of having to go to bed and fall asleep first, such a vulnerable stage of life, all alone.

And now, now I was alone. With those thoughts again. Knowing the dreams were waiting. The ones filled with guilt and grief and regret. The ones that made me a little more scared of myself, a little crazier, day by day.

As I fell asleep, I could still smell the blood I had spilled. It worked as well as a sleeping pill.

CHAPTER FOUR

Esteban

Fucking animal, Esteban Mendoza thought to himself as he surveyed Javier's office. Blood was absolutely everywhere, even on the walls, which meant Juanito would be spending all hours of the night wiping that shit down, not to mention disposing of the body. He had to do the exact same thing the other day, after Javier got carried away with a piece of barbed wire. The pigs he kept out back were getting fatter by the minute.

It wasn't that Este really felt bad for Juanito, it was more that it would steal his time away from *him*. After all, Este was having him do all sorts of things that in some ways were far worse. Juanito wasn't even gay. Not that Este was either, he just liked to get off and it usually didn't matter who was sucking his dick. It was more about the power. The control. And that need to humiliate someone the way he used to be humiliated himself, back when he was a little punk hanging on the corners of the *colonias* of Juarez. When he told Juanito to get on his knees and put his cock in his mouth, he felt like a king. The king he always should have been. The *patron* he'd dreamed about.

He'd bided his time long enough. Put up with Javier long enough. He had to act now, before Javier really went to the dark side. It wasn't that Javier would slip up. Este had told Luisa that her husband was getting sloppy, but that wasn't really the case. Ever since Alana's death, he'd become sharper, like a new knife. He'd become more focused on building his empire and taking the jagged pieces of what was once one federation of *narcos* and putting them back together again, with him at the helm.

Javier was lost, yes. Grieving, no doubt. But he wasn't letting go of the business. And if anything, he was becoming more dangerous. Unpredictable. Inhumane. Este had never, ever feared Javier before. He had no reason to. He knew Javier had always looked at him like a lackey, a joke, and that was something he purposely cultivated. Because who would ever suspect Este of really using his brain? He was smart enough for the techie stuff, but no one would expect him to be devious. Or calculating. In fact, Este grew tired of the surfer look a year ago but kept it up because appearances were everything in this place. He fucking *hated* wearing flip-flops.

But now, Este wasn't so sure that Javier wouldn't snap one day and have his own head chopped off, for no real reason at all. What Este had wanted to accomplish by offing Alana – (he had offed her, hadn't he? He wondered that sometimes at night, the image of the boat exploding in the background again and again. Were the female remains Alana's? The DNA findings on Alana were faked to bring certainty to Javier, but Este wasn't quite certain himself.) – was to bring Javier to his knees and make him vulnerable. In a sense, it had worked. But Este had to act fast now before it took a turn for the worse and Javier became harder to manage.

His grace was gone. His elegance was still there, but when Este looked into those golden eyes, he only saw rage, and behind that rage, madness. The old Javier would never have killed a whore without reason, and now he was just doing it out of this newfound bloodlust. The old Javier probably wouldn't have cheated on his wife (even though the old Javier did have a habit of cheating on *other* partners, and later, beheading them, so maybe this wasn't new). And the old Javier would *never* have been so ambitious as to kidnap a *federale* as a means to assassinate another cartel leader.

The first step was Luisa. He was almost there. Even though Javier's behavior surprised him, he wanted him to keep pushing his wife away. He wanted Javier to cheat on her. He wanted Luisa ruined and helpless and looking for love and affection anywhere.

Este wanted Luisa to come to him. He would show her what she was missing, how a real man fucked. He would give her everything that Javier couldn't. He would do this, in secret, for a long time, until the secret came out. He would then take her for his own, and when he was bored of her one day, kill her. Make sure Javier knew about that, too. Maybe give him a front row seat.

Of course, he would take the cartel as well. The plans were being set in motion for that. He could have kissed Javier for being so ballsy and ambitious.

It was all pretty much perfect.

But if he didn't act now, he could end up dead.

And death was something Este feared. Death before

getting to show the world what a fool Javier Bernal was. Death before getting to show the world it had underestimated Esteban Mendoza.

Esteban left Javier's office and strode down the hall, down the stairs to the basement. This was where Juanito lived. He actually had it pretty good, at least in Este's mind he did. He had more money than he knew what to do with, but because he was under Este's command (and yes, Javier's, as he had so recently demonstrated), he couldn't have his own fancy house with fancy cars and fancy hookers. He was told he could have all that later. It was always later. Now, his job was just to do as they said, no matter what it was, and in time he would rise in the ranks.

What Javier didn't know, though, was that Juanito was loyal to Esteban and not to him. The minute that Juanito joined the cartel, Este had taken him under his wing. At first Este had explained everything as a bit of hazing. He'd had his own little torture session on Juanito – pulling off toenails with a clamp, waterboarding, using a heated hammer to make burns on his back. Things that Javier would never notice. But Juanito sure did. And fear of Este was built into him from the start.

It made him so much more compliant. The rape came later (though Juanito was willing to go through with it, Este liked to think of it as rape – it turned him on even more). More torture here and there. Pretty soon Juanito was willing to do whatever Este asked of him. And one of the first things he had asked was to help orchestrate the murder of Javier's sister.

If Juanito had any objections to that, he didn't dare

voice them to Este. He went through with it. Took Alana's phone call for help and instead of patching her through to Javier, told her help was on the way.

Este picked up Alana, and the rest was history.

Now Este wanted Juanito's help with the next phase of the plan, and he knew he could get it. But just in case Juanito was starting to fear Javier like Este was, he needed to put that fear back into him.

Este opened the door to Juanito's room without knocking. It was dark, so Este flicked on the lights. Juanito was in bed, sleeping, but sprang awake in a second. No one knew how to sleep through anything in this compound.

"What is it?" he asked, wiping the sleep from his eyes. Juanito was such a young kid. Este forgot at times until he saw that emptiness instead of youth in his eyes. But that loss of innocence was pretty much all his fault and he might as well take pride in it.

"I made a mess in Javier's office, hey," Este said. "I need you to take care of it. After you take care of me."

Este made an elegant gesture with his fingers for Juanito to turn around. A current of fear passed over his eyes, and it made Este immediately hard.

Juanito knew the drill. He shuffled out of his boxer shorts – a stupid pair with bananas on it – and got on all fours, his small, flabby ass facing Este.

Este didn't admire his body, didn't admire anything except his compliancy. He knew he was going to cause him a lot of pain and that helped with the hard-on.

Thank god the room was soundproof. Este slammed into him, his grip merciless on his hips. Juanito cried out in horror, in pain, a scream that would have made anyone's dick shrink in an instant, but it did the opposite to Esteban. Besides, now he wasn't even thinking about Juanito. His thoughts were all on Luisa. On what he would do to her. This same thing. She was going to go along willingly at first – that was part of the plan. Get her desire, her trust. But in time, that desire would turn to fear.

And when Este tired of the fear, he'd fuck her with his gun. He did that to a woman once, the only woman he remotely had feelings for. He would do it again. Luisa would love the danger of it all. He knew she liked fucked up shit like that.

And then Este would pull the trigger while it was deep inside her.

And then he would rule the world.

CHAPTER FIVE

Luisa

Sometimes, lately anyway, when I thought back to the day I had married Javier, my mind got all lost and jumbled. Confused. I brought up images of my wedding to Salvador Reyes. Perhaps because I was terribly nervous before both.

Of course I was nervous with Salvador, because I knew how powerful he was. I knew he had the capacity to hurt me, I knew I wasn't in love – or even "in like" – with him. And I was a virgin. But I hadn't expected to be nervous with Javier.

It was only a month after he killed Salvador and I joined Javier at his compound – this same compound – that Javier proposed to me.

We were in bed one Sunday morning. Sundays were the best days. We'd awake when the sun rose in the east and streamed in through the windows, then we'd spend a few hours under the covers. Sometimes we'd make love right away, other times we'd wait until coffee was delivered. But we never got out of bed unsatisfied.

That morning, Javier was in a quiet mood. This was nothing new – sometimes something dark and heavy would befall him. I could see it in his eyes. They didn't quite have that intensity anymore and he seemed to be tortured subtly by some inner demons. I knew he had a lot of them.

We made love slowly. He took his time, not in a torturous, teasing way, but as if he were trying to memorize me, hold on to every second, every moment. It unnerved me because I wasn't used to it. I was used to dangerous, rough, wild sex, or quick and passionate sex. But not this forlorn, pensive emotion. Not from him.

After we both came with soft cries, he slid out of me from behind then flipped me over so that I was on my back. He climbed on top of me, his weight on his elbows on either side of my shoulders. He brushed my hair off my damp face, the sun and our sex heating up the room, and those wonderful eyes of his peered down at me.

They were searching, like a hawk, golden in the light, but they were sad. I didn't think I'd ever seen him sad. It made me hold my breath and I wrapped my hands around the small of his back, brushing gently against his skin, holding his body to me.

"Do you love me?" he asked, his voice low, almost hesitant.

I stared up at him in surprise. Of course I loved him. With everything I had. Didn't I tell him that all the time? Even though I had yet to hear it back, I still told him because I was unashamed of the truth.

"I love you," I told him.

"Do you want me to love you?" he asked, fainter now. He ran the tip of his fingers along my forehead, down my cheekbones, across my jaw, more gentle than a feather.

I didn't know how to answer that. Did he not love me?
Could he?

Would he?

So I said, "Yes."

He carefully licked his lips, brows furrowed slightly in thought.

"Do you want me to marry you?"

Now I was really surprised. I felt like the wind had been knocked out of me. My mouth dropped open and my brain and heart battled each other for a moment, wondering if my answer would set me up for some sort of humiliation.

But still, the truth. "Yes," I whispered.

"Good," he said, and only then did he give me the quietest of smiles. "Because I love you, Luisa. Even when I thought I didn't have it in me, I do. I love you. And I want you to be my wife. My queen. My everything. Rule with me." He leaned closer and kissed me delicately on the lips. "Marry me."

And I said yes. The room grew brighter. The sun filled my soul. And I thought I could never be happier.

We laughed, drunk on love, on the future, and we made love several times that morning. He wouldn't stop. He was insatiable. I couldn't stop either. I was just so taken with him that I wanted him to keep taking me. Forever.

The wedding happened a week later. Needless to say, there wasn't much planning. When most *narcos* get married, it turns into a nationwide celebration. Mayors and Sinaloan officials are supposed to show up, as well as the *narco* families whom Javier had good relations with.

They are supposed to be huge feasts, real traditional parties. I should know – I had just that with Salvador.

But maybe because of my past, Javier opted for something quiet. In fact, it was just me, him, a minister, and Este as the witness. In a small, thick-walled church out in the middle of the hills. At least it had a beautiful view of the valley and Culiacán in the distance. A view of everything that would belong to me.

And yet I was nervous. Tapping my foot, picking at my simple white dress that was as delicate as a nightgown. I was nervous, because to me, this was it. Javier was it. If anything went wrong, if it all went south, there wouldn't be anyone else. I wanted him forever or I wanted nothing.

I had reason to be nervous, it turned out. Because now, as I sat alone at the kitchen table pouring myself another glass of wine, the evening breeze sweeping through the screened window and bringing with it the smell of rain and relief, I realized I had nothing.

The other night, when he finally succumbed to me, I knew I wouldn't get another chance. I don't know how I knew it, but I did. I saw it in his face after we were done. I didn't care about the pain. I didn't care about the scarring or the blood. I didn't care if he hit me (which he didn't, and wouldn't, it wasn't his style). I knew that made me sound like a pathetic, lovesick woman, but it was the truth.

I just wanted something of him. His attention. Even if it meant his wrath. I wanted it. The feel of his body, his touch, his desire. And I got it. I knew he wanted to make people hurt, so I gave him the chance to hurt me. The conflict showed in his eyes, the slight hesitations he made. He was so afraid of really hurting me, but I wasn't, because I knew he wouldn't. He was more afraid of himself than I was of him.

But with whatever I got, it was even worse when it was taken away. Now I was aching for more and saddled with this uncomfortable feeling that there never would be. That it was over between us. And there would be nothing left for me.

Juanito strolled into the kitchen to get something from the fridge. Dinner had been served by our cook, Alberto, but I had eaten alone. Esteban ate elsewhere. I'm not sure the last time Javier had dinner with me, and Juanito seemed to fend for himself.

"Hungry again?" I asked him as he pulled a plate of leftovers out.

He looked sheepish. "I didn't eat earlier."

I'd never seen him have dinner with us. I wanted to ask Javier how he was being treated – lately his young face looked years older, gaunt and ashen, and his eyes were dull. But I didn't dare approach Javier with this stuff now. Before Alana, yes. But not after. Funny, I had started to think of life as Before AD and After AD (Alana's Death). Besides, Juanito was probably getting high on his own supply. Many of the *narcos* did, though the worst Javier did was drink. Even now, it was only booze that Javier occasionally dipped into.

That, and murder.

Juanito was in charge of our finances after Javier was through with them, just going over the boring stuff like an accountant. There's a price to dealing with large sums of money when you're trading in a billion dollar industry:

you pay the *pisa* to plazas, dock handling charges, shipping costs, trucks, labor, equipment, security. Juanito was learning where the money went after it came to us. I knew that Javier had plans for him when he was ready, but I didn't know what they were. For now, he just did whatever Javier passed down to Esteban.

I patted the seat next to me. "Sit down." He stared at me, hesitant. I flashed him a smile, which I knew was relaxed and easy, maybe even sloppy, thanks to the wine. I'd already had three glasses.

"Okay," he said. He seemed jumpy. He sat down beside me, and it was then that I noticed he had rope burns around his wrists. I stared at them for a moment, trying to figure out what they could be from. He caught me looking and gave me a sheepish look. But he didn't explain.

"I don't think I've talked to you much lately," I said, trying to put him at ease. "How are you?"

"I'm good," he said flatly. He smiled and nodded, as if to convince himself. "Very good. Excited about the move."

"The move?" I asked, then remembered what Este had said about bringing us to a ranch somewhere when the *federale* was captured. I'd wanted to talk about it more with Javier but, well, that didn't happen.

"Oh," Juanito said slowly, reading my face. "I meant *our* move. You're staying here. Right?"

I frowned. "I don't see why I would."

He blinked, now unsure. "We're leaving *tomorrow*."

"What?!" I exclaimed, nearly knocking over my glass. I saved it just in time and swore under my breath.

"You don't know?" Juanito said, and now there was fear in his eyes. I was too angry to coddle him.

I got up, my chair sliding noisily across the tile floor. "Do I look like I know?"

"Please don't tell Este I told you," he pleaded to me, his eyes now filled with fear.

I pursed my lips for a moment. Why would I tell Este? Juanito should be fearing Javier. And I was sure he would after I was done with him.

"I'm talking to my husband. Your *patron*." *And your patron*, I thought to myself, *who wants to keep you in the dark for as long as he can.*

Not if I could help it.

I marched out of the kitchen, hearing Juanito curse to himself as I left. I went straight down the hall to my husband's office and nodded at Diego standing guard outside of it.

"I need to speak with him," I said, seething, my heart racing wildly in my throat.

I couldn't see Diego's eyes behind his dark aviator shades which he liked to wear, even inside. I only saw my reflection. I looked like a mess of a woman. I *was* a mess of a woman.

"He asked for no one to disturb him," Diego said calmly.

"Is he busy getting some *puta*?" I asked, and he balked slightly at that.

"I don't know what Javier does," he said, even though I bet he knew exactly what Javier did. Bet he handed out the condoms. "But I have my orders."

"And you realize I'm not going to obey them," I told him. "I pay your salary too."

He seemed to fall asleep on his feet before I realized he was probably staring at me and thinking. Then he took in a deep breath and knocked on the door.

Javier immediately barked, "I said fuck off!"

"He is in a bad mood, *senora*," Diego said to me in a low voice. "Things didn't quite go as he planned today."

I raised my brows. "Today?"

"With the *federale*."

I stared blankly at him. He tilted his head then nodded, realizing I didn't know anything.

To his credit, he continued. "Javier was adamant that no one get killed. One of the *federales* reached for his gun and our *sicario* reacted. The *federale* is dead. But we do have Evaristo Sanchez now, as planned. Javier will get over it."

"And me," I said. "Do you know what happens to me? Sanchez is in the desert somewhere, right?"

"Yes," he said simply. He didn't care that he was the one informing me. Perhaps because Diego didn't fear Javier. Diego certainly worked for him – for *us* – and was a man to be trusted, but Diego was at least twenty years his senior and had more experience in the cartels and in life, more than Javier had.

And Javier needed him.

He went on. "You will have to check with your husband about the details. But if I were you, it should wait."

"It can't wait. Juanito just said they are leaving tomorrow. You're going too?"

His lips came together in a thin line and he didn't answer, so I knocked on the door instead.

"Jesus Christ, Diego," Javier swore from the other side. "What part of *fuck* and *off* do you not understand?"

I knew that Diego was giving me an "it's your funeral" look under those glasses but I didn't care. I put my hand on the knob and opened the door.

I stormed into the room, slamming the door behind me.

Javier wasn't with another woman, not at the moment. He had just been standing at the window and staring out at the jungle and the craggy hills that rose above it in the distance, barely visible now in the dusk. An open bottle of tequila and a full highball glass were on the table.

He whirled around, ready to rage, his amber eyes flashing, but when he saw it was me, he stopped, stunned.

"Luisa," he said. Just the sound of his voice made me realize that I hadn't come to find him in a long time.

But I wasn't there to make nice, not now. He might have been mad over some dumb mistake one of our men had made, but I was even more so.

"Why didn't you tell me!?" I yelled at him, marching right over to the window.

He swallowed and took his time before he answered. "About what?"

I gestured to the room. "Everything. You already got the *federale*?"

He swallowed then raised his chin to look down on me. "What's your point?"

"My point?" I repeated, flabbergasted. I could feel my throat getting thick, my face growing hot. I prayed I wouldn't cry, wouldn't be weak. "My point is , . . is . . .

Javier, I'm sick and tired of you pushing me away like this. Not telling me anything. We used to be a team."

His eyes didn't change. His face became expressionless, like stone. "There was a place for that. Things are different now."

"But I am still your wife!"

"And you knew what you were marrying when you agreed to become my wife," he said, an edge now in his voice. "And sometimes, you have to accept that. Accept this."

"Accept that you kidnapped a *federale* without telling me about it, and are now holding him in the desert somewhere, where you are going tomorrow, all while I'm supposed to stay here?!"

He raised a brow ever so slightly. "It is no place for a lady."

"Oh, we both know I am not and never will be a lady," I said, almost sneering. "You're just trying to get rid of me."

"So what if I am?"

I froze, caught off-guard. He'd said that far too easily. "Just like that . . . I'm suddenly someone to be thrown away. You used to *love* me!" I pressed my hand hard into his chest where his heart should have been.

With a slight narrowing of his eyes, he said, "This is for your own good. Don't try and twist it around with some feminine woe-is-me bullshit."

"Woe is me?" I repeated incredulously.

"There are bigger things going on here than just your *feelings*," he said, stepping back and away from my hand, like he couldn't stand for me to touch him at all. "Things that affect us all."

"Well how the fuck am I supposed to know that when you don't tell me anything?!"

He turned around, chewing on his lip briefly. "You want to know what's going on?" he asked, his smooth tone suggesting I shouldn't even be informed. "Our *sicarios* took Evaristo right out of his apartment outside Tijuana. He's now at one of our *fincas*, outside the shithole town of La Perla, where he will stay until he gives us the information we need. When I get that information, I will take control over the Tijuana plaza."

"It's too risky," I said.

"And that's why I never asked for your opinion," he stated. "Because I knew that's what you'd say."

"Kidnapping a *federale*, Javier . . ."

"It's already been done," he snapped. "And he will talk. And we will get what we want."

"But I won't get what I want." I let my words hang in the air. I wanted him to snap at them. He didn't, though. Because he knew.

He looked away. "Is that it?" he said softly. "You wanted to yell at me because I'm trying to keep you safe?"

"How is keeping me here safe? You think because Artur and some of the guards will protect me? The only person who can really protect me is you." And what I didn't want to say was that I was afraid that if he left me here, he'd leave me to die. That it could all be part of some plan to get rid of me. Not the best thing to think about your husband, but I couldn't help it. I felt lost with rage and rejection, and everything seemed like a threat.

"The *federales* could come for Evaristo. They may track us. You would be safer here."

"I don't believe you for a second."

"Fine," he said. His voice was calm, but I could tell from the way he spun his watch around his wrist, the way the muscles in his neck looked strained, that he was close to erupting. "Don't believe me. All I ask of you, as my wife, is to stay out of my way."

I couldn't help but scoff. "That's all you ask of me?"

"Do you see me asking anything else?" His glare, his words, were knife sharp.

My head shook slightly as I folded my arms and took a deep breath through my nose to try and steady everything that was about to blurt out. "How about turning a blind eye on all the women – the prostitutes, whores, whatever they are – that you've been fucking behind my back?"

To his credit he kept his mask on, but his eyes flinched slightly. He didn't say anything.

"You think I didn't know?" I said, coming up to him until I was inches away. His spicy scent filled my nose, something that would normally turn me on or bring me peace, but now it was bringing me nothing at all. All my rage was making me feel hollow, like it was carving me out from the middle. Still, I wouldn't let it go. "You're practically doing it in public, flaunting it, as if you want to prove that you can get away with it, as if you can get away with anything! You don't care if it hurts me, or maybe it's that you *want* to hurt me. Well, you're doing it. It kills me, Javier. *Kills me* to know you've been unfaithful."

I watched him closely, my breath heavy, wanting to see something in his eyes, in his soul.

But he only swallowed and said, "You don't understand."

"Fuck you!" I yelled, my hands going against his hard chest and shoving him back. "I understand! What the fuck is there to understand?"

"Calm down," he said, putting his hands over my arms, but I swatted him away and pushed him back again. The fact that he was basically immovable made me angrier.

"At least admit it! Admit it!"

"Fine," he said, his hand coming over my wrist and holding it hard, the pain almost hard to bear. "I admit it. Is that what you want to hear? Does that make you feel better?"

"No," I practically spat at him.

"Does the fact that most of them don't walk out of here alive, does that make you feel better?"

"It makes it worse." I grimaced, shaking my head vigorously. "You're using your sister's death as an excuse to be an asshole, a monster."

That got his attention. His pupils turned to tiny pinpricks in the amber. I regretted it, but there was too much anger and adrenaline rushing through me to back down now. I would not cower to him.

"What did you just say?" he said through clenched teeth.

Of course, now he was mad. He was upset. I practically had to throw rocks at him to get him to feel something.

I straightened up and looked him dead in the eye. "Sometimes I wish your sister died long before I met you, as at least then I could have had an idea of what kind of husband you were going to be."

I didn't see the hit coming. There was just a crack

across my cheek, then stars, then black swirls at the edges of my sight. But I didn't fall down. I think I was too stunned to. I just held my cheek, the skin throbbing, the bone screaming, and stared wide-eyed at Javier.

He had hit me. It was a slap across the face and I probably should have expected it, but he'd never hit me before. For all the painful, twisted things he'd done to me – that we'd done to each other – he'd never done this. It wasn't his style to hit women, a slap or not.

I didn't know what his style was anymore. But now, now I feared it.

I feared him.

He stared at me in a rage, nostrils flaring, his chest heaving, and he jabbed his finger at me while I stood there, holding my cheek, trying to breathe through the shock of it all.

"You do not disrespect my sister like that," he growled, his voice rough and hard and frightening. "She is my family. She was my family. And that's the one thing you obviously are not, because families do not disrespect each other."

I had nothing to say to that. No protests. And the apology I had, because really, I meant Alana no disrespect, was caught in my chest, unable to come out. I just stared at him, wondering what this meant now that I was no longer family.

He watched me for a few moments, the two of us locked in our gazes, with so much anger that the air was electric between us. Then he winced as if pained, and turned away from me.

"Get out," he said quietly. "Please." He paused before screaming, "Go!"

I snapped to it and turned from him as quickly as I could, scuttling out of the room. I didn't even look at Diego as I passed him and ran down the hall, hot tears burning behind my eyes.

I couldn't stay inside, couldn't stand to feel the walls constricting around me. I rushed out of the house and into the dying light. Through the kitchen window I could see Esteban laughing, his hand on Juanito's shoulder, who was smiling. At the time I barely registered it, but I would go back to that image later and wonder why Juanito wasn't in trouble.

I'd wonder about a lot of things.

But as it was, I could only think about myself at that moment and how I was nothing more than a wounded animal. My cheek throbbed but the pain inside was far worse. It was debilitating, hindering my actual movement. I practically staggered all the way to the pond.

The minute I was behind the cover of the palms and reeds, I collapsed to the ground, just feet from my usual spot. The look in Javier's eyes, the sincerity in his words, kept flashing through my mind, stabbing me over and over again.

It wasn't that he wanted to hurt me. It's that he wanted me to hear the truth.

That horrible, bitter truth that seemed to be stuck in my throat, and I was unable to dislodge it no matter how hard I tried to fight.

The tears came, broken at first, just like me. Fragments of sobs. I felt like a little girl, curled up on the floor of the closet after a fight with my parents. My mind even wanted to hold on to the hope that Javier would feel bad for what he'd said, what he'd done, that he would show remorse, worry, that he would come out here looking for me. That he'd scoop me up in his arms and tell me that we would get through this. That we could survive.

That he loved me.

But I knew that wouldn't happen, because he was right. I knew what I was getting into when I married him. I knew he wasn't like most men; in fact, I'd never known anyone like him. So ruthless and cunning, but with tenderness, loyalty, and a twisted code of morals hidden deep inside him.

All the good in him vanished with Alana, and the Javier that was left was a walking ghost. And I had promised, for better or for worse, to stay by his side.

So I was stuck with a man who no longer wanted me to be a part of his life. But there was no way I could up and leave either. How do you leave one of the most powerful men in the country? You don't. You stay and you keep quiet.

And the worst part was, as much as I was falling out of love . . . I still loved him something terrible.

Love was a terrible thing.

I lay down in that grass, mosquitos buzzing at my ears that I didn't bother to swat away. Let them suck me dry, let them take the last of me.

"Luisa?" I heard Esteban's voice in the dark. Footsteps and his presence over me followed. I didn't want to move, didn't want to acknowledge him.

I felt him crouch beside me, and he put his hand on my arm. His skin was soft and warm, and the contact seemed to bring comfort. I would have taken anything as comfort at that point. I realized just then how starved for affection and attention I was.

Before I opened my eyes, I realized that Esteban had been the only person to offer me anything recently. I wasn't sure how I felt about that.

"Luisa," he said again, gently now. I looked up at him and saw nothing but concern in those green eyes of his. They stood out in such sharp contrast to the scar on his cheek. Like Javier, he was a man comprised of both good and bad, with the bad side often pushed to the extreme. But now, when I needed it most, he was offering me the good.

I was such a fool.

"Hey," I said softly.

"What happened?" he asked, hand now on my hand. I didn't brush him away.

"Marital problems," I managed to say. I sighed and slowly lifted myself so I was sitting up. Bats began to fly overhead, snatching up the evening's insects.

"I figured as much," he said, settling down to sit beside me. "I talked to Juanito, hey."

"Oh," I said, suddenly wary. "It wasn't his fault he told me. He thought I knew."

"As you should have. I thought Javier would have at least informed you on when we were leaving and that you would have to stay behind."

I swallowed hard, feeling the pinch again. The rejection.

"I'll talk to him though," he went on. "Let him know how ridiculous he's being. You're a team, you two. You're just as much in this business as he is. You've made some incredibly insightful moves, you know, and I know he needs to be reminded of all this. If it weren't for your own plans and ideas, we wouldn't have the cocaine pipeline from Columbia."

I nodded absently. It was true that I had been contributing to the organization, even finding ways for us to expand. But that was all past tense now. Still, it was nice that Esteban remembered.

"No need to talk to him," I told him. "He won't listen. He doesn't care. He says he's keeping me safe but . . . it's not just that. He doesn't consider me part of the family anymore."

"Then he's an idiot," Esteban said. "There's a time to grieve and there's a time to move on. He can't treat his own wife like she's no longer a part of him. He can't just kick you to the curb. Doesn't he see how wonderful you are?"

His words made my heart flip, just a little. It was jarring to hear anything nice about myself, especially coming from him.

"I don't think he cares if I'm wonderful or not. I'm just in the way."

Esteban shook his head and grabbed my hand again. "Luisa, I wasn't kidding when I told you that you deserve better than this. You do. And you know it. That's what pains me."

I eyed him. "I don't think you know anything about pain."

A stiff smile came across his lips. "No? Maybe you don't know much about me."

He was right about that. I actually knew very little about Esteban Mendoza. Maybe it was about time I started.

He seemed to lean in closer as he said, "You could let me in, hey? I'd like that. I would like you to get to know me. You might like what you find. You might find we have more in common than you think."

There was a glittering intensity in his eyes that I had a hard time looking away from. I tried to remind myself that this was Esteban, the man who decided it was fun to taser me at one point. Granted, I had been trying to escape at the time. Perhaps now, in the position I was in, I couldn't say I'd do anything differently.

Maybe we were alike.

Finally I had to look away, my gaze directed at the base of the palm in front of us. In the grainy twilight I could barely make out tiny red ants scurrying up the tree. They had absolutely no interest in the brutality of our compound, the screams or the breaking hearts or the ending marriages or the lives full of bad choices in order to live selfishly. They didn't care. We were insignificant to them.

Suddenly, Esteban reached out and tucked a strand of hair behind my ear, a disarmingly tender gesture. I couldn't help but freeze, afraid for my eyes to meet his again, afraid that this weird electric current in the air was more than it should have been.

"I won't leave you behind," he said. "You're coming with me tomorrow."

With us, I wanted to say. But I didn't. Because at that moment, what he said sounded real.

I wanted real.

I just wasn't prepared for how real it was going to get.

CHAPTER SIX

Javier

I wouldn't admit many things to people, but I would admit a lot to myself. And when I hit Luisa, I knew I had done wrong. Taken it too far. That I'd become less of a man for doing that.

All my life, I thought I could operate under my own code of morals and ideals. It was no different than most, I supposed. The cop who had to shoot someone in self defense. The soldiers that go to war and raid villages in the name of freedom. Everyone made excuses for what they did, because they believed in it. Because they believed they were in the right.

I had always thought of myself as a somewhat civilized, almost classy, *narco*. I, at least, wanted to bring purpose and grace to what I did. I didn't believe in killing mercilessly. I believed in mercy, in forgiveness, in giving people second chances. I believed in letting people go after I got what I wanted from them.

I believed that to snitch was an outrage, even though we were dealing and fighting and killing each other to work in a billion dollar industry. I believed that religious celebrations were to be respected. I believed that family came first. I believed that women and children were not to be harmed.

I believed a lot of things. I also believed that I would never hit any woman. I knew that it didn't make sense, considering that I could carve up their backs without a sweat. But there was something elegant and sexual about knife play. Whips, chains, ropes? Sure. But to hit was ugly. Brutal. Unbecoming.

Cheap.

So when I found myself striking Luisa across the face, I thought for a moment that perhaps I had lost my mind. Never mind the needless, senseless deaths that were at my hands over the past few months. Never mind that I had broken promises to others and to myself. Dirty, filthy promises. It was then and only then that I knew I had lost who I was. That every moral fiber that I based myself on was threadbare, and I was close, oh so close, to losing all sense of myself forever.

It scared me. I watched her leave the room, and though I was reeling from her own words, the callous ones that reached deep inside me and left a scar, I knew I might have damaged her beyond repair. I could heal myself in time, but could she? Would we? I didn't think so.

I tried to tell myself that it was for the best. That things were so strained between us that we never had a chance of coming back. But the fact was, I didn't want her near me anymore. Not because I didn't love her, but because I didn't want to do that again. I didn't want to see that look in her eyes, the betrayal. Not just because of how I slapped her, but because the truth was, I was a terrible, horrible husband. Unfaithful, cruel, and cold.

I knew she wouldn't be in my bed that night; regardless, I decided to sleep on the small couch in the office.

Perhaps a mistake, considering the big day I had ahead of myself. I needed as much sleep as possible.

But who was I kidding. I didn't even close my eyes for a second, and it had nothing to do with the couch. I kept seeing Luisa in the black and did what I could to absorb the guilt that was threatening to eat me from the inside out. So I did what I always did when it came to those kind of feelings – I blocked them out, shut them down, and told myself I didn't feel a thing.

The next morning there was a knock at the door. I'd just finished doing my morning exercises, push-ups and sit-ups to get the blood flowing, and a small part of me was hoping it was Luisa, perhaps here to apologize, maybe to spare me from apologizing to her.

But it was Este. He came in and gave me the once over.

"You look like shit, *esé*," he said, and though his tone was juvenile as always, he didn't smirk. In fact, he looked rather grave.

"Even on my best days, I'd rather look like shit than you," I answered quickly, reaching for the hand towel and dabbing the last vestiges of sweat from my face. "What do you want? We don't have much time before we push off."

"It's about Luisa," he said. He was hesitant, probing.

I made sure I gave him nothing to go on. "What about her?"

"I don't think . . ." He paused then seemed to compose his thoughts. "It's not safe to leave her here, Javi. I know you trust Artur and the others, and I do too, but I just don't think it sends the right message."

I eyed him curiously. "And what message is that?"

"That you're afraid to bring her along," he said. "Or that you just don't care for her anymore." He seemed to watch me closely. "That makes you both more vulnerable."

"She'll be fine here," I said, even though I was starting to doubt it myself. What if I came back and she was gone? I remembered everything I'd said to her last night but it all still scared me. I wanted to push her away, yet at the same time the thought of losing her entirely wasn't something I could handle at the moment.

"Will she?" He folded his arms across his chest. "How do you know that?"

"Because I would kill anyone who would let harm come to her."

"Be that as it may, she would be dead. And all you'd have is the chance to kill someone who fucked up, which isn't anything new. Listen . . . do you really want that blood on your hands?"

I cocked my head, appraising him, wondering what his angle was here. "Why do you care?"

"Because you're a lot easier to deal with when she's around," he said. "And you listen to her. At least, you used to. She might be a good person to have during the interrogations of Evaristo, just to keep you in check. You don't want to bring out your machete on him, not right away."

"Not ever," I said quickly, knowing we'd already done enough damage when one of the *sicarios* – who was lying in a dusty grave somewhere – took out a *federale* during the raid. "Look, what's been happening . . ." I ran my hand through my hair then shook it off, standing up straight. "I will stay true to my word with Sanchez. I want him because I want someone else. When I get the info, I'll let him go. I'm not stupid enough to anger the *federales*."

"Well, then I believe you," he said. He stepped closer to me and put his hand on my shoulder. I eyed it warily. "I don't often get hunches, Javi, but when I do I listen to them. Trust me when I say that leaving her here would be a big mistake. You need her still, even though you think you don't. She's more than just your wife – she's good for all of us."

Well, here was something fucking new. Esteban being sincere and somewhat emotional. I wasn't sure I liked it. In fact, I didn't like it at all. Emotions got you killed in this business. But he was making sense, and I knew that if something happened to Luisa, I'd never forgive myself. Besides, the ranch was no less safe than here.

I just nodded and stepped away from his hand. "You go tell her, then. She needs to be packed up in twenty minutes."

He grinned at me like he'd won the lottery and quickly left the room. I stood there in the middle of my office for a good minute or two, my brain trying to focus on something in Este's smile. When I couldn't figure out what it was, I started packing.

Helicopter travel comes with some risks, but you can't beat the immediate payoff. I hopped into the craft with Diego, Esteban, Luisa, and our trusted pilot, and headed off to the *finca* in the Chihuahuan Desert, while the rest of the crew would come via a protected convoy of armed SUVs.

Luisa was sitting beside me, staring out the window at the scenery below with wide eyes as the landscape changed from the verdant mountains of Sinaloa into the fawn-colored desert as we headed deeper inland.

To me, there was nothing more beautiful than the desert. While others found it boring, I found it stark, rough, and relentless, filled with a million hidden things that wanted to kill you. The desert demanded our respect, and in return, it would clear your head and remind you how damn insignificant you really were.

I needed that sometimes. Sitting here in one of my nicest white linen suits, being chauffeured by one of the many helicopters that I owned, a whole world at my feet, sometimes it was good to humble me, just a bit. Humility only made me want to work harder.

Luisa shifted in her seat, trying to get a better look at one of the craggy canyons that opened wide and long below, rust, taupe, and coffee-colored sands stretching into the distance. She was wearing a short but simple black dress that lifted as she strained to see, and her perfect legs, toned and golden brown, were on display.

I felt my dick twitch in my pants and took a deep breath through my nose. Aside from the other night, I hadn't been this close to her in what felt like forever, and it was hard not to just flip her on her knees and maul her right here. It didn't matter that we weren't alone, the *patron* could get away with more than just murder.

Luisa would have allowed a public fuck under normal

circumstances, but today she wasn't even looking me in the eye. I couldn't blame her. Even though she did a good job with her makeup, you could still see the puffy red mark on her cheek. She kept her hair on it, flowing dramatically over that side of her face, but I knew it was there. We all did.

Besides, it was still for the best to keep her as far away from me as possible. Even though she was coming to the ranch, she would be put in her own room, and I would be spending as much time with Evaristo as needed.

I wondered how long and what it would take to make him talk. Perhaps he'd be a pussy like so many agents and cough it up right away. After all, what was it to him if we nabbed Hernandez? One less *narco* to deal with – isn't that what they wanted? Though the thought of him giving in made the whole situation a little less fun.

I looked at the rest of the cabin and saw Esteban leering over Luisa in the same way that I had. I frowned, watching him carefully, waiting for him to remember where he was and that he wasn't supposed to ogle the *patron*'s wife.

Eventually, the corner of Este's mouth lifted slightly, as if he were smiling to himself. The expression in his eyes, though, was anything but happy. It was carnal, something I wasn't used to seeing from him. I swallowed the slight sense of unease I had, telling myself that I was prepared for anything.

It wasn't long until I spotted the ranch on the horizon. I nudged Luisa with my shoulder, and she glanced at me with hardened eyes.

I nodded at it. "There she is. Your new home for the next while."

She nodded, silent, and looked back.

The ranch was located down a five kilometer dirt road off the desolate highway sixty-seven. The closest town – La Perla – was nothing more than a few houses and dusty shops, a hard place where the locals would lean back against their adobe houses and squint into the sun, beer in hand, wondering where the years had gone.

We flew close to the sandy road, following it as it led to the compound, the dust whirring beneath the rotors. I'd picked out the spot myself last year when we snatched the property from a *narco* who wasn't following the rules. There were other *fincas*, properties to hide in, but I liked this one the best. It wasn't all harsh desert either. There was a wash that had some water trickling through it during the winter, and mesquite trees lined it, providing shade. The rest of the property sat beneath the rocky crag that hid a family of coyotes at its base and a golden eagle's nest at the top.

The chopper touched down on the landing pad, which was located between the long garage and the barn. The horses in the outer pasture ran away from the sound, their tails flying in the wind.

"Oh," Luisa said excitedly, and when she turned to look at me, I saw the woman I fell in love with. "I didn't know you had horses."

"*We* have horses," I told her, tempted to put my hand on her leg, but not willing to risk public rejection. "Evelyn takes care of them and she will take care of us."

Evelyn Aguilar was the mother of one of our *narcos* who was captured and tortured last year, probably by the Zetas. After he was found, I made a vow to keep his mother safe and employed. Evelyn lived by herself out here, looking after the ranch and the horses, and filling in as a housekeeper and cook whenever the ranch was being used. So far, I'd only come out here once and just for a few days, but her debt to me was deep, and she had waited on me hand and foot.

Luisa seemed to remember that she despised me, so her look became hard and she turned away, as if she was too stubborn to let herself get excited. I'd known she was that stubborn but I hoped later on when I told her she could go riding that the look would come back into her eyes again.

The chopper landed in a cloud of dust and was quickly approached by Borrero and Morales, two members of my security team and the top *sicarios* who carried out the kidnapping of Evaristo. Aside from Diego, they were the best of the best. It's too bad that *federale* had to die during the event, but I knew that hadn't been their fault. They were far too smart for that.

Borrero, tall and lanky with a skinny moustache and a penchant for wearing red, shook my hand as I got out of the helicopter. "You got here quicker than we expected."

"Is that bad?" I asked as I walked away from the whirling sand. I nodded at Morales who was standing with his arms folded and he nodded back. If Borrero was red, Morales was black. He'd grown up in the desert and then later spent his formative years as a chief instructor for the military training camps that took place out in places like this. His skin was dark and weather-beaten, and he always wore a black cowboy hat and leather boots. Like Diego, he had a sordid past I didn't care to know much about and was the kind of man you wanted – *needed* – on your side.

"Not bad," Borrero said, following me. "Sanchez is still unconscious though."

"I'm sure I'll find a way to wake him up." I looked over my shoulder to make sure Luisa was all right. Esteban had her hand and was helping her out of the helicopter, her hair flying around her like a black cape as the rotors slowed. "Where is he?"

"In the tunnel," Morales said as he fished a cigarette out of his front pocket. "Thought it would be a more agreeable place for him to wake up. Especially for whatever you have planned."

All *fincas* have at least one escape route. This ranch had a tunnel leading out from behind the hot water tank in the basement that went all the way behind the mountain and into the wash. The other end opened up by a crop of prickly pear on the riverbank and under a camo net, shielded by *nopales* and tarbush. There was a black, bulletproof truck, tank full and ready to go the distance.

Remembering my manners, I stopped and waited for Luisa and the rest before approaching the house. There, on the long wraparound porch out front, was Evelyn, waving at us like an old frontier wife. Her greying hair was pulled back in braids and she wore a long peasant dress.

"Welcome," she said, clapping her hands together. She had to be excited that she had company for once. Living out here must be lonely, though the solitude was one of the reasons I liked it so much. Having an entourage around you twenty-four seven was exhausting and I wondered if I could ever truly be on my own without someone watching me, whether for my own protection or otherwise.

"You must be Luisa," she said to Luisa as she came forward, holding out her hand in politeness. Evelyn pulled her into a tight hug, and I had to chuckle at that. Evelyn was round and fluffy, like a stuffed pancake, and about sixty-four, though she looked much older. Nothing aged you as much as grief. Even now I was seeing more silver hairs at my temples and a line between my brows that hadn't been there before.

"The place looks great," I said to Evelyn respectfully. "I can tell we are in good hands."

She beamed at that, ever grateful to me, and then to my relief she took Luisa and started giving her a tour of the sprawling ranch house. Luisa didn't need to be a part of what would happen next.

After they'd gone, I looked to Borrero and Morales. "Show me to the *federale*." I glanced at Esteban and said, "You should get yourself settled."

He raised a brow but didn't say anything to that. Esteban wasn't new to the interrogation process, but still, I felt better not having him there.

I followed Borrero and Morales, with Diego behind me as always, down the hall and stairs to the basement. It was clean, dark, and cool down here, with a metal chair in the middle of the room and rope coiled underneath it. Two other chairs were stacked in the corner beside a sink and a storage chest. There was an arsenal of depravity in that chest; I had spent a full day here last time picking out the best means of torture and filling it up just so.

The closet that contained the hot water tank looked like any other, complete with a mop and bucket – crucial for washing away the blood – and you could barely fit inside it. But Borrero squeezed past the heater and pushed at the bricks on the wall behind it. A hidden door opened with a groan, the grating sound of bricks grinding against each other, and soon he disappeared.

We followed him – Diego grunting because his stomach could barely squeeze past the heater – and then we were in a long, dirt tunnel that stretched straight out for a few yards before curling around to the left. Faint lights lined the ceiling, and in the middle of the tunnel was Evaristo, hands and feet bound, tied with a metal leash to a chair. He had a ball-gag in his mouth, and his head was slumped over, his eyes closed.

In person he looked a lot younger than I had thought. Maybe everyone looked a bit younger when they had their eyes closed. Innocent, almost, though I knew the boy-man couldn't be where he was with the *federales* and still maintain his innocence. They might have been fighting on the other side, but they were still capable of being as twisted and immoral as the cartels were. At least we had a code of conduct. They pretended they had one and called it justice.

Beside Evaristo on the ground were two buckets of water and a large metal toolbox. I wondered what my *sicarios* had selected for me and what they'd already used themselves.

As Diego closed the brick wall behind us, I went over to Evaristo and looked him over closely. One of his eyes and the corresponding cheekbone was black and blue, and there was a trail of dried blood beneath his nose. His dark hair was matted down, maybe with sweat, maybe with blood. Other than that though, he didn't look half bad.

"He got a little frisky when we first took him," Morales explained. "I roughed him up a bit, knocked him out."

"He's been out ever since?"

He shook his head and puffed on his cigarette, the smoke wafting down the tunnel, trying to find fresh air. "He came to but we put him back under. The more disoriented he is, the better. It's been a few hours though since we last gave him a hit, so I'm sure you can wake him and get him talking."

I was sure about the first part but not the second.

Before I did anything to wake him, I crouched down and inspected the tool box. At the top was a small battery pack and rod. It was the typical narco route for interrogations, but it was a staple because it worked so damn well.

I picked it up then nodded at Borrero and the bucket. "Wake him."

Borrero came over and tipped the water over Evaristo's head. He immediately jerked in his seat, blue eyes wide and crazed, the gag sucked into his mouth as he inhaled hard. Now he looked older. This was good. I didn't like the idea of having to torture a boy, even though I would do it to get what I needed.

As Evaristo jerked against the metal leash and fought against the bonds, I stooped over in front of him and looked him in the eye.

"Welcome," I said to him. "I think you know who I am. And I know who you are. And we're going to play a little game, you and I. I think you're very good at playing games, aren't you *federale*?"

Water streamed down Evaristo's face. His eyes widened at first then narrowed as he seemed to recognize who I was. Of course he recognized me. I was their number one target, and it had just been his rotten luck that he was dispatched to go after the Tijuana cartel instead. Too much pressure from the DEAs in California. They wanted the drugs to stop appearing in their backyards but hadn't quite figured out that all the drugs came from somewhere.

"Ah, you do know me," I said, reaching out to brush his hair off his forehead. He flinched at my touch, as he should, and I was briefly, uncomfortably, reminded of Luisa. I swallowed that down and kept my focus on him. "So, the question is, how long do you want to play this game? You can make it really easy for yourself. You can talk right away and I won't even have to use this." I lifted the battery pack. He didn't seem affected in the slightest, which was admirable considering he *knew* what it could do. "I also give you my word, and you should know my word is good. If you give me what I want, I will let you go. I won't drive you up to the PFM building in Mexico City, but I will let you walk out of here alive. You understand?"

Evaristo didn't nod but I could see in his eyes that he did understand. And he didn't like it. He was already prepared to put up a front and he had no idea what I was going to ask of him.

"We're not interested in your organization," I told him. "We're interested in your information. I want everything you have on Angel Hernandez. I know you know where he is, but you haven't been given the bureaucratic authority to capture him yet. What a pain in the ass bureaucracy is, am I right? They couldn't even save your own sorry little ass. You wanted Hernandez and you got me instead." I put one hand on the ball gag and the other held the battery in view. "Are you ready to talk?"

He gave me nothing. I pulled down the gag and he gulped in air.

"Well?" I prodded.

When he caught his breath, his eyes sliced into mine. "Fuck you," he said, spittle flying.

I raised my brow. "They've trained you well." I sighed and straightened up, looking down at the battery pack. "I think I'll keep you ungagged. Screaming gets me off." I shot him a smile. "And you will scream. They can't train that out of you."

I looked over my shoulder at my security team. "Any of you bothered by screaming?" I asked them, knowing they didn't mind it at all. Morales grinned eerily.

Within minutes, Borrero and Morales stripped Evaristo naked, threw more water on him, and I had attached the *picana* prod to the battery pack. Diego held the pack, in charge of the voltage, and I waved the prod at Evaristo's neck. It was a good, sensitive place to start. "Let's see what you've got."

What Evaristo had was a huge capacity for pain and screaming. Can't say it didn't turn me on.

CHAPTER SEVEN

Luisa

"This is where you will be staying with Mr. Bernal," the kindly Evelyn Aguilar told me, opening a door to a very spacious master bedroom that seemed to take up the whole end of the house. I stepped in gingerly and looked at the rustic furniture and terracotta tile floors. It was simple, yet I knew that the furniture only looked shabby and probably had cost a fortune. The view was of the south and the crooked mountains rising from the desert floor. The windows were small and deep-set into the adobe walls, so the view was partially obscured. I knew it was that way for our protection, from intruders and from the desert sun.

I gave Evelyn a small smile. "It's lovely. But I'm afraid I require a room of my own."

Thankfully she just nodded and said, "Oh yes, come with me," and didn't question why I wouldn't be sleeping with my husband. Perhaps this was normal to her. Perhaps when Javier had stayed here before, he hadn't quite been alone.

My stomach clenched at the thought. Even though I had known about his callous infidelity before I confronted him, the fact that he fessed up to it so easily, and without any remorse, continued to make me sick. He knew he'd hurt me and he just didn't care.

Or perhaps he did. After all, he decided to allow me on the trip to the ranch in the end. But it had been Esteban who told me that this morning, not him, and I was starting to think it had been Esteban's idea as well.

I couldn't pretend that I hadn't noticed his roving eyes on me, either. Just this morning as I sat outside on the front bench and sipped my coffee, wearing just a camisole and shorts, he couldn't keep his eyes off me as he told me the news. Same with on the helicopter. Esteban had been ballsy to do it in front of my husband as well. Not that I felt bad about it – Javier deserved that and then some – but it made me a little uneasy about being around Esteban now. He'd been my closest companion over these last horrible months, but the sexually charged looks threatened to push our relationship in another direction.

It scared me. It also made my heart flip and my thighs clench, just a little bit. Enough that I noticed. Enough that I liked it. And that scared me even more. I wasn't in the right frame of mind to handle any sort of temptation like that.

I wasn't really in the right frame of mind to handle anything. And now I was in the middle of Mexico, in a hot, unyielding desert, wondering if it had been the right decision to come here, even though it's what I had wanted. I had felt trapped and isolated at home, but at least it was still my home. This place was a stranger to me and I felt like I was at its mercy.

"Here we go," Evelyn said, pushing open another door further down one of the halls. It was much smaller, but it had an en suite bathroom, and the heavily locked French door looked like it opened to the wraparound porch. I could already see myself having my morning coffee here and watching the horses run in the distance. At least there was that.

"Thank you, it's perfect," I said and her face lit right up. Minutes later she returned with my bags – I didn't know how to pack light but she was surprisingly strong – and I shut the door behind her, collapsing onto the bed. The mattress was on the firm side but I found myself drifting off within minutes.

I'm not sure how long I was out but the screaming woke me up. I knew it had been coming – I'd learned to accept the screams as progress – but they still rattled me. I lay there, breathing hard, having a hard time seeing the progress in any of this. I felt like I was just spinning my wheels.

And the screaming didn't stop, no matter how long I tried to wait it out. I'd been filled in by Esteban about the man in the tunnel, *federale* agent Evaristo Sanchez, and I still thought the risk we were taking was too great. I didn't take any pleasure in this, because whatever horrible things Javier and his men were doing to the young agent, I knew that it would be used against us one day.

Finally, I'd had enough. I couldn't fall asleep, and my heart would not stop racing. I got up, slipping on a pair of suede, low-heeled boots and hat, and headed out into the hallway. I passed by the spacious kitchen with white-washed walls and exposed wood beams on the ceiling.

Evelyn was busy chopping vegetables and cheerfully

humming a *corrida* tune to herself. I told her I was going for a walk, and she warned me to be careful about rattle-snakes. I merely pointed at my boots. The desert hills around San Jose del Cabo where I grew up were equally as dangerous and I knew how to handle myself.

The moment I stepped outside, the thick air blanketing me like an open oven, the screams began to fade. I headed straight over to the peeling wood fence that housed the horses. The fence seemed to go on forever, dipping over a low hill and fading off into the distance.

I leaned against it, careful not to get splinters on my arms, and a breeze swept off the hills, hot but smelling of hay. A dapple grey horse grazed on tufts of dry grass, its tail swishing. I smiled despite myself. For a moment, I imagined what it would be like to hop on its back and get the hell out of here. Just me and the horse and the desert, no fear, no constraints. Just freedom.

I knew I wouldn't get far. If I didn't succumb to the relentless heat and the fact that my cell phone didn't work out here and I had no idea where I was going, Javier and his men would find me in minutes.

Unless he didn't, I told myself, and before I knew what I was doing, I was stepping through the fence. *Unless he couldn't care less where you went. Don't be so naïve.*

I picked up some hay that was gathered near a shanty at the gate and headed across the paddock, hoping I wouldn't scare the horse. There were other horses here, spread out in small herds, maybe twenty in total, but this horse was the closest. And alone.

"You and me both," I said under my breath as I quietly approached him.

He kept his eye on me as I came close, but only raised his head at the last minute. I held out the hay, perhaps too fast, and the horse took off, spooked.

I sighed as I watched him gallop away until he disappeared over the hill. I looked behind me at the house and clenched the hay in my hand. I had nothing better to do.

I set off after the horse, determined to win over something in my life. I went over the hill and saw the land gently slope toward a dried up riverbed where mesquite and acacia grew. The horse had paused down there, grazing on yellow flowers that grew in the sparse shade.

I headed after it, watching my feet carefully as my boots navigated the loose rocks and hard sand. Scorpions scuttled away from my shadow.

It was cool down by the wash, even with the water all dried up. The horse had his head up, watching me, but I thought I saw some kind of understanding in his large dark eyes. I decided to stay put, holding the hay at my side.

"It's okay, boy," I told him softly. "I won't hurt you."

The horse watched me then slowly resumed chewing before it lowered its head again and went back to plucking the flowers off the shrub, its lips nipping them delicately.

I didn't know how long I stood there for, just watching the gorgeous animal. If I couldn't hop on his back and ride off into the sunset to start a new life, maybe I could convince Javier to bring him back home with us. We had the barn that had the pigs back on our compound, and we could easily use one of the stalls for him.

I was just about to come up with a name for him – *Bandito* – when he slowly took a few steps toward me, head down, seeming to hone in on the hay. I carefully held out my hand and he took the hay from me.

"Aren't you handsome?" I asked him, wondering if he'd run if I tried to pet him.

But before I had the answer, he suddenly raised his head, the whites of his eyes showing, and then turned on a dime, galloping off and leaving me in the dust again.

I coughed and turned around, wondering what had startled him.

Coming down the slope was Esteban, his eyes sharply fixed on me.

"What are you doing?" he asked, jogging the last little bit. I was having a hard time pretending not to notice that his shirt was off and slung over one shoulder. He was fit, all sculpted abs and a deep tan. I looked to his feet and saw that he had slip-on sneakers instead of flip-flops on for once.

"I was getting to know the horses," I told him as he stopped right in front of me. He smelled liked sweat. It wasn't a terrible smell, it was actually rather primal. His skin glistened and I looked up at his face, the brim of my hat shielding me from the intense sun.

"You shouldn't wander too far," he said. "The desert is no place for a woman like you."

My brows rose. "A woman like me? And what kind of woman am I?"

"One that shouldn't be so bold, not in places like this. There are many things out here that can kill you, hey."

I rolled my eyes and turned, heading down to the wash,

seeking the shade. "Oh please, you think I didn't grow up with the desert in my backyard?"

"I'm sure you did," he said, and I could hear him trailing after me. "But you're not a little girl on the Baja anymore. You're a queen. And you need to treat yourself like one."

"Queen," I muttered, and sat down on a large, wide rock beneath a tall mesquite. "I doubt a queen would have contemplated escaping on a horse across the desert."

He sat down beside me, his arm pressing against mine. I stiffened, trying to relax with him so near but I couldn't.

"Oh, I bet many queens try to escape. Few make it. Didn't you ever see *Roman Holiday*?"

I gave him an incredulous look, trying not to smile. "With Audrey Hepburn? Badly dubbed in Spanish?"

"Yes," he said, grinning at me. "She was a princess, and she wanted nothing more than to escape. I think it's very common." He leaned in closer, his gaze suddenly intensifying. "I could be your Gregory Peck, hey."

I managed a weak smile. "You're not handsome enough," I told him.

I thought he would have looked insulted at that, but instead he put his hand on the back of my neck, holding me there. "I may not be handsome, but I sure can fuck better than him."

I couldn't respond to that. I couldn't do anything as he leaned in and kissed me hard and wet on the mouth. His tongue slipped in through my lips, and I found myself opening my mouth to let him in.

This was so terribly wrong and I knew I had to stop it.

It was wrong.

It shouldn't happen.

It couldn't happen.

But for that one second, I kissed him back. The feel of his tongue against mine was slick, hot, and electrifying, and every nerve in my body was on fire, like the sun above the mesquite.

I couldn't remember the last time Javier had kissed me.

Just that thought made my heart knot up, bringing me back to reality. I put my hands on Esteban's shoulders and pushed him back, breaking off the kiss.

I wouldn't play this game with him.

I wouldn't give in to my urges, the same urges he was preying on, trying to get me to break, to offer me affection and attention when I'd had none.

His gaze was just as intense as before and he was breathing heavily. "Don't tell me that you didn't want that. That you haven't thought about it." He took my hand and placed it on the crotch of his shorts so I could feel how thick and hard he was.

I felt dizzy, out of breath. The sun, the heat; it was too much.

I couldn't let this happen.

I pulled my hand back and got to my feet, unsteady. "I have to go back."

He got up too, grasping my wrist tightly so I couldn't walk away without a fight.

"Let go or I'll scream," I said, wishing my voice didn't sound broken.

"We both know no one will hear you," he warned. "We also know that you won't. Because I'm not doing anything wrong. And neither are you."

"I'm married," I said feebly.

I took my vows under oath, under god.

If I didn't have my morals, what did I have at all?

"I *know*," he said. "And is this what you want for the rest of your married life? The lonesome queen who pines in her castle for someone she can't have – her husband? All while the king has his share of whoever he wants to fuck."

The truth hurt. And it didn't matter how many times I heard it, it still had that fatal sting, like the scorpions in the shadows.

But I couldn't do this. I had to be good. I had to honor my vows. Without them, I had nothing. Someone had to believe in love.

I had to believe.

Even if I was a fool.

"I have to go," I told him, but Esteban held tighter, till my wrist began to ache. Why were all the men around me so set on pain? Why did I always feel so powerless against them?

Why did they stir up trapped, dark feelings inside me, the ones I always wanted to bury?

"I wouldn't go back if I were you," he said, his look cautioning. "Not while Javier is occupied."

The mention of his name made me flinch a little, and I wished I couldn't still feel Esteban's rough lips on mine, taste his sweat. So much guilt already for so little.

"I can handle it," I told him. "Sadly, I'm used to torture."

"Oh no, Luisa," he said, tilting his head sympathetically. "He's done with Evaristo for today. It's the women . . ."

My throat felt like it was starting to close up. "Women? What women?"

"You didn't see the cars pull in?" he asked, and when I shook my head he sighed. "I guess it was good you were out here, then."

"What cars? From where?" I asked, alarmed.

"He had them brought in from Durango. Can't have a proper *finca* without the *putas* for everyone. Especially your husband. Don't take it too personally, though, I'm sure it's no reflection on you."

It was stupid and foolish to feel as devastated as I did, like my heart was being cut from my chest. I didn't even know I had a heart left after everything already.

I looked away and Esteban tugged me toward him. "Hey," he said softly, finally releasing my wrist and putting his hands on both sides of my face. It took everything I had not to break down. "I'm sorry. I shouldn't have told you. I didn't think this would bother you anymore. But your heart, Luisa. You have such a good, big heart. And it breaks me to know you wasted it all on him."

I couldn't meet Esteban's eyes. I didn't want to see my reflection in them.

"Javier is *patron* now," he said. "He's got everything he wants. And what do you have? What do you deserve? I've seen him around you. I know you sleep in separate rooms. He won't even touch you. It's like you disgust him."

"Esteban, please," I cried out, feeling my eyes fill with tears. "I'm hurting enough."

"I agree," he said. "And it's time to stop. Look at me." I couldn't. I shook my head and the tears spilled.

"Look at me, Luisa." The pressure on my face increased,

and finally I let my blurry vision meet his intense stare. "Javier is a changed man and he's not coming back. You're stuck in this marriage with him for the rest of your life, chained to a monster. His pride is too big to let you go, and if you go anyway, you won't last long."

I didn't want to believe any of that, but I knew it was true. I was sewn into this life now.

"And no other man is going to want to fuck you, to be with you, when you're married to one of the most powerful and dangerous men in the country. No other man but me."

My eyes widened and his gaze seared like the desert heat. "I can give you everything that he can't," he said. "I can give you more than he ever could."

He kissed me again, holding me in place, and this time I fought more, because to give in would be to believe all the horrible things he'd just said. But Esteban was relentless, his tongue fucking my mouth as he pressed his erection against my hip. One hand reached under and pulled up my dress, his fingers trying to slip between my legs.

But I couldn't, I couldn't.

"No," I told him, my words muffled against his lips, realizing we were in the damn desert of all places.

"There is no more *no* anymore," he said. Suddenly he shoved me down so I was on my knees, and I cried out in pain as the rocks cut into my skin. "Shut up," he said, and I raised my head to see him take his cock out of his pants. "Suck it. See what I taste like."

I was too stunned, my knees throbbing, but he made a fist in my hair and yanked me forward. Nearly powerless to protest, I took him in my hands and into my mouth. His salt hit my tongue, but he thrust his hips forward until he was as far in me as he could go. I nearly gagged.

"God, you're fucking beautiful," he said through a moan. "Such a queen. You suck so good but I'm going to fuck you so much better. So much better than him."

It was then that I realized how little choice I had. How little choice I'd always had. For my whole life I'd been stuck between a rock and a hard place. Working tirelessly for my parents – I'd had no choice in that, not really. I either did it or they died. Marrying Salvador, I'd had no choice either. He would have killed me and my parents if I had said no to him. Going off with Javier had been the best choice I'd ever had, because finally I had been in the position to go off on my own and live my own life.

But I was an idiot who fell in love.

Love turned on me and broke me. I lost the love of my husband along with his desire and respect.

And now I had another impossible choice. I could protest, I could try and walk away from this situation and pretend that I didn't want it, that I hadn't thought about it, that I didn't need what Esteban was offering me. I could walk away . . . if he let me.

Or I could give in. I could let that bad, dirty part of me come out to play and toss my morals out the door. My morals that had done nothing but keep me frozen in time, a loser of the heart. My morals were nothing more than a fucking cage.

My morals would hold me hostage for life.

You don't have a choice, I told myself, though deep

down I knew I did, and I knew the one I was about to make was the bad one – the wrong one.

I thought about Javier and the women and the love I'd never have again.

That touch.

That intimacy.

I had something like that now.

To take it was my choice. Finally, *I* had a choice.

The guilt went and slithered off somewhere, like the snakes on the desert floor, taking my morals with it. My soul went on leave.

I took Esteban in, my hands pumping him, unsurely at first, but then my grip tightened as I shed all inhibition, filled with the perverse need to continue. I was getting off on this, despite how badly I needed to stop.

"Oh, so good," he went on, slamming in harder, my teeth razing him, but he only seemed to get thicker. "Is my big cock making your little cunt wet? Is it? Don't get too slick though, gorgeous, I want it to hurt a little. I want you to feel every single inch of me from the inside. I want you to scream."

Suddenly he pulled out of my mouth, and with his hand on my forehead, shoved me backward into the dirt. My head struck the edge of a rock and I cried out again, feeling wetness in my hair. As everything swung around me in a dizzying wave, I looked at the rock to see blood on it. I was bleeding from the head.

But Esteban didn't care. He was pushing up my dress around my waist and pushing my thong to the side, ready to enter me.

"Stop. I hit my head," I tried to say, but then he was

on me and my head was pressed back into the rough sand.

"You won't care about that soon," he said, his lips on mine and kissing me feverishly as he guided himself into me. He was right; it did hurt. The friction was painful as he jammed himself inside to the hilt.

I gasped, trying to breathe through it, but he was merciless and thrust harder, the rocks digging into my back, my ass, everywhere. I was aching sharply and all over until he put his fingers in my mouth, getting them wet, and then placed them at my clit. Just the simple pressure made the pain melt into pleasure.

"I've wanted you for so long," he groaned against my neck, biting me. All I could think was that I was going to look like a real wreck after this, like a truck had hit me. I wondered what Javier would say. And then I realized how much I wanted him to say something; I wanted him to care.

My wants were very dangerous.

"So fucking long I've dreamed of this and all the things I wanted to do," he said, nipping my lower lip between his teeth. "You do realize this is just the beginning and not the end. I will own you, Luisa. And you will be mine."

I didn't know how to feel about that. I didn't know how to feel about anything until desire was throbbing through me, and all I knew was that I wanted it more, more, more. The sex, the wanting, the needing. I welcomed it through my veins, swept away by the passion, the delirious lust. It was making me feel something good for once. It was erasing all the pain on my skin and the pain deep inside.

I put my hands on Esteban's firm ass and drove my nails in, wanting him in deeper, wanting the feeling to never end. I felt wild and free and righteous. I had been owed this. The sweat poured off him and onto me, soaking my dress, the sun high in the sky behind him, waiting to dry it off.

Somewhere in the distance I think I heard a rattlesnake, but there wasn't even fear anymore. There was just this yearning that might never end, and I was lost, lost, lost in someone else as they were lost in me.

"Fuck," Esteban grunted, and I felt him strain as he came. "Fuck, fuck, fuck."

It was enough to set me off. I came hard, crying out a bunch of nonsense that seemed to soar up into the sky, feeling so much heat expand on me and in me. I was yanked into an undertow, not knowing which way was up and which way would have me drown.

I was so sated that I didn't care if I drowned or not. I just lay there, bleeding and broken and bruised on the ground, while Esteban lay on top of me, sweat pooling between us. We both tried to catch our breath, the air dusty and dry and filling our lungs. I felt like my heart would never slow down.

Finally Esteban raised his head and peered at me, a sloppy smile on his face. He tucked my hair behind my ear and said, "You certainly don't look like a queen right now."

I couldn't help but smile back. "Some queens like getting dirty."

"Dirty queen," he mused. "That's you all right. But from now on, you're my dirty queen. No one else's."

I swallowed hard, trying to figure out just what he was expecting. Was this not just a fuck, a heat of the moment thing? Or did Esteban expect this to continue? Was I to keep him as a lover just as Javier kept lovers of his own?

I wasn't prepared to entertain that just yet. Not now, when my emotions were high and my intentions were running away on me.

And then the guilt hit me straight on like a freight train.

I panicked and quickly got to my feet, pulling down my dress and wiping off the dust. I tried to get myself looking normal, but the dirt clung to me, as did the pebbles which were nearly embedded in my skin. I couldn't get it off, couldn't get clean. My hands whacked all over my limbs.

"Hey," Esteban said as he got to his feet. "Luisa."

I kept wiping at myself and everything started to spin.

He reached out and grabbed my arms.

"I can't get clean," I said, my voice shaking. "I can't get the dirt off."

"Calm down," he said. "Turn around, I'll help you."

I turned around, my eyes fixing on the bloodstained rock. What had I done? How would I explain the wound on my head? Javier would know, he'd *know*.

Este wiped down the back of me then said, "There. Some cuts and scrapes, but you can tell him you fell down, *if* he even notices."

"He'll notice," I said. He'd see the guilt on my face, the guilt that was pouring over me like thick black tar. "Esteban, we can never, ever tell him. We can never tell him what we did."

He zipped up his shorts and gave me a wry look. "You think he'd be hurt?"

I shook my head, even though I wasn't quite sure. "He can't know."

"I know," he said calmly. "If he knew, he would kill you."

I swallowed, wondering if that was the truth. "He'd kill you too," I pointed out.

But Esteban just smiled.

I reached behind my head and looked at the blood on my fingers.

He reached out and grabbed my hand, sticking my bloody fingers in his mouth. He slowly drew them out and said, "All clean. Shall we head back?"

Going back now sounded like the most dangerous prospect in the world. "I can't," I said. "I can't."

"You can, and you will. If he asks, if anyone asks, tell them you took a tumble." He jerked his chin to the hill. "You go back first. I'll follow later."

I took in a deep breath and wished the pain inside me, that knot in my heart, would have stayed away after the sex. But it was back. "Okay." I paused. "We won't ever tell."

"No, we won't," Esteban said. "Now go. And remember what I told you about him. Just go straight to your room and take a shower. It will be easier on you that way."

I nodded, staring at him for a moment before I turned and headed up the hill. It took me a while to head back to the ranch house, but then again it felt like I was sleep-walking or in a dream.

I couldn't believe what had just happened. How weak

I had been to commit adultery, and with Esteban no less. How foolish and stupid I was to take such a dumb chance. I had a good life. Maybe I didn't have love anymore, or sex without having to practically beg for it, and maybe my husband was a totally different person. But I had money and security.

But it was amazing how little money and security mattered in the long run when your own heart wasn't being loved.

I had no illusions about Esteban loving me. I knew he didn't. I knew that he might hold some affection for me and that perhaps his attraction to me was based more on one-upping Javier, having what he had, that envy he felt for his boss.

I also had no illusions about loving Esteban. I didn't. I didn't even know if I liked him. But he had been there out in the desert, and he knew what I had needed before I did.

The fact was, I still loved Javier even though it was futile and painful to do so. I was also sure that a part of my own heart was breaking over what I had just done. But despite that, I also knew that I would eventually come to terms with it. And one day I'd be forced to make another choice: to make peace with my life the way it was.

Or to do it again.

I was too afraid of what my answer would be.

When I got closer to the house though, the guilt and dirt I felt on my soul waned a bit. Because there were cars parked outside, and from somewhere in the house I heard a girlish giggle.

I carefully walked down the porch, my footsteps heavy from the boots, and went into the kitchen. Evelyn looked up at me in concern.

"Luisa, what happened?" She quickly put a plate away then scurried over to me.

"It's fine," I said, surprised at how calm I suddenly felt. "I was following the horses and I slipped on the hill, tumbled for a bit. I'm okay. Just embarrassed."

She didn't seem to believe me so I deftly changed the subject. "Who came in the cars? I thought I heard a female laugh."

Evelyn looked grave. "You know how boys are," she said. "They wanted company."

I gave her a stiff smile. "I'm going to go shower. I might skip lunch if that's okay with you."

She nodded, seeming to understand.

As I went down the hall, I heard the laughter again. Two girls now. Thankfully they weren't coming from Javier's room but someone else's. I quickly went into my small bedroom, locked the door, and went into the bathroom. I avoided my reflection in the mirror and stripped, then got in the shower.

I couldn't get the water hot enough. I turned it hotter and hotter, until the air filled with steam and I was sure it was scalding me.

But still, I felt like I couldn't get clean.

CHAPTER EIGHT

Esteban

E steban watched as Luisa climbed up the hill and out of his sight. Though she didn't know it yet, she really did look like she'd been ravaged. It pleased him to no end to know that it was all because of him. That he finally had done it. And even though fucking her was a means to an end, it wasn't half bad.

Actually, Luisa was better than he had expected. Sure, she wasn't wild, but he hadn't really given her much choice out here. And she protested, which he liked the most. In some ways he wanted her to really fight back. The fact that she hadn't meant that she'd been thinking about him, needing a good roll in the hay, something he'd only hoped for once.

In time, because they would do this again and again, it would become too much for her. It sickened him to think that Javier had probably screwed her six kinky ways from Sunday, with all his affinity for ropes and knives and asphyxiation. Because of that, Luisa was a hardened champ when it came to pushing boundaries and limits. But eventually Esteban would take it too far, and he relished the moment she became afraid of him, the moment she'd ask him to stop and he wouldn't.

That would be the moment Luisa realized how truly fucked she was. Because then he would hold all the power. She'd be his dirty queen and she'd get even dirtier, because he'd probably make her sleep with the pigs at that point. He saw it in her face, that former beauty queen, the girl who was a twenty-three-year-old virgin with loving parents and a moral outlook on life. She thought she was above scum like Esteban. Hell, she felt things like *guilt*. He didn't even know what guilt felt like.

He couldn't wait to wipe that smug, righteous look from her beautiful face and make her uglier, inside and out, day by day. It was what got him out of bed in the morning. That, and the look on Javier's face when he realized how much he had underestimated him. The look on his face when he saw how everything else had been taken away.

Oh, Luisa was playing into his plans so well. He hadn't counted on her still smarting over Javier's infidelities, but the woman felt far too much. In that respect alone, she would never cut it as a true *narco* queen. The real queens of the country knew to turn a blind eye to their husband's affairs. It was just the price you paid for being married to a *patron*. Everybody knew it.

But Luisa, she hurt and bled over it. She had a soul and a heart that were so woefully out of place, but at least they made her gullible and easier to mold. She believed everything that Esteban told her about her own husband. She ate up every lie that came out of his mouth.

It was genius of him to mention the whores that had been driven in. The women weren't for Javier, though, not this time. They were for Borrero, Artur, and whomever else. Maybe even Esteban, if he felt like it. But Javier had Evaristo now, and he was in his zone and wouldn't be distracted by women at this point. He was terribly single-minded at times.

Esteban had wanted Luisa to believe the opposite and so she did. And that led her right to him, aching and vulnerable.

The sound of hoof beats came from behind him, and Esteban turned around to see the dapple grey stallion that had enraptured Luisa so much. For no real reason other than an extremely misplaced sense of jealousy, Esteban hated that damn horse even though it had, in some ways, helped with the plan.

The horse stared at him cautiously, and Esteban fancied he could almost see the wheels turning in its head, trying to decide if he was friend or foe.

"If I had a knife on me, I'd slit your throat right now," Esteban said to the horse. He wasn't joking either. Killing animals meant nothing to him. It had probably all started when he was ten years old and tied his neighbor's beloved dog to their truck and watched as the owner, unaware, dragged the animal to its death. Esteban laughed at the horror of it all and felt thrilled that he, just a little boy, had the power to end a life so easily.

He would do it again and again.

Later, the puppies and cats and rabbits, they would become people. And it felt even better.

The horse seemed to decide Esteban was a foe after all. He snorted once and then took off at a trot, leaving Esteban behind. He had the brief fantasy of finding it later, slicing its head off, and delivering it to Luisa, blaming it on Javier. It was a little too *Godfather*-esque for Esteban's tastes but he thought it might be fitting.

He watched the horse go and then slowly headed back up the hill, toward the ranch. He knew he had to keep it casual between Luisa and himself for the next day or two, to give her space and time to realize that what she wanted was him. But he couldn't let it go too long. He had a schedule to keep, and it all depended on the man in the tunnel. The longer he could hold out, the better. He could only hope the agent was stubborn as all hell, and that Javier took his time. That was one thing he could count on. Javier didn't like to rush. He enjoyed the art of it all.

What a sick fuck.

Though it was hard to practice patience, a virtue Esteban never had in spades, he did what he could to keep Luisa at bay. It wasn't that hard. She was staying away from him. She wouldn't even look at him. He didn't know if it was out of guilt or the fear that Javier would see something in her eyes.

But of course Javier never saw anything because Javier was rarely seen above ground. He spent most of the day in the tunnel with Evaristo. Esteban only went down once or twice, to deliver news about a shipment to Javier or something else of importance – far from Evaristo's ears of course – and sometimes he caught Javier at breakfast before he went on his morning run across the desert.

Other than that though, Javier was caught up in his obsession. He didn't suspect a thing, and to Esteban's relief, he was taking things with Evaristo slowly. He was still using the battery pack, and Evaristo wasn't talking, but Javier was in no hurry to brutalize him beyond mercy. This was a day by day event that consumed the *patron*.

One evening after a dinner of Evelyn's heavenly *nopales* and chicken stew, Luisa got up and headed out into the desert on her evening walk. Esteban knew now was the time to strike.

He waited and then followed her out there as she climbed into the horse pasture. All the animals were out of sight so she kept going. He was glad he had brought his knife this time.

She went down into the wash but then headed up out of it and to a ridge, disappearing behind clumps of *yucca* and *agave*.

When he found her, she was sitting on a bunch of smooth boulders and staring off into the distance. If you squinted beyond the mirage of sun shimmer, you could see the faint line of the highway. Other than that, it was desolation.

She knew he had been following her. She didn't turn around or even flinch when she heard him call her name.

She knew and she had been waiting. This was what Esteban had wanted.

They didn't talk much. She held a world of sadness in her big eyes, but anger too, and it was the anger that fueled her. Esteban didn't even need to add anything to that fire.

He sat down on the rock and unzipped his shorts. He pulled her on top of him, and she was ready to go.

They fucked like that in the desert, the sun searing

their shoulders and the wide open spaces around them swallowing their cries.

Esteban didn't think it was as good as last time, maybe because she wanted it and was wet and willing. There was no pain and no blood. But he saw the pain inside her, and that alone was enough to make him come.

Later, he'd pull Juanito into his room and inflict the pain on him that he couldn't inflict on her. Juanito took it like a champion and Esteban made false promises that he wouldn't do it again as long as Juanito behaved.

Then he was back to Luisa, hauling her out under the moon and pushing her to the dirt.

They carried on like that for a week.

One full week out in the middle of nowhere. Fucking in the dry earth, amidst the snakes and scorpions and other horrible, dangerous creatures, just like themselves. All the while, underneath that same earth, Javier worked away on Evaristo, wanting answers.

He'll get them soon enough, Esteban thought to himself.

The clock was ticking.

CHAPTER NINE

Javier

"Are you ready to talk?" I asked Evaristo calmly. I was sitting in my usual chair in the corner, running a file over my nails. They were getting awfully damaged over the work of last week. Torture would do that to you. Sometimes it was as hard on me as it was on them.

Not that I was being too hard on the *federale*. I had been taking it slow and easy, warming him up. But now, now I felt as if I had been far too nice to him. The agent wasn't talking, he wasn't even close to it, and I had to step it up a notch.

He'd been trained almost too well, and he was as stubborn as fuck. He could take the voltage and not talk, even when applied to the bottoms of his feet. His dick was a last resort, but there was something crude about shocking the genitals. Not to mention they often shit a brick after, and I sure as hell didn't want anything other than piss and blood around here.

I would prefer to remove a finger or toe with a thin, jagged saw rather than shock him there. But before I would even consider that, I'd apply some heat.

"Evaristo," I said, louder now. My voice echoed down

the tunnel. I was starting to feel like a snake, like this was my burrow, my new home. The few times I had gone outside here I was almost blinded by the sun.

Evaristo, still naked, always naked, turned to look at me. He was always silent. I really admired him for that. He had no reason to put up such a front with me. After all, the information had nothing to do with him or his organization. I tried to reason with him, to tell him that my taking out Angel would only help them. One less *narco*. But he wouldn't have it. He didn't speak – at least, he didn't give me information – because his loyalty and sense of righteousness was that strong.

But he would break. I could see it in his eyes. He was tired. Weary. And I was starting to make the other side look good.

I eyed Diego who was leaning against the dirt wall. Borrero and Morales were elsewhere, perhaps partaking in the women in the house. I had no interest in that anymore. All my rage and violence was getting a daily outlet now.

"Let's see, what might give our young friend here some . . . motivation?" I said to Diego. "Do you have a lighter?"

He nodded and tossed one to me which I caught in one hand. Diego brought a small can of gasoline out from beside the toolbox and found the t-shirt Evaristo must have been wearing when he was brought in. He dumped the gas on the shirt, soaking it through.

"Why are you spending so much time with me?" Evaristo asked, his voice hoarse yet somehow strong.

I cocked my head at him. "Because you're being a pain in the ass. Do you really think you're going to win any favors with your peers because you held out long enough? Does it matter when you're going to give in, in the end?"

He shrugged even though the movement made him wince. I walked over to him, flicking the lighter as I went.

"I don't care what my peers think," he said.

"Oh, is that so? I totally would have pegged you for a brownnoser from the way you're holding out on me. I figured back at work you're nothing better than a dog with its nose up someone else's shithole, taking whatever comes your way."

"Then you don't know me at all."

"I think I know enough of you," I told him. "You want to be looked at as a hero. A self-righteous little prick and example for all the damned *federales*."

"Maybe," he said, eyeing me. "Maybe I don't give a flying fuck about them. Maybe I'm trying to see what *you* are made of."

I exchanged a look with Diego. He lifted up the soaked shirt, ready to follow through. We both knew it got dangerous when the captor got too personal. I couldn't help but be fascinated though. I subtly shook my head at Diego to keep him on standby.

"You should know what I'm made of," I told Evaristo as I crouched down beside him. I flicked the lighter on and pressed it into his thigh. "Sugar and spice and everything nice." He began to sweat and his skin started to burn beneath the flame. "Or is it worms and snails and puppy dog tails? Yes, I suppose the last one suits me better."

He clamped his eyes shut, face contorted in pain until I took the lighter away.

"So tell me, why do you want to know what I'm made of?" I asked him.

He didn't open his eyes. He breathed in and out harshly before he said, "You said you're going to let me go. I'm going to make sure that I know who I'm dealing with in the future."

I laughed. "I gave you my word and this is the thanks I get. Well, go ahead and tell your boss all about me, I'm sure he'll be impressed. More by me than the fact you got this information."

"Maybe it wouldn't be for my boss," Evaristo said. "And just for my own knowledge."

I really didn't know what this kid was getting at now, but I had a feeling he was just trying to waste my time. I nodded at Diego who came over and manhandled Evaristo, undoing the ties around his chest and pushing him down so that his head was between his knees. Evaristo struggled and Diego slammed his elbow into his cheekbone with a loud crack.

I winced at the brutality, knowing that it could make talking more difficult for the agent now, but didn't say anything. When Diego was done tying him in this new position, his bare back exposed, Evaristo spit out a tooth.

"You're merciless," he said, his words a thick jumble as blood pooled out of his mouth. "That's good. It would be even better if you didn't let me walk at the end."

I couldn't help but chew my lip for a second as I raised my brows at Diego. Was it our luck that we had kidnapped some sort of masochist? God, wouldn't that be just a fuck in the ass.

Diego wasted no time. He threw the wet shirt across Evaristo's back and pressed it into his skin. I walked up and flicked on the lighter, holding it inches away.

"Tell us how to get Angel Hernandez and we won't have to do this."

"You will have to do this," he answered.

And so I did. I held the lighter to the shirt until it caught fire, then stepped back and watched as the flames spread along his back. Evaristo screamed and screamed until the fire naturally went out.

"That wasn't even the bad part," I told him as he gasped for breath, sweat dripping off his face and mixing with the blood on the ground. "Do you want to talk before that?"

He groaned, panting, but managed to say, "You think I don't know this game? You'll have to do it anyway."

He was right about that. Only a fool would think it was over at this point.

"Fair enough," I said. I grabbed the edge of the charred t-shirt that was now seared to his skin and ripped it right off. It took a layer of burned flesh with it.

Evaristo's screams were deafening and seemed to go on forever. I didn't feel anything but hope. Hope that when he calmed down, maybe he would finally talk. This was starting to become something of a chore, and if he was a masochist, that was going to take most of the fun out of it.

But every masochist has a breaking point. I wondered how much of a sadist I'd have to be to find it.

I didn't want to do the burn method again. The chance that he could go into shock was too high, and generally most people died after the third try. By then the internal organs are fried.

So Diego lifted his foot and very slowly I began to saw off his pinky toe.

Evaristo still didn't talk, despite the excruciating time I took to cut through the gristle and bone, and we had to inject him with adrenaline to keep him alert and conscious.

Finally – *finally* – as his toe rested on the ground in front of him, severed from his foot, and after Diego had taken off his own shirt to soak with gasoline, Evaristo muttered, "Please . . ."

I motioned for Diego to pause and pulled Evaristo back by the hair. "Please what?" I asked, staring down at his face, puffy, black and blue. He'd aged centuries at my hands, and I was shocked to find that the need to hurt, maim, and destroy was still inside me.

He opened his eyes and stared right at me. They were red, all his blood vessels having burst at some point. "You're worse than they say you are," he said slowly, painfully.

I tried not to smile. "Then you'll talk? Or do you want more?" My eyes slid to Diego and back.

Evaristo breathed in and out, thinking. I nodded at Diego who slapped the shirt down on his raw back.

I kept my fist in his hair as he cried out, screaming again. "No, no more. No more, please! Don't light it. Don't light it! I'll talk." He shut his eyes, and for a moment I thought he might cry, but when he opened them again he said, "If you keep your promise."

"That I let you go?" I asked. "I gave you my word

and that's the truth." If Evaristo ended up dying in the desert, food for vultures, I didn't really care. But I *would* let him go.

"Okay," he said. "Okay. I want water."

"You'll get water after you talk. In fact, I'll have my wife take good care of you." That was one reason why I brought Luisa along – she was very good at tending to captives after they'd been tortured. It made them feel safe. Sometimes I had her do it during the whole process, as a way of playing good cop and bad cop. She probably didn't want to do it, but I knew she would. Her heart was too good to let someone suffer.

Evaristo slowly nodded and tried to breathe through what was left of his pain. Then he opened his mouth and began talking.

Half an hour later I had all the information I needed to successfully destroy Angel Hernandez, to do the things that Evaristo's very own agency wouldn't come right out and do because of bureaucratic tape and involvement in the DEA. He still didn't believe we were doing his organization a favor. In fact, he didn't seem to have much faith in them at all.

I couldn't blame him.

"Well," I said to him as Diego finished writing up everything in his notebook. "I'll go get Luisa and some water." I started to walk away but paused, looking at him over my shoulder. His eyes were drooping shut and I had an odd twinge of respect for the young man.

"Evaristo," I called out. He lifted his head and stared at me. "You proved yourself today, what you're made of. Your agency is lucky to have you. And you are far too smart and valuable to be a *federale*. If you ever want to fight for the other team, you have a place here. Just keep that in mind when you return. You may think you'll be in their good graces, but they will shun you. They will wonder what you told me and call you a snitch. And sooner or later, you'll be working a desk job in some office in Mexico City, because they won't trust you after everything you were put through. They won't show you any respect. All this pain will be for nothing. But you have my respect."

He watched me for a moment. Then he said, "Fuck you," and closed his eyes.

I shrugged. "As you wish."

I left the tunnel and went upstairs. I had totally lost track of time. I had lost track of days. It was almost dark outside, the light fading to a bruise, the color of Evaristo's cheek.

I found Luisa in the kitchen, sitting at the table with a cup of tea in front of her. She was alone.

I stopped in the doorframe and watched her for a moment. I couldn't tell if she was lost in her head or ignoring me. Her hair fell across her face as she stared out the windows at the darkening desert.

Something beat inside me quietly. And for once it wasn't rage.

It was regret.

"Luisa," I said softly.

She looked up at me, so startled that she spilled some of her tea on the table. Her eyes held something dangerous in them. It was fear of me. I couldn't blame her.

"Sorry," I apologized. I came over and sat down beside

her. She seemed so small all of a sudden. I felt like I hadn't laid eyes on her for a week and that might have been true. "Are you okay?"

Now the fear changed into something that looked like guilt. I didn't like that look. It made my chest feel hollow. It made me feel like a million things were about to go very wrong.

She nodded and picked up a napkin from the middle of the country table, dabbing at the tea. I reached out and put my hand over hers. I half-expected her to snatch hers away but she held it there as if frozen. In fact, it appeared she was holding her breath.

"I mean here, on the ranch," I said, clearing my throat. "How have you been doing?"

She watched me for a few moments as if trying to gauge my sincerity.

"I'm fine," she finally said, her voice barely above a whisper. I licked my lips as I watched hers, so full and soft.

"Where is everyone else?" I asked.

She shrugged and slowly moved her hand out from under mine. "They went into La Perla. Evelyn is with the horses."

"She runs a tight ship around here. She's a good woman," I said. "So are you."

She flinched as if I'd hit her again. "Luisa," I said carefully. "Has something happened?"

She rubbed her lips together then looked me dead in the eye. "Why do you care about me all of a sudden?"

Now it was my turn to act like I'd been backhanded. But I couldn't get mad, even though I wanted to, because she had a right to say that. She had a right to say anything she wanted.

"Because you're my wife," I told her, wishing that meant something to her. "So, has something happened?"

She shook her head. "There is nothing."

She let that word hang in the air. Nothing.

Nothing at all.

Nothing between us.

The shame came over me like a tidal wave. At one point she had been everything to me, and now, now I was realizing how close I'd come to losing her, if I hadn't already.

I had pushed her away and away and away, but I didn't want to do that anymore.

I just didn't think I could get her back.

The look in her eyes told me that she hated me. She was hard now, like a woman carved from stone, and I was afraid that no matter what I said or did, I could never bring her back to the way she had been before. I had broken her in too many pieces, and what had been pieced back together had no room for me.

"Are you happy?" I asked her despite myself. It was a stupid question.

She gave me a sharp look. "What do you think?"

I pressed my lips together and nodded. "I'm sorry."

But she didn't seem to understand that I was sincere or appreciate how sorry I was. I knew sorry meant nothing anymore. In fact, the words that came out of my mouth made her tense up even more.

Annoyed, she brushed her hair back from her face and looked down at her cup of tea before taking a sip.

Her neck was covered in small bruises.

My heart stilled but I made sure concern wasn't showing on my face. I stared at them for a moment, memorizing the shape, before she could catch me looking.

They looked like fucking hickeys. Or bite marks. They looked like what I used to do with her when I was feeling particularly bloodthirsty and crazed with lust.

My mind raced, trying to come up with an explanation. She also had bite marks on the backs of her hands, so it's possible something in the desert air had been biting her.

It was possible.

But unlikely.

I pushed it aside for now.

"I have good news," I said. She didn't look at me but I went on. "Evaristo talked. We'll keep him for a few more days." I paused. "I need a favor from you."

"Oh?" she said.

"He's pretty beat up," I explained. "It wasn't pretty, what I had to do down there."

"But I bet you enjoyed it," she muttered quickly.

I appraised her, the sharpness of her words, the burning in her eyes. "Yes, I did," I admitted slowly. "Does that still surprise you even now?"

She looked right at me. "He never did anything to you. He didn't deserve it, what you did. He was an innocent bystander. That used to be something you believed in."

"I used to believe in a lot of things, Luisa. Myself, included."

"That makes two of us."

Ouch. I managed a smile, as if it didn't sting. "Back to the favor though . . . can you tend to Evaristo?"

She rolled her eyes. "Play nurse again?"

My expression grew grim. "This isn't a game, Luisa. You know that. I'm not asking you to put on a nurse's uniform and give him a pity fuck." My eyes narrowed as I watched her freeze up again. "That's not something you're willing to do, is it?"

She got out of her chair abruptly, nearly spilling her tea again. "Of course not," she said, taking the cup to the sink. Her actions were entirely deflective.

"Good," I said, rising up. "Now you don't have to do anything you don't want to, but I thought it might appeal to your good side that there's a wounded, innocent man down there who needs your help."

"My good side?" she repeated, keeping her back to me.

"We both know you've got bad in you as well."

But just how much bad has come out to play lately? I wondered. *And with whom? I had an idea.*

"Fine," she said, turning around and walking past me. "I'll go help him."

I reached out and grabbed her arm. Her eyes widened as I pulled her close to me.

"You look different these days," I told her.

She held her ground. "Maybe it's the dry air."

I smirked at her. "Maybe it is. Maybe it's a lot of things."

Our eyes were locked intensely, another game to see who would look away first.

I chickened out first.

I leaned down and kissed her, hard and flush on the

lips, my grip still firm on her arm. I'd forgotten how well my lips knew her. I realized how long it had been since I'd last kissed her. I realized how damn much I missed her.

She barely kissed me back. She made a sound of surprise and pulled back, and when she looked up at me, she looked more scared – and confused – than ever.

All she saw was a monster.

She swallowed, her eyebrows coming together, trying to process it. You'd think she had just been doused in acid.

"Don't worry," I told her gruffly. "I won't ask anything more of you."

I let go of her and she stepped back, still looking shocked, as if it hadn't been her husband at all that had kissed her. It took all of me to not feel even remotely humiliated.

With her head down, she slowly turned away, as if to run.

"Oh," I said lightly before she could leave the kitchen. "I'd appreciate it if you didn't say anything to Esteban about the interrogation process."

"Why . . . why Esteban?" she asked, slowly turning around, hand at her chest.

I frowned, not liking her reaction. "Because I know you two are close. And I also know he thinks he has a right to know my business. *Our* business. He doesn't. So as far as you know now, I'm still interrogating Evaristo and he hasn't said anything. Can you do that? Can you *lie*?"

I swear I saw relief wash over her. She nodded quickly and left the room, leaving me alone.

Of course she could lie. I knew she was lying to me already.

I just didn't know about what.

But I knew I'd get it out of her.

And that it was going to hurt.

CHAPTER TEN

Esteban

That night, Luisa didn't come out to see Esteban. He sat on the fencepost for a while, then thinking perhaps he was being too bold, he headed along the rails until they dipped over the hill. He waited in the wash, at the base of the acacia. He went over the ridge and waited on the boulders until the moon was halfway across the night sky.

She never came.

This didn't worry him. It angered him. How fucking dare she stand up their tryst already, leaving him hanging out to dry? If Javier weren't around, he'd give her a black eye to teach her a lesson, and that would be getting off easily. Hell, he thought he should give her a black eye anyway. How would she explain it? That Esteban hit her for no reason? Not damn likely.

It didn't really matter now. Tomorrow he was making the call. Tomorrow he would set everything in motion and things would change, for the better. For him and Luisa, at first. And then just for him.

He dusted his hands off on his shorts and headed back to the house. Maybe he could sneak into her room and have a quick fuck there before escaping out the door to the patio. Maybe that's what she was waiting for.

He had to admit, he was starting to look forward to their escapades. Sure, she didn't respond in the same way that Juanito did. She didn't have that fear of him. She didn't mind pain so much. But he knew she would in time, and just picturing that was enough to get him going.

Besides, Luisa really was beautiful. In any other life and at any other time, he could imagine himself being with her. Not forever. Not really for any length of time. And he certainly wouldn't love her because he could never feel that emotion, let alone be that selfless.

But he would have a good time with her. She would fulfill his needs. She was stunning to look at, beautiful to feel, and he'd enjoyed corrupting her once pure soul bit by bit. He would have shown Luisa proudly on his arm to anyone who looked his way, and he would feel like the king of the world to have such a rare creature in his possession – smart, funny, gorgeous. She was beautiful and yet he hated it at the same time.

And then in the end, he would say goodbye and move on. He probably wouldn't even kill her. He'd just let her leave and that would be the end of it. It was almost noble of him in this imaginary future.

But that's not the way his world worked, and it wasn't the hand he had been dealt. This Luisa wasn't really his. She didn't really care for him at all – he was just a cock and an excuse to exact her own brand of revenge on Javier. He didn't care one way or another what her feelings were because the damage had already been done.

Soon Javier would find out, when Esteban allowed it.

The day after tomorrow. When everything else in the *patron's* life went to shit. He would know and Esteban would become king.

Smiling to himself, he walked down the hallway and stopped at Luisa's door, about to knock.

"What are you doing?" Javier asked, voice cold as steel in the dark.

Esteban turned to see Javier at the end. He had blended in with the shadows a little too well, the light from the kitchen failing to illuminate him until he walked forward and stopped just as the light hit his eyes.

God, his eyes were some scary ass shit at times, Esteban thought. *Like a snake's.*

"I was seeing if Luisa was awake," Esteban said, knowing it would only make Javier suspicious if he tried to cover it up.

"Why?" Javier's eyes locked on him in that very hawk-like way. They burned amber under his black brows while the shadows played up his high cheekbones and wide mouth.

Esteban shrugged and gave him his trademark stupid grin. "Bored, I guess. You're not around much."

Javier's jaw tensed. "I've been busy."

"Has the fed talked yet?"

He shook his head. "Soon though."

It better not be until the day after tomorrow, Esteban thought. *I need Evaristo here.*

"And what's the plan after that?" he asked, just to keep him talking, to get him to forget that he was ever about to knock on Luisa's door because he was "bored."

"You'll see," Javier said. He eyed his wife's door and

said, "If I were you, I'd let her sleep. She's had a long day. Goodnight."

As Javier turned around and disappeared into the dark hall, Esteban frowned. Had Javier been with Luisa today? When? And why?

Had she talked?

He was tempted now more than ever to go inside and wake her up, if she was asleep at all, but he had a feeling Javier would be watching.

Always watching.

Esteban would just have to be a bit more careful.

One more day, he told himself as he strolled toward his room.

One more day.

CHAPTER ELEVEN

Luisa

Despite my better judgement, I couldn't help but be captivated by Evaristo Sanchez. Of course, it was my first time laying eyes on him in the flesh, and I knew there was a handsome man beneath the bruises and blood. Javier and Diego had really worked him over.

But he still had this quiet charm and tenacity you rarely found in these situations. When I first introduced myself, he looked at me through slits for eyes and said, "You must be an angel. I must be dead."

I told him if I was an angel, I was a dirty one and he certainly wasn't in heaven. He said he wasn't in hell anymore, and we agreed he was in a kind of limbo, that though the torture was over, it didn't change the fact that his back had been brutally burned and he was missing his pinky toe.

I had played nurse before so I did what I could without acting too squeamish about it. I anointed his wounds with antiseptic and wrapped his toe and foot. I gave him antibiotics that were always lying around, along with a small dose of morphine for the pain.

Evaristo didn't do or say much else, but he watched

me closely. There was a cot set up in the basement so Borrero and I helped him squeeze past the hot water heater and into the room.

"Your husband is an interesting man," Evaristo said as he eased himself down onto the cot. His blue eyes were bloodshot and glazed from the drugs, and I knew he wasn't feeling any agony at this point. I'm not sure if I'd be so stoic after a week-long torture session, especially if I didn't have my toe by the end of it.

I also wouldn't be using the word *interesting* to describe Javier.

I stared at him for a moment. "Interesting? You should be calling him a monster."

"Oh, I'm sure I did for a moment there. But he can't be so bad, if you're married to him."

That felt like a gut punch, and I instinctively wrapped my arms around myself, aware that Borrero was watching our exchange. "I'm not as good as you think," I said quietly.

"No?" he asked. "And is your husband as bad as I think? As the world thinks? You survived Salvador Reyes before, didn't you? I guess this is just a lesser of two evils."

"It depends if you believe evil is absolute or not."

"And do you believe that? You were raised Catholic, weren't you?"

So many questions. So personal. I straightened up, not wanting to get into religious beliefs with him. I didn't want to think God had been looking over my shoulder for the past week, watching me commit sin after sin.

And in some ways, loving it.

In some ways, hating myself even more.

The way Javier kissed me today . . . I didn't know what to do. It was so unexpected. It bruised my heart and soul and left me reeling, aching. Because he was giving me what I'd been craving, what I'd been looking for in Esteban.

And in that kiss, I realized the horror of what I had done.

Yes, I also knew the horror of what he had done. The women he'd been with. The innocent lives he'd taken. But even though I wasn't willing to forgive him, I could at least understand what was happening to him.

I couldn't understand what was happening to me. I had sex with Esteban over and over again while my husband was down here, torturing this poor man for information.

We were both so fucking dirty.

And today, today was the first time I'd seen Javier try and pick himself up out of it. He hadn't killed Evaristo. He was letting him walk when any other *patron* would have offed him. And he had reached out to me. Kissed me. Made me feel useful for once, even if it was just to come down here and take care of a tortured man.

I wanted Javier to try again. To keep trying.

I wanted to forget all the bad that I had done. I wanted to remove it from my heart.

"Are you crying?" Evaristo asked.

I ran my fingers under my eyes and saw that I was. Borrero stepped away from the wall, concerned, but I just waved him off. "Oh, I guess it's the air here. So dry."

Evaristo nodded though I knew he didn't believe me.

"I'd say you could do better than him," he said softly. "But that's none of my business, what goes into a marriage. Or a business. Just tell me . . . do you believe in him?"

He watched me with open curiosity.

"Do I believe in him?"

"Yes. Do you think he'll take over the Tijuana cartel and then proceed to take over whatever is left?"

"Javier is very ambitious," I stated.

"I'm not talking ambition. I know he's ambitious. Everyone in the world knows that. Do you think he – you all – will succeed in the end? That you will rule absolute. Does he have what it takes to take this as far as it can go?"

"Yes," I said, without hesitating. "Unless he gets killed, I think he will go as far as he possibly can."

He nodded, seemingly satisfied. "Then there isn't much the *federales* can do to stop him. Except kill him."

I blinked and quickly exchanged a look with Borrero, who was standing at attention. Was that a threat?

"They won't kill him," I said, raising my chin.

His eyes managed to stay kind. "Let's hope they don't." He let out a long breath and closed his eyes. "Thank you for being an angel." Then he seemed to drift off to sleep.

I watched him, puzzled at our exchange, until Borrero came over and laid his hand on my shoulder.

"Let's go, Luisa. You've done enough," he said, and led me up the stairs.

After that, I went straight to the kitchen to down what was left of a bottle of merlot, then I went to my room. I rested there for a while, tossing and turning under the covers. It was a cold night and I felt even colder inside. I was supposed to go meet Esteban for our nightly tryst but I wasn't in the mood.

I wouldn't be in the mood again. With a simple, impulsive kiss, Javier had sealed himself as mine again. I had done something terrible, but I was ready to put that behind me now. Hope was so very dangerous, but at the moment it was blooming inside me, like the desert wildflowers after a rain.

I was almost asleep when I heard voices outside my door.

Javier.

Esteban.

They didn't sound like they were fighting. In fact, they sounded as they usually did. Javier, dry and calm, Esteban, easygoing, like everything in life was one big joke.

Except Esteban wasn't easygoing at all. In fact, the more time I spent with him, the more I started to realize there was more to him than met the eye. For one, he was pushy and violent. Enough that I could see him going to a dark place very quickly, a place where no rules applied. The attitude he had most of the time was just a front, covering up something darker. The only problem was, I didn't know if this was common knowledge and I was just slow to catch on to it, or if he was someone I needed to watch closely.

Of course, now he was. I had made it that way.

It grew silent, and I heard footsteps disappearing down the hall.

I sat up in my bed and listened, trying to make sure

he was truly gone. The last thing I wanted was for Esteban to come and find me tonight.

I got out of bed, just wearing a camisole and my underwear, and crept over to the door. I opened it a crack and looked up and down the hall. It was dark and empty.

I took in a deep breath and silently closed the door behind me before I tiptoed down the hall. From one room I heard manly grunts, from another I heard a woman's giggle. I didn't know where Esteban was.

But I knew where my husband should have been.

I stopped at his door, noting that Diego wasn't on duty. This house was half the size of the mansion back at home, so either Diego or Artur was probably patrolling the perimeter of the building.

I tried the knob but of course it was locked. He would never leave his bedroom door unlocked unless Diego was there.

I knocked as quietly as possible, not wanting to draw attention to myself to anyone but him.

The door opened slightly and Javier stared at me through the gap, backlit by the lamp in his room. His eyes were shadowy but I could tell they were surprised.

"Is everything okay?" he asked, looking over my shoulder with concern.

I nodded, feeling almost nervous, like a girl on her first date. "I'm fine. Can I come in?"

"Sure," he said, holding the door open for me. I brushed past him, feeling the air between us intensify as he quickly looked out the door, checking again for who knows what, before closing and locking it.

I stood in the middle of the room and looked around,

as if I hadn't seen it before. The truth was, I didn't know where to look or what to say or why I was really here.

"What is it?" he asked. His voice was lower now and smoother than scotch.

I turned to face him. He stood by the door, his hands at his sides, though his fingers were twitching slightly as if he didn't quite know what to do with them. He was shirtless, wearing loose black pajama pants, this very thin material that left nothing to the imagination if he got a little excited, and he often did. His shaggy hair was messy for once, across his forehead, making him look years younger. But his eyes burned the same. His eyes never lied.

Did mine? I wondered what he had seen in them early.

Had he seen the truth?

I chewed on my lip but didn't answer him.

He frowned, a deep line between his brows.

His nostrils flared slightly. His shoulders tensed up.

Eyes blazed like the sun.

Then he strode toward me and took me in his arms.

His lips found mine, hot and feverish, and one of his hands was in my hair and the other was wrapped around my waist. His strong fingers dug into me like he was incapable of letting go.

I wished he never would.

I whimpered in his grasp, at the desperation as his body strained against mine. He was kissing me so deeply that I could feel it in my toes, and my nerves were razed and raring, filling me with a need so strong it was almost violent.

"Luisa," he said, breathing hard as he pulled his lips off of mine and licked down my neck, behind my ear. Just the sound of my name was making my knees liquefy. "I need to fuck you, claim you. My wife."

His wife. I was so close to drowning in my guilt.

I decided to drown in him instead.

"I'm all yours," I said breathlessly.

He grunted at that and wrapped his hands under my ass, picking me up and ravaging my neck as we moved backward toward the bed. He threw me down on it, immediately ripping my thin camisole in two while I slid out of my shorts.

While one hand slipped between my legs, the movement silky smooth, his other arm pressed down on my windpipe. With less air coming in, every sensation was heightened. The feel of his stubble as his chin raked against my skin, his large tongue lapping around my breasts, the hardness of his erection as it pressed against my legs, the blissful intrusion of his long fingers finding purchase inside me.

I moaned, lost in lust, and the pressure on my neck increased. I couldn't tell if it was the lack of oxygen or my desire for Javier that was making the world seem smaller.

Finally I had to put my fingers on his arm to try and release some of the pressure. He pressed harder for a second, then raised his head to look at me. I couldn't speak, I had to tell him with my eyes that it was too much and I couldn't breathe.

For one frightening second there was a look in him that told me this was his intention, but just like that, it melted away and there was softness instead. He took his arm off of me and gently kissed down my windpipe before coming up to my ear.

"I don't wish to hurt you anymore," he whispered.

I inhaled deeply, letting it expand in my lungs, and nodded.

He kissed me long and hard, and I felt myself stealing his breath. His tongue was wet and probing, and I suddenly needed that tongue elsewhere.

He knew this. He knew me too well. He moved down and off the bed until his head was between my legs. His lips found me, his tongue slow and teasing. He moaned into me. This was his favorite thing, my taste, my very essence. It fired Javier up like nothing else, and I knew he was stroking himself as he did so. I could make his cock harder than cement.

"Oh god," I whimpered, my back arched and my hands gripping his silky hair as I pulled his mouth deeper into me. His tongue thrust inside and I automatically clenched around him as he pushed it back and forth, revving me into a frenzy. I ground my hips, wanting more, more, more.

"What did I tell you about being greedy?" he murmured into me, taking the chance to lick up the insides of my thighs.

"Something about how I could be as greedy as I wanted," I said through a moan.

"You're right. You want it all and I will give it to you."

He razed his teeth over my clit then plunged his tongue inside me again while two fingers dipped into my tight ass.

I came immediately, hard and wild, my body bucking like a runaway horse. I shouted out his name, moaning like a woman possessed.

"How many times can I make my queen come?" he challenged, his voice sounding far away as I rode through the orgasm, my soul splintering out into shards of light. It threatened to let loose a million emotions I was trying so hard to cage.

Luckily Javier was fast. He stood up, completely naked now, his gorgeous cock jutting out, and yanked my thighs toward him and up, so my hips were raised and my legs were hooked over his shoulders.

He thrust into me, grinding his teeth, the muscles in his neck corded.

"Fuck," he muttered, closing his eyes as he slowly pulled out. Achingly, teasingly. Then he pushed in again to the hilt.

My breath hitched as he sunk in deeper, and I was enraptured by the intensity on his face, the desire and lust that seemed to smolder throughout him. His eyes lifted to meet mine and held me there. I was his hostage, his captive, all over again.

I wouldn't have it any other way.

I gave myself to him as he pounded in and out. Open, vulnerable, exposed, he could have all of me if I could even get a taste of all of him.

Just when the strain seemed too much and his eyes pinched shut, about to come, he somehow had the nerve to stop. He pulled out and I was suddenly bereft without him inside me.

"I need you closer," he said, and he got on the bed so

that he was sitting up, and then pulled me on top so that I was straddling him. "Much closer."

I eased onto his cock, reveling in how full he made me feel, and while one arm went around my waist, holding me close to his own sweaty, hard chest, the other disappeared into my hair. He held me softly but firmly in place, our bodies fused.

He kissed me, mouth open and insatiable, then stared deep into my eyes. There was so much I wanted to see in them.

"Luisa," he murmured.

"Yes?" I asked as I fell deeper and deeper.

Javier started nibbling across my jaw and I closed my eyes to take it all in.

"I want a son," he whispered, voice ragged against my neck.

I pulled back and faced him, stunned. "What?"

It was the way of life here in Mexico, and that was no less important in the cartels. Family was everything, and the *patrons* always wanted big families with sons who would eventually take over the family business.

When it came to children though, it was something that Javier and I discussed only once. While I wanted a family at some point, he was hesitant. He had once confessed to me in the middle of the night that he feared he would be just like his own father, deadbeat and horrible. I couldn't convince him otherwise.

I didn't have a womb that demanded kids or ached for them. I ached for him. But I also knew that Javier was talking nonsense when it came to his fears. Though there was no denying that he, at times, was not a good person and could very well be the monster that everyone feared, I knew he would make a wonderful father. He was fiercely loyal and protective, and our baby would grow up to be the most spoiled brat in the land.

But I never pushed the issue with him, because I wanted what he wanted, at least for now, and if I ever started feeling the urge, that ticking clock that enslaved women, then I would let him know. I would stop taking the pill and we would start trying.

I never dreamed he would let me know first.

But now I could hear it in his voice, raw and choked, that desire.

I stared up at him, locked in the intensity of his gaze. "You want a baby?"

He swallowed and brushed the hair off my forehead. "Yes, Luisa. I do. For us. For the future." He paused, seeming to get lost in himself, his face contorting slightly with want and need. "I love you. And I am so, so sorry that I haven't been there. I am so sorry for what I've done to you."

"No." I spoke softly, unable to handle this.

"Yes," he said. "It is the truth. And I know the truth doesn't mean much from me. But . . ." He closed his eyes and rested his forehead against mine, "I want it to matter. I want to start over. All of this, all of us. Will you do that with me? Will you love me again?"

My heart shattered beautifully, shards flying everywhere inside, landing soft, and I was filled with nothing but warmth.

I ran my hands through his thick, soft hair. "Of course I will. I never stopped, Javier. It didn't matter what you did. I tried, but I couldn't. You're embedded in my skin."

"And you're embedded in mine," he said. "Deeper than you will ever know."

At that, he moved his hips, pushing himself deeper inside. I welcomed him with a greedy groan.

CHAPTER TWELVE

Luisa

The next morning I woke up in Javier's bed. I was alone – I had prepared myself for that. But the space next to me was still warm and I could hear his shower running.

I sighed happily and rolled over as the bright sunshine streamed in through the deep-set windows. Everything looked white-washed and clean. I felt clean too, as if I'd been stripped of everything dark and toxic, and all that was left was a new me.

I knew it was naïve and wishful thinking but I didn't care. I needed to cling to the belief that we could start fresh, start anew. I needed to believe that our love was strong enough to survive anything.

The shower turned off and Javier strode out of the bathroom, towel wrapped around his waist, his athletic and toned upper body showcased in the morning glow. He gave me a quick smile as he walked over to the closet, completely in business mode.

It was his demeanor that reminded me of exactly what was going on and what was at stake. Last night may have been everything I'd needed and wanted, and it could have been the same for him. But he was a man with a job to do and that was the kind of thing that couldn't take a backseat.

"Big day?" I commented. I realized I was just trying to make conversation, and that in turn made me see that despite everything that had happened, nothing was back to normal.

"It is," he said, slipping on a black dress shirt and facing the mirror. "Another day of fixing up our *federale*, if you don't mind so much."

I shook my head. "It's fine. I kind of like him."

"Well, don't get too attached," he warned. "Tomorrow he's out of here."

"What exactly do you plan on doing with him?"

He shrugged. "Not sure yet. We'll play it by ear. Diego thinks that we should kick him out of the chopper in the middle of the desert. I'm more inclined to get Juanito or someone to drop him off in Monterey. The city has always been so neutral anyway."

"Sounds like you've got it all figured out," I said, running my hands over the soft sheets.

"I've got that figured out," he said as he pulled on white linen pants. Always commando. "What I've really got to focus on is what to do with the intel on Hernandez. We can't screw this up. We get one shot to get him, and anything after that we are fucked right up the ass."

I nodded, feeling privileged to be let in on this information again, feeling a part of his life, like a true partner. "Well, other than making sure Evaristo is comfortable, whatever you need from me, just ask."

He smiled at me in the mirror's reflection. "I'm glad

you asked that. Because there is something I would like to ask you."

"Yeah?"

"And Esteban."

My blood turned to ice. My lungs froze right over.

Oh fuck.

"Oh?" I said, and Javier slowly walked over to me as he slipped a belt through the loops on his pants.

"Yeah. I would like to ask something of the two of you."

I plastered the fakest damn smile on my face. "What is it?"

He smiled right back but I couldn't be sure if it was fake or malicious, or what it was. I was so paranoid that my heart was threatening to fly right out of my chest.

He knows. He knows. He had to know.

"It's something that can wait for now," Javier said, putting his hand on my shoulder. He leaned down and kissed me lightly on the lips. I had to force my body to break the freeze and kiss him back as I normally would.

I wondered if he could taste the fear on me.

"I've got a busy day," he said, turning around and walking back to his dresser to slip on his watch. "I think I'm going to head with Diego to La Perla or maybe Durango and see if we can get some work done. It's better to do the work in the car and pilfer someone's wifi. It won't leave a trace, just in case our systems are being watched."

I nodded absently. "Is that possible?" I asked, just wanting him to keep talking.

"Anything is possible, my queen," he said, shooting me a wicked smile. "You should know that more than anyone."

I couldn't swallow the brick in my throat. I smiled again and slowly got out of bed. "I should get dressed," I said, willing my voice to remain steady.

"I'll see you later. Bring Esteban back here around nine tonight," he said before he strode out the door and into the hall, closing it behind him and barking at Diego who must have been outside.

Oh shit.

SHIT.

What the hell did this mean?

I felt like I was about to have a full-blown meltdown. Panic was creeping up my body, worming its way into my chest. I had to remind myself to breathe in and out, to not let my guilt get the best of me. The fact that he wanted to talk to both of us didn't have to mean the worst. It didn't mean he knew.

It didn't, it couldn't.

I had to find Esteban right away, but I had to wait until Javier and Diego were gone, so I practically forced myself to shower and spend time getting ready before I went out to look for him.

I didn't have to look far. Esteban was on the porch, staring off into the distance, a cup of coffee in his hand. It was a lovely beautiful morning, the sky saturated blue and stretching as far as the eye could see. There wasn't a single cloud.

It's too bad I couldn't take the time to fully appreciate it.

"Esteban," I said warily as I walked across the porch

to him. He didn't turn to look at me. He was probably mad about me standing him up last night.

I stood beside him, watching his gaze. That favorite horse of mine was in the distance. Esteban seemed so focused on him, and not in a good way.

"Where were you last night?" he asked me, voice hard. He still wouldn't look at me.

"Sorry about that," I said.

"But where were you?"

I hesitated. "With Javier."

He nodded. "I see. In what way were you with him?"

"Esteban, I think he knows," I said, skirting the issue.

Finally he looked at me, and his eyes were smoldering with hate. "What did you do?"

My chin jerked back, surprised that he would blame me so fast. "I didn't do anything!" His look intensified. I shook my head. "I swear to god, I didn't do anything or say anything."

"Then why do you think he knows?"

"He asked if the both of us would come to his room tonight. At nine. That there was something he needed to ask us."

He stared at me for a moment. "Did you fuck him last night?"

"Esteban," I warned, stepping away from him. "That's none of your business."

"You're wrong," he sniped, and reached out to grab the back of my neck, his fingers squeezing the skin as he yanked me to him. "Everything you do is my business now. You're not his anymore, you got that? You're mine.

And there's nothing you can do to change it. It's happening."

What was happening? I wanted to ask, but he squeezed my neck harder and I winced from the pain.

"Hey," I heard Borrero say as he stepped out from the kitchen to the porch. "What's going on here?"

Esteban immediately let go of my neck, and my hand flew back there to press on the pain. "Nothing you should worry your pretty little head about," Esteban said to Borrero.

Borrero glared at him and walked over to me. "You all right, Luisa?" he asked as Esteban stomped off the porch and headed toward the barn.

I nodded, trying to catch my breath. "I guess I said the wrong thing."

Borrero watched me curiously for a moment before his eyes drifted off to Esteban in the distance. "You know I'm supposed to keep you safe. If Javier had seen what I had just seen . . ."

Javier would have probably chopped Esteban's arm off.

"I know," I told him, trying to smile. "It's fine."

"I'll be watching you, you know," he said, and now I couldn't figure out if it was for my own protection or because Javier might have told him about his own suspicions.

"I'll be staying out of trouble, don't worry," I said to the *sicario* before heading back inside the house.

I stayed out of trouble by staying near Evelyn the entire day and helping her with her chores. The more we talked, the more I realized that she was far smarter than I had initially thought, and we had a lot in common. We both had to hide behind a mask. I wore a beauty queen one and she wore one of an old maid, but we both were so much more than we appeared to be.

Evelyn told me that the ranch had been used a lot recently for the sole purpose of training. While I knew that Javier was trying to set up his own army to battle against those crazy Zetas, I didn't realize so many of the camps took place here. It was good to know that we were improving the army we already had, the ones who could battle it out against the Gulf Cartel and whomever else declared us their enemy.

Speaking of enemies, the only time I was away from Evelyn was when I was with Evaristo in the basement. He looked only marginally better than he did yesterday and he wasn't as talkative, but he still watched me with almost reverence as I applied the ointments and fed him his pills.

It was around eight o'clock when Diego and Javier returned home from wherever they had gone. They quickly corralled Morales and went walking around the property as the sun was dying in the west. I guessed they were discussing whatever it was they had learned that day, the next steps in the plan to get Hernandez.

When it was close to nine, I quickly finished the wine I was having with Evelyn – I'd had more than I meant to, my nerves getting the best of me – and headed to Javier's room, hoping to find Esteban.

I didn't. It was empty. I wondered if I should go looking for him or if Javier would.

But before I could answer that question, Javier walked through the door, Esteban in tow.

"Please sit down. Both of you," Javier said, gesturing to the bed with an open palm. His tone was light and I started to have some hope that he wasn't about to kill us.

That was until he went and locked the door.

"What's this about, Javi?" Esteban asked, seeming more bored than intrigued. He was good at pretending. I knew he had to be at least shitting himself a little bit. Even sitting next to Esteban felt electric and dangerous.

Javier eyed us coolly. "I'll get to that. You're not armed, are you Este?"

Esteban exchanged a quick glance with me then shrugged. "I'm always armed."

Javier held out his hand. "Give it to me."

Esteban didn't move. "Why?"

"Because we're all friends here, aren't we? And friends – real friends – shouldn't need to arm themselves when they're with each other. We are real friends, the three of us, right? Don't you dare prove me wrong."

I swallowed and watched with bated breath as Esteban nodded and slowly pulled out his pistol from the back of his shorts. Javier snatched it out of his grasp and walked over to the dresser, placing it on top.

"Doesn't that mean you need to disarm yourself too?" Esteban asked.

Javier smiled like a snake. That panic in the pit of my stomach started to squirm.

"Of course," he said, and he brought his gun out, putting it beside Esteban's. I didn't dare mention that I knew Javier had a small pistol strapped to his leg and a knife on the other. I saw him strap them on before he pulled on his pants that morning, like he always did. *Patrons* believed in extra protection.

"So why exactly are we all gunless pussies now?" Esteban asked.

Javier leaned against the dresser. "I didn't want anyone to freak out from what I'm about to ask you. A favor."

A favor?

"What is it?" I said, trying not to sound scared.

He cocked his head slightly and appraised me for a moment. "A little fantasy of mine."

I frowned, not sure what he was getting at.

"Esteban," Javier said to him, "as I'm sure you are aware, I've been having some issues lately. Alana's death . . . hasn't been easy on me. And I've been taking it out on the wrong people. You, I'm sure, plus others. Many, many others. But mostly my poor wife." Javier gave me a quick smile. "I've been unfaithful to her. I've been rude and rough and disrespectful. I have failed as her husband."

The fact that Javier was admitting this troubled me. I knew he had a hard enough time admitting his faults to me in general, but to Esteban? He was the last person he wanted to look weak in front of, but that's just what he was doing here.

I glanced at Esteban out of the corner of my eye. He was sitting rigid, looking about as worried as I felt.

Javier went on, hands behind his back. "But I don't want to be that to her anymore. I want to be a better man, so to speak. We're going to start a family."

Esteban's eyes widened and he swallowed hard. "Congratulations."

"Thank you," Javier said simply. "Of course, she's not pregnant yet. At least, I don't think so. We made love last night but these things can take time."

I didn't know where this was going, but it was wrong. Everything that Javier was saying, even though it was the truth, was wrong. He wasn't acting like himself. He had some ulterior motive, some.purpose, and I didn't know what it was.

"But an heir, particularly a son, will do wonders for us and the organization. Don't you think?"

Esteban shrugged again though this time it seemed forced. "I guess. It's the way."

"It is the way," Javier said with a sharp nod. "And the way is about family and responsibility and doing what's right to protect that unit. It's not for frivolous acts. It's not for degenerates. There is no place in the family unit for . . . uncouth urges." He eyed both of us. "I guess I'm not being very clear. I admit I'm having a hell of a time just coming out and saying it. I've done this many times before, sorry Luisa, just not with you both."

I stared at Javier, waiting for him to put an end to my confusion.

He smiled something wicked. "Before I become a father, I want one last fantasy out of my system. One last *rotten* immoral urge." He paused. "I want the both of you tonight. Together. Right here."

I blinked. Did I hear that right? I glanced at Esteban who was staring back at me with matching confusion.

He couldn't mean what I thought he meant.

"Uh," Esteban said, scratching at the scar on his cheek.

"Correct me if I'm wrong, *patron*, but . . . are you asking for a threesome?"

My brows raised and I looked anxiously at Javier for his answer.

"It sounds so juvenile, doesn't it?" Javier said. "But yes, that is exactly what I'm asking for. As a favor to me. Do you have any objections?"

"Yes," I said at the same time Este did.

Javier clapped his hands together and stood right over us, peering down. "I thought you would. But you're going to be a part of this regardless. There is no saying no to me, you should know that by now."

I knew that, but it didn't mean I wouldn't try. Because nothing good could come of this. And I think that's exactly what Javier had in mind.

Esteban cleared his throat. "I didn't think you were the kind of guy who would easily share his woman."

Javier gave him a cutting look. "Oh, I assure you I am not. But because I'll be having a piece of you as well, I think it evens out. Now, strip."

There was no way this was about to happen. Esteban wouldn't allow it. Forget about the affair, he still wouldn't allow it. Esteban seemed to spend his days fighting the authority that Javier had over him. He wouldn't just let Javier call the shots now, especially in a sexual manner. It would humiliate him.

Which was the whole point. Now I knew what Javier was doing.

But why I was involved, I didn't know.

To my complete surprise, Esteban stood up, and with his eyes on Javier, pulled his shirt over his head and threw it to the ground. Then he undid his shorts, sliding them down until his bare ass was right beside me.

No. No, no, no.

No.

I looked away. I couldn't do this. It should have been a million girls' fantasies but there was something so inherently wrong about this. If this had come from a genuine, organic place, then maybe I would have been more than up for it. But there was no way in hell this was ever one of Javier's fantasies and I was completely on edge.

Javier barely gave Esteban the once over – he didn't look too impressed – and then fixed his gaze on me.

"My queen," he said, and I wished I could see the glimmer of tenderness in his eyes, what I had seen last night when we made love. But I didn't see anything there except something wicked.

Devious.

He smiled at me and jerked his chin to Esteban. "Isn't this what you want?"

I shook my head, my hands gripping the edge of the bed.

"No?" Javier asked, leaning over and putting his hand into my hair, making a fist. I stiffened, my eyes locked with his as I silently pleaded for this not to happen. "You never fancied having a fuck with your friend Este here?"

Oh Jesus. He knows.

He knows.

He grinned at me. It was beautiful. It was terrifying.

"Well, if you've never fancied Este, I know he sure as hell has fancied you." He looked to Esteban briefly. "Isn't that right, you little shit?"

Esteban, stark naked, just shrugged.

The bastard just shrugged.

"Of course," Esteban said, so carefree that it grated on me. "Who wouldn't want Luisa? I mean, look at her."

Javier nodded, seemingly satisfied. "See, Luisa, he wants you. And if you say you don't want him, well I guess you'll just have to pretend. Now, take off your clothes before I make Este do it for you."

I kept staring at Javier.

"Why are you doing this?" I whispered.

He yanked my head forward and put his lips to my ear.

"Because," he said softly, drawing out the word before biting my earlobe.

A shiver rocked through me.

He pulled back and released my hair. His fingers curled around the hem of my dress and started tugging it up my legs. I understood that this was for my own humiliation now. He was looking for guilt. He was searching for truth.

I had to pretend, just as Esteban was, that this was okay.

My life depended on it.

I took in a deep breath, managed a small smile that gave Javier a bit of pause, then I raised my arms over my head to help him. Javier pulled the dress off, and then I was just sitting on the edge of the bed in my bra and underwear. The set was black and lacy, and the minute I felt the eyes of both men on me, taking me in like a feast, I couldn't say I wasn't turned on. Maybe I wouldn't have to pretend in the end.

Maybe I could get out of this alive.

"Stand on the bed," Javier commanded. "Then take the rest off. Slowly."

I took in a deep breath then stood up, going to the middle of the bed in a few shaky steps. I faced them while I slowly unhooked my bra, my breasts bouncing free. The air felt cool against my nipples, but they were already hard. The more they stared at me – my husband and my lover – the more turned on I became. I knew that Javier wanted all the control, but the more I owned it, the more that control belonged to me.

I eased my panties down my legs and stepped out of them. Now I was completely nude and on display. I kept my eyes on Javier, not wanting to look at Esteban, too afraid to give anything away.

"Get on your knees," Javier said. "Come to the edge of the bed." He jerked his head at Esteban. "Get him off."

I swallowed hard and tried to play it cool. Esteban certainly was. He was grinning like a fool as he came to the edge of the bed, his cock already hard and upright.

I didn't move, not yet. "And what will you do?"

Javier, still in his clothes, said, "Watch." He paused and gave me a tight smile. "For now." He moved over to the dresser, the guns still on top, and leaned against it casually, folding his arms. "No more stalling, my queen. Do it."

And so I did. I dropped to my knees and crawled to the end of the bed. With one shaking hand, I wrapped it around Esteban's hard length and prepared to put it in my mouth.

"Make sure you watch him," said Javier.

I was hoping I wouldn't have to look at Esteban at all. I took his cock in and met his eyes. I was hoping I could go out of focus and not really look at him, at the smug intensity, but Javier barked, "Act like you're enjoying it!"

I tried. But Javier wasn't buying it, I could tell. He let out an aggrieved sigh.

Suddenly he was climbing on the bed behind me, his hands grabbing my ass and squeezing it, kneading it. I began to melt into the motion and I started sucking Esteban with more passion. I was starting to become insatiable.

Javier spread my cheeks apart and I briefly tensed as I felt his tongue slowly, laboriously, licking around the pucker before trailing down my crack.

"You're wet as sin," Javier murmured into me, and the vibration of his low voice alone made my head spin. He rubbed his fingers along my slick folds, teasing my opening, my body begging for his penetration. "Maybe you like this after all."

He pushed two fingers, three fingers, four inside me, deep as he could go, while his mouth and tongue ravished me over and over again. I gasped, losing my concentration on Esteban, his shiny, hard cock bobbing in front of me. Javier then pressed his thumb into my ass, past the joint and I lost all control of my body.

The orgasm ripped through me like a tidal wave. I cried out as every part of me quaked and shuddered. Javier barely slowed down, forcing me to come again quickly.

The bliss was nearly unbearable. It took all that I had to keep tending to Esteban, who was now holding my head and pulling me back to him, forcing his cock into my mouth again.

Javier brought his face and hands away and then I heard his fly unzip. Next thing I knew he was rubbing wet fingers around me before his cock slowly eased into my ass and I expanded around his hard width.

With his hands tight, gripping my hips like he was trying to break me, he pushed himself in to the hilt and groaned.

"So fucking tight, my queen. Dirty fucking queen," he said between gasps as he began his rhythmic pumping.

I felt like I was on some kind of drug, some kind of trip. Every nerve was a live wire, and I was drowning in this symphony of flesh, sandwiched between two crazed, possessive men that would normally never share me.

I only belonged to one of them. Even though Esteban's cock felt good in my mouth, in this wild, hedonistic heat of the moment, it was Javier as he thrust himself deep inside, who was mine.

My king.

And the man in control.

As I was on the verge of coming again, Javier fingers stroking me now, Esteban began to tense up. He grabbed a fist of my hair, pulling sharply, and I could feel his ass muscles squeezing.

"Fuck me, fuck, fuck," he cried out softly as he came into my mouth, his hot cum dripping down my throat and out the corner of my lips.

"You come like a girl," Javier remarked to Esteban as he continued to fuck me from behind, my breasts swinging. I didn't know if Esteban took offense to that jibe or not, because I was coming all over again, an explosion of stars that took me somewhere very far away.

I could barely catch my breath. Letting go of Esteban, I collapsed onto the mattress, trying to muster reality from a lustful high. Javier slowly pulled himself out, still hard. For whatever reason, he hadn't come yet. That wasn't his style.

"Now we're just getting started," Javier said. He climbed off the bed, walking around to where Esteban was. His hard cock was in his tightly fisted hand, but otherwise he was still dressed. He gestured at Esteban who was still reeling from his orgasm.

"You, get on the bed and fuck her," Javier commanded.

I blinked. We weren't done?

Esteban seemed to hesitate as well. He'd just come after all, though he'd proved to me before that he was something of a machine. It wasn't sex that turned him, it was the violence and danger of it all and there wasn't anything more dangerous than what we were doing now.

"Take her on her back, edge of the bed, right here." Javier was determined, his tone flinty. "Be rough with her, I don't mind. I'm sure she doesn't either."

"Do you want to give me a minute," Esteban muttered. "I don't really get a fucking boner on command." He started stroking his cock while Javier watched him with cold eyes.

As I'd thought, it didn't take Esteban long to get somewhat hard again.

"Get on with it," Javier commanded.

"What's the hurry?" Esteban said but obeyed nonetheless. He reached for me and flipped me over so that I was on my back, and even though he'd just come, the man was ready for me all over again. He climbed on top of me, and while taking a rough grip of my hips, thrust his cock inside me. I had barely recovered, my body still throbbing.

"That's right," Javier said, now standing right above me, his own cock poised straight out. "Just like that."

Esteban's expression intensified as he pinned me to the mattress, smoothly grinding his hips into mine, his cock diving in and out between my legs.

Then Javier said something I'd never expected him to say.

CHAPTER THIRTEEN

Javier

E steban gave the whole show away. He was just a little too into it, too much acting. Then there was Luisa who was trying not to meet his eyes, looking guilty as hell. They both thought they were acting, but their actions didn't match. It shouldn't have been this way. It shouldn't have been the truth.

It wasn't easy having to watch it all unfold. Seeing her with him and having all my darkest, most destructive suspicions confirmed.

But it had to be done. If I had called either of them out on their affair, they would have denied it anyway. Here, here, in front of my goddamn fucking face, I could see their connection. Her guilt. And his smug smile, the one that silently told me he'd had his way with her before. That this was just the icing on the cake. That he thought he had pulled a fast one on me.

I tried not to think about the timeline, the logistics, when this had started between them. Was it before Alana's death? The beginning of our marriage? Or had it started here at the ranch? Maybe it was somewhere in between.

Regardless, by the way they worked each other's bodies, they knew each other very, very well.

I wanted nothing more than to let the rage enslave me. I wanted to kill the both of them, right here, right now.

And on top of it all, on top of the anger that was choking me, causing my lungs to burn and my vision to swirl, there was hurt.

Stupid, foolish fucking hurt. I didn't think I had it in me anymore. To feel. To bleed. More than that, I deserved this hurt. I knew I did. But it didn't change a thing. It didn't stop my heart from plummeting to its death.

But I couldn't do it now. Couldn't kill them now. I wasn't ready yet. I wasn't done.

"Esteban," I croaked out while he continued to fuck my wife just inches away. Luisa peered up at me as I stood right above. "It's my turn."

Esteban slowed his thrusting, the sweat building on his back, and then looked up at me. His eyes were feverish with lust, and he was annoyed I was interrupting his little fuckfest. Luisa giving him head wasn't good enough for him – he wanted to be deep inside of her. He wanted his claim.

He wouldn't get it.

I stroked my cock, my eyes locked on Este's in challenge, and I smiled.

"Suck me off. Return the favor."

Now I had his attention. He looked like he wanted to murder me, which made my smile wider. He thought he was in control here? He was wrong. In this play, I had all the power. I always did.

"Didn't know your gate hinged that way," Esteban said, trying to sound cool, but I could see the disgust in his eyes. He wasn't disgusted by the fact that I was a man and he was a man, but because submitting to me was the last thing he was prepared to do. But he would do it.

"It doesn't," I told him. "But you seem like you were born to suck my dick. I'm just giving you the chance to live up to your potential."

His glare deepened, his face growing red.

I was enjoying this far too much. He should have been glad I wasn't flipping him over and fucking him in his hairy ass. Maybe he was too afraid he'd enjoy it. At least this way I could watch every agonized moment on his face.

I quickly reached down, shoving up my pant leg and pulling out my gun. Luisa gasped and Esteban froze, mid-thrust, as I waved it in front of their faces. I cocked the hammer for impact, the sound sweet.

"I don't have all night," I told him, and I pressed my cock in his face. "Don't make me ask you again, or I'll be putting this gun in your mouth instead."

"Javier . . ." Luisa protested softly.

I gave her a wry look. "Shut the fuck up. You want to play the game, just take what he's giving you, and I'll take what he's going to give me." I looked back to Esteban. "Now, open up, sunshine."

If looks could kill, I'd have been a dead man twice over. But I was the man with the gun, not him.

With great reluctance, Esteban opened his mouth and took me in. I'd be lying if I said it didn't feel good, but the humiliation on his face made it so much better.

"You suck dick like a girl too," I told him with a grin. "Where'd you learn to do that, hmmm?"

He paused and I pressed the gun against his forehead, trying to make a mark. "Keep going, you fuck, and act like you like it."

He went back to it and somehow managed to keep fucking Luisa at the same time. But of course he managed, because the two of them had an ease with each other that made me physically sick. That was all I really needed to know the truth. It's all I needed to see.

"All right," I said after a minute, grabbing him by the hair. "I've had enough. You're so good at sucking cock, Este, it's a bit concerning. And while I really would enjoy coming all over your goddamn ugly face, I think you've gotten my point." I pulled out of his mouth, gripped my gun, and pistol-whipped him across the face.

Luisa screamed and Este fell on top of her, blood spraying everywhere.

"And that's just in case you didn't."

He looked up at me, moaning and holding the side of his cheek where the blood rained down.

"You think I don't know," I said, trying to stay in control, to keep my voice from shaking. All I could feel was the tar-black rage threatening to consume me.

Luisa quickly crawled out from under Esteban, but I caught her arm before she could run to the door. I whipped her backward onto the bed, keeping the gun trained on her.

"Don't think I wouldn't put a bullet in your brain, you lying fucking bitch." I gritted my teeth and black dots filled my vision, pulsing with the spreading anger. Though I had told myself I wouldn't harm her, seeing the truth in their eyes hurt more than I thought possible. It didn't

matter what I had done before, or that this was some sick
karma.

Because, beneath it all, I *knew* I deserved this and
worse.

But knowing didn't stop the rage. It only fueled it.

"Javier, please," she said. She didn't say more than
that. There was nothing else she really could say, and
she knew it.

I shook my head. "And with him. God, Esteban, you
must have thought you were so fucking smart doing that.
Trying to one-up your *patron* again." He sat beside Luisa,
naked and pathetic, holding his face while his eyes danced
between agony and fear. "But you know you're not leaving
this room alive. You know it. How does that make you
feel?"

"Okay, knowing I'll die with a bigger dick than you,"
he answered.

I shrugged and aimed the gun at him. "Whatever makes
you feel better." Then I paused and aimed it at his dick.
"On second thought, I don't want you to feel better at
all. And what could feel worse than having your dick shot
off, hey?"

My finger pressed against the trigger.

And suddenly the room shifted to the left as an enor-
mous roar filled my ears and everything was aglow,
shrapnel flying everywhere. I hit the ground as parts of
the roof rained down on me. There were screams, I could
smell smoke, and I didn't know which way was up until
I heard Diego's voice, so small and tinny, and then his
hands on my shoulders, pulling me up.

"Come on," he said, maybe he was shouting, I didn't

even know where I was for a second. As he hauled me out of the room I looked back in the room to see Luisa and Esteban gone and embers falling down from the ceiling like snow.

"Luisa," I said before I broke into a coughing fit.

"Borrero is on it," Diego said and he brought me into the hallway, shielding me as we went. Blasts of gunfire came from the kitchen but there was no time to dwell on it as we headed for the basement door. Between staccato shots, a man screamed in agony. I had no idea who it belonged to.

We quickly ran down the dark staircase and into the basement. The single bulb swung from the commotion, casting the room with an eerie glow and beneath it all was Evaristo, bound to the cot and looking at us with wide eyes.

"Get him!" I yelled at Diego, my voice struggling to be heard above the gunfire upstairs. "We can't afford to leave him behind."

Not because I had any sentiment for him but because he knew too much about my escape route and if he was questioned by anyone for a second, he would give it all up. After all, I was the monster that tortured him.

Diego gave me a look and then pushed me forward so that I was in the closet. I squeezed past the hot water heater and pushed on the brick wall as I heard him undo Evaristo and they quickly followed.

Once on the other side, Diego closed the door behind him and there was only the tunnel in front of us leading us to freedom.

"What the fuck is going on?" I asked them. Diego had

Evaristo by the scruff of his neck and I noted with a strange pang of sympathy that the man could barely walk.

"I'd ask you the same thing," Diego said and nodded down at my crotch. My fly was unzipped, my cock just poking out.

I grimaced and quickly did it up. I eyed Evaristo. "Is this the *federales*?"

Evaristo didn't say anything at first and Diego pulled him along as we hurried down the tunnel.

"Could be Tijuana," Diego said, "if they got wind of what you were after."

"Could be the Zetas too," I said.

"Could also be my guys," Evaristo managed to say, struggling to keep up. "Bomb blast to get you running, not uncommon."

I eyed him sharply. "Seems like you could lose innocent lives that way."

He smiled, his lips still puffy from the beating, his cheeks black and blue. "No one is innocent in Mexico, *patron*."

Unfortunately, he was right about that.

"And you didn't see this coming?" I asked him.

He shook his head and then winced, a piece of matted hair falling on his forehead. "I've been with you. And even if I did know something, I wouldn't tell you. You're not torturing me anymore."

The tunnel curved to the right, the thick dirt walls blotting the view in front of us, and for a moment there I feared that perhaps there was no way out. I'd never actually done a test in this *finca*, let alone any of the other ones.

But then it straightened and you could see the end, a rough wooden ladder heading out of the ground. The lights above flickered as the ground shook from another blast, albeit further away, and then went out.

Diego's flashlight went on in a second.

"Almost there," he said, and now I was thinking back to Luisa. Even though I had threatened to kill her moments earlier, now that I was faced with the possibility that she might be back there, she might be hurt, I couldn't even bear it.

"Are you sure Borrero has Luisa?" I asked Diego as we came to the ladder.

He nodded. "I saw her run with Esteban out the door before I got there. Borrero was right behind me. He and Morales, it's their job to keep her safe."

I tried not to grit my teeth at the mention of Esteban. Just the fact that the two of them ran out of the room before I could even get out added insult to injury.

Had this been their doing somehow?

"Did . . ." I tried to think of a way to phrase my fears without losing face, "did it seem like Esteban was taking her."

"I'm sorry Javier, I do not know," he said. "But what I do know is that you are safe. This ladder here will lead you to safety. That is my job."

I nodded and gripped the ladder for a moment, before climbing up.

The top of the hole was covered in planks of wood. I pushed them up and to the side as the cool desert night assaulted my face and stars gazed down.

I slowly got out, seeing silhouettes of trees. We were

on the other side of the small hill, the *finca* obscured from view, even though the hill's outline lit up with another bomb blast or gunfire fight.

There was no time to panic. To worry about my empire. To be concerned about my wife.

There was no time at all because the heavy, clattering sound of many AKs being aimed at you seemed to make time slow.

"Put your hands above your head, Bernal," a deep voice game from the direction of the trees. But they weren't just trees. They were people.

The blinding red dot of a sniper's rifle shone in my face.

I was surrounded by *federales*, each of them with a weapon trained on me.

I couldn't move, couldn't even think.

I heard Diego swear from beneath me on the ladder, still in the tunnel, and I knew he was running the other way, back to the *finca*. Maybe with Evaristo, maybe alone. He wasn't abandoning me. He knew he wouldn't have a shot.

He knew I still needed him.

"Javier Bernal," that deep voice came again and foot-steps seemed to echo through the earth. A wide-set man stopped feet away from me, his gun taking the stage. "You're under arrest by the PFM. Surrender or we will take you in dead. We will gladly do it."

I swallowed and slowly put my hands up in the air, knowing I was caught and there was no way out of it.

"Ah the *federales*," I said. "I finally get to meet Mexico's finest *puta*."

Next thing I saw was the butt of the rifle.

Heard the crack of my nose.

And everything went black.

When I came to, I was being brought to my feet by a man who had horrible BO and being forced into a helicopter.

"Get him in," someone yelled and it was then that I felt the heat of the fire. I raised my head, my vision swimming, and saw the ranch burning down. *Federales* were everywhere and everyone that belonged to me was gone.

Everyone except Esteban and Luisa.

They were a few yards away, beside a convoy of SUVs, their faces lit by fire.

For one beautiful instant I was so damn grateful that Luisa was alive.

But then I became aware of what I was really looking at.

I was in handcuffs, being hauled into the helicopter, *federales* and their guns trained on me.

Esteban and Luisa were uncuffed. They were free. They were wrapped in rescue blankets, as if the *federales* had tended to them, fucking kissed their boo-boos and put Band-Aids on them. They weren't even being watched, except for an agent who walked past Esteban and put his hand on his shoulder, whispering something in his ear.

Esteban kept his eyes on me, ablaze in the flames. His mouth curled in a slight smile.

He wore a look I hoped I'd never see.

The look that said, "I win."

Then he turned and walked away toward the SUVS, pulling Luisa with him.

She was staring at me in utter horror, throwing the looks over her shoulder, as if she couldn't quite believe it all.

I'm not sure if the horror was meant for me and my fate in prison.

Or for what she'd just done.

It wasn't enough that they'd had an affair.

The two of them had set me up.

They'd turned me in.

And they'd rule the empire – my empire – together.

The chopper lifted off and as I stared blankly at the ground below, the two of them got smaller, along with the blazing ranch and the desert hills. It didn't feel like I was flying though.

It felt like I was falling.

I was heading for rock bottom.

And if the impact didn't kill me, it was going to fucking hurt like hell.

After everything I'd worked so hard for, in the end, love could have been my ruin.

CHAPTER FOURTEEN

Luisa

I t had all happened in the blink of an eye. My world shifted from one horrific scene to another. One moment it looked like Javier was going to kill the both of us, the next moment the whole world exploded.

I didn't even have time to react. Even though Esteban had seemed shocked, he acted right away, scooping me up and throwing me over his shoulder as we headed for the door. I screamed for Javier. I knew he'd gone down but I couldn't see him in the darkness, the power all out and the only light coming from the flames licking the hole in the side of the room.

But Esteban didn't stop. He kept running until we were in the kitchen. Even though it was late, Evelyn was there, with a rifle in her hands and she was telling us we were under attack, to get to safety. She didn't even blink at the fact that we were both naked and together.

Esteban pulled me outside to the porch and I looked inside just in time to see Evelyn firing at men in black, masks on their faces.

The *federales*.

Many of them, one of her.

I turned away before I saw the result.

Esteban still had a stronghold on me and led me out to the dirt road that would take you to La Perla. In the distance, headlights and flashing sirens lit up the sand, coming our way.

"What are we going to do?" I asked him. "We have to get Javier."

"Javier is gone," he said, coming to a stop but still holding on. "He's going to try and escape out his tunnel. Notice that you weren't included."

"We left him on the floor!" I yelled and suddenly reality hit me, that he could have been hurt or dead. I tried to run back but Esteban swung me around until I went flying into the dirt.

"I just saved your fucking life," he said, nearly spitting at me. "You think he wouldn't have killed us both in there?"

I got to my knees just as the cars pulled up, their headlights illuminating our naked bodies. "We need to run!" I told him, trying to run but he was fast and pulled me up by my hair.

"There's no running Luisa, not anymore," he said.

I gasped from the pain, my eyes wild as I looked over at the masked *federales* getting out of the cars, their guns aimed at us. I felt like it was all going to end in a second.

Javier Bernal's wife and right-hand man in custody? Game over.

The *federales* yelled at us to get our hands in the air and we complied, even though the darkness, the distance, was calling my name. I could run. Find Javier, make sure he was okay. I could save myself at least.

But to move would mean death.

A man stepped out of the first car, tall and extra forbidding with his bullet proof vest, the black helmet, the mask.

"Esteban," he said.

Esteban nodded. "If he's anywhere he's in the tunnel."

My mouth dropped. How quickly he sold him out!

"We already have our guys on the other end," the soldier said. "It should be a clean capture." He turned his sharp eyes to me. "Luisa. I'm Adan Garcia Ruiz. We're sorry it had to come to this. But you'll be better off this way. We've promised Esteban his protection and yours."

I stared at them for a moment while one of the soldiers approached us, holding out silver emergency blankets to cover us up.

"Protection, why?" I asked as I snatched the blanket, taking a step away from them and quickly wrapping myself up.

Ruiz and Esteban exchanged a look. "We made a deal," Ruiz explained. "We didn't want to but we saw an opportunity. Your husband for your freedom."

I stared at Esteban, my heart picking up speed. "You set this up? You sold us out!?"

"I sold out Javier," he said calmly, wrapping the blanket around his waist, like it was a towel and he was just stepping out of a spa. "It was the right thing to do. He had too much power and the cartel was bound to collapse in time. I just speeded it up." He gave me a wry smile. "I was tired of the business. Figured this was the only way I could retire and live the simple life on a beach somewhere. Spend my days surfing."

I couldn't believe it. I just shook my head, my fingers curling over my heart.

Javier.

All this time, Esteban had been setting him up.

"That's bullshit," I sneered at him. "You just want to take over."

"We'll be watching him. And you," Ruiz said. "To make sure that doesn't happen. But at the same time we're grateful. Let's just hope that Evaristo is still alive."

"He is," I said feebly. "Javier only wanted information on Hernandez and the Tijuana cartel. He kept to his word and let him go."

God, at least I hoped he let him go. If the *federales* captured Javier, it could be the difference between life and prison and killing him on the spot.

And still, I couldn't believe any of this. I closed my eyes and prayed that Javier would somehow escape, that maybe Diego saw the tunnel had been compromised, that he got wind of a snitch. Javier had already done prison once in America, before I had met him, but now if he were caught, he'd be put in Puente Grande. Where the worst of Mexico's worst would go.

And with so many *narcos* in there already, families torn apart and lives shattered by the drug trade, by our cartel, Javier could be fair game.

He would get no special treatment, the *federales* would make sure of that.

He was in for many years of hell.

And me, I was free.

For the first time in my life, it wasn't what I wanted.

I wanted to collapse right on the ground. I guess the soldier closest to me saw that because he put his arm out and led me over to the SUV, placing me inside and giving me a bottle of water. He was saying something to me, but I didn't remember what it was because all I could think about was Javier.

After everything, he was still everything.

I don't know how long I was sitting there for. The ranch house went up in flames. I never saw Evelyn again or Borrero, Morales, Diego, Juanito. Javier. It was like Esteban and I were the only ones who got out alive.

Then there was a roar of crunching tires and headlights appeared around the small hill behind the blazing house. They pulled right up next to a helicopter, the blades slowly starting to rotate.

The doors of one of the SUVs opened and that's when I saw Javier. Seemingly unconscious and being dragged by two beefy soldiers, but he was there and he was alive.

He was alive.

And he was about to be taken from me forever.

Without thinking, I suddenly jumped up and out of the car, running toward him, my blanket trailing behind me. The sharp rocks and cacti pierced my bare feet but I couldn't feel them.

"Javier!" I yelled but he didn't stir and I could hear soldiers running after me. Esteban was the first to catch up.

He put his hand on my shoulder, nails digging in and pulling me back. One of the other soldiers stepped in front of my vision briefly, yelling at me to forget it, turn around and head to the cars.

I stopped and watched and hoped that Javier would wake up and see me. The soldier backed off and I shrugged off Esteban's hand.

Look at me, Javier, look at me, I thought. *Please be all right.*

But when he did come to, just as he was being put into the chopper, I realized my wish had been dangerous. Whatever confusion he felt was gone as his gaze sharpened and he saw me. He saw us.

We were free. He was captured.

His eyes broke my damn heart.

His eyes that told me that he knew what I had done and that he would never be the same. His eyes that told me I ruined him to the very ground.

As the chopper lifted up, I knew I was dead to him.

And I would most likely never see my husband alive again.

I didn't remember much after the *federales'* raid. Three days passed in a blur and I was high as a kite on some kind of pills that the *federales* kept giving me. Every moment that I was coherent, I collapsed into rage or a sobbing fit, unable to get it all out, everything that was killing me inside.

I couldn't stop blaming myself. I couldn't stop bleeding over Javier.

After a while, I welcomed the pills.

Though Evaristo had been tortured, damaged, the fact that he was alive seemed to soften the *federales* attitudes toward us. Then again, Esteban told them that Javier wanted to kill him and Esteban went out of his way to ensure that wouldn't happen.

It was a lie that did my head in but in my drugged state, I couldn't do much but sleep and cry.

Esteban and I had been taken back to an unmarked facility in Culiacan that seemed to be half medical facility, half intelligence offices. I spent my days in a small room, with a nurse, and I only saw Esteban on occasion or sometimes Ruiz. On my last day, I saw Evaristo who had been recovering nicely and had backed-up Esteban's story, that he was the reason he was alive.

"Why are you lying?" I asked him, slurring my words as I tried to sit up.

Evaristo put his hands on my shoulders, holding me steady. "Because it doesn't make any difference to your husband now. And believe it or not, Esteban's lie is saving your life. You'll walk out of here soon a free woman."

"The *federales* never would have killed me," I told him.

He smiled but didn't say anything more.

Finally I was allowed to leave with Esteban. We were set loose on the streets and though it didn't take long for Esteban to quickly wrangle up a car for us, I couldn't help but feel that we were being watched with every step we took. Esteban might have traded Javier for our freedom but what kind of freedom would it be. I needed to escape somewhere far away, to get out from the shadow of the *federales* and the cartels.

But I couldn't even do that. Because I was a useless mess.

For the first time since I left Cabo and walked off with Salvador Reyes, I knew I was nothing more than a lost little girl, powerless at the hands of men.

An SUV pulled up on the busy street and for a moment I thought Esteban would just let me walk away. Maybe I could disappear into the crowds and start my life over again. It wouldn't be easy, but it would be real and it would be mine.

As if he knew what I was thinking, Esteban quickly grabbed my arm and then opened the back door to the SUV, roughly shoving me inside. The doors all immediately locked and I was surprised to see Juanito in the driver's seat.

He didn't seem ashamed in the slightest. In fact, he looked proud as he glanced at me in the rear-view mirror, his posture straight and chin high.

As we drove through the city and then toward the hills, I couldn't figure out if Juanito was acting for me or Esteban. After all, though Javier was in prison and none of us would probably see him again, as long as he was alive he would still run his business. That's just how it worked and why so many government agents from both Mexico and America would rather the kingpins be dead. Dead was dead but prison hardly hampered their career.

It wasn't until we arrived at the compound, my home, that I knew the stone cold truth.

This was no longer my home. It was no longer my compound.

I was no longer queen.

On the fence at the entrance, where the guard house was, the gardener Carlos's head was on a post. He had been decapitated, blood dripping from his severed neck, his once genial face frozen in fear, in anguish, a warning of all that would happen to me.

I could only watch as we passed by, my stomach sinking as six or seven men with AKs swarmed the vehicle, following us down the driveway. When we came to a stop, Esteban opened his door, then reached across for me and grabbed me by the hair. I yelped as he dragged me out of the car, threw me down on the cement.

The ground cut my knees and elbows and I tried to get to my feet but Esteban kicked me squarely in the shoulder. Pain radiated from my bones as I fell backward to the ground.

"You're home, Luisa," Esteban sneered. I brushed my hair away from my face, feeling like a panicked, cornered animal as the men gathered around me, Esteban standing in the middle of them all and staring down at me with a look of such utter superiority it made me sick.

There was no way he could just take over the cartel like this, not with Javier in prison. My husband had far too many people loyal to him to let this happen.

Yet, as I looked around wildly I couldn't see a single familiar face. Only Juanito and from his eager, completely unapologetic expression I knew he wasn't the Juanito I'd known.

Everyone was a stranger and I was in a hell of a lot of trouble.

I didn't know what to do or say. I tried to scramble to my feet but Esteban was quick and kicked out again, this time the tip of his shoe catching my chin. My jaw slammed together and more stars began to spin outward from my vision. Somehow I didn't collapse to the ground, though blood immediately filled my mouth. I had a few seconds to make a decision as the men seemed to close in on me, Esteban laughing now, everything sounding like I was underwater.

I could plead for my life, for my place here. I could try and reason with Esteban.

Or I could fight.

The thing was, I knew either choice would end more or less the same way. And even though "more or less" sometimes meant the difference between life and death in our world, both options were bleak.

I chose to fight.

I got to my feet, unsteady and lilting to the right a little, but I did it. Holding my jaw, I raised my chin and look at Esteban right in the eyes.

"I am still queen," I said, though it was more of a mumble, though moving my mouth made me nauseous. I said it as proudly as I could, looking at the depraved and ugly faces of the men around me. "And by law, this is my land, my home, and you are all still employees of my cartel."

There was a pause before the men all glanced at each other and started laughing, as if it were the funniest thing they'd ever heard. So much machoism in this country, it didn't matter if I was in power of a cartel or just a simple woman wanting a job. The men always treated you like a joke if you were anything more than a whore or a mother.

Esteban wasn't laughing though. He was glaring at me as if he couldn't believe I had the nerve to stand up to him. He didn't want to hear the truth, that by my marriage to Javier, everything was really and truly all mine.

The truth hurt. And now I knew he was going to make me pay for it.

"Is that so?" Esteban finally said, unable to hide the

irritation in his voice. "You must think you're in the wrong country, hey. There are no laws here. You should know that more than any of us, beauty queen." He eyed the men and jerked his chin at me. "Get her."

My body turned on instinct and I immediately began running for the house, the front door just twenty feet away, but before I could, someone reached out and tackled me from behind, sending me flying into the gardenia that lined the edge of the wall.

I screamed but it was futile. Hands, so many hands, grabbing my body, pulling me up and then seeming to pull me apart.

One of the men, the biggest one, lifted me up by my throat, his fat, thick fingers pressing into my jaw. The pain was so intense, I prayed I'd pass out but I didn't. By some sick, cruel world joke, I didn't.

"We don't bow to no queen," the man said, his nose swollen with purplish veins, his breath so sour I could have gagged if I wasn't being choked already. His grip tightened until I was sure my windpipe had been crushed in. Light danced before my eyes.

"Don't kill her," I heard Esteban calmly say in the background. "Just teach her a thing or two."

The man grunted and then marched forward, still holding me by the throat, until I was up against one of the white pillars by the door. He banged my head against it, hard, the pain shooting down my spine, while my arms were pulled behind the pillar by someone else and hand-cuffs were placed around my wrists. Two men grabbed a hold of my legs so I couldn't move.

He pulled a knife out from a holster around his waist,

the sun glinting off the sharp, narrow blade, and placed the tip at the neckline of the cotton dress the *federales* had given me to wear. Pressing the blade in until I felt it lightly puncture my skin, he began to drag it down, slowly. I stared as blood spilled down my chest, the dress ripping down the middle as he went.

The pain was intense, almost sickly. I sucked in my breath, trying not to scream, trying so hard to hide my fear, but when he got to the soft of my stomach and pressed the blade further in, I couldn't hold back.

I cried out, turning my face away from the sight as he quickly brought the knife down, ripping the rest of my dress. Without undergarments, I was completely exposed, naked and bleeding before them like I was about to be burned at the stake. My gash stung from the air, causing tears to well in my eyes.

"Spread her legs," the man said to the men below him.

I wouldn't plead. I wouldn't ask them to spare me. I would take it like I had taken it from Salvador, from his men, once upon a time when I thought life was a worse fairy-tale than this.

I'd been wrong.

Nothing had been as bad as this.

My legs were wrenched apart.

The man undid his fly, took his disgusting appendage out and started stroking it in front of me. I looked away. The other men started hooting and hollering and I shut my eyes, praying that Esteban wouldn't want to share me this way, that he would have a change of heart. But I knew my wishes were useless. Esteban wanted this and

I, I brought this all upon myself when I believed he was better than the person he was.

"Look at me bitch," the man said, grabbing my face with one hand, sending me into a swirl of pain. He forced me to face him as he grinned at me and his grubby fingers thrust between my legs. With an angry push of his cock, he entered me and I felt as if my body were being torn apart. More than that, I felt my soul was too and that I might never be able to piece it together again. I felt stolen. My insides were nothing but dirt.

The man licked up my face with his sour, wet tongue as he thrust hard in me, the pain almost splintering, like it was breaking off into slivers that dug deeper and deeper. I closed my eyes tight and did what I could to go off into another place, like I had done before, but that place felt out of reach. As he jabbed himself inside me over and over again, like a sweating, fat pig, his greasy hands clawing painfully at my breasts, only then did I hear Esteban.

"That's enough," Esteban said loudly from behind me. "Pull out of her, you fuck. She's not getting fucking pregnant by someone like you."

The man sneered at me, on the verge of coming, but did as he was told. He then proceeded to jack off until he was coming all over my body, his semen mixing with the blood. After a satisfied grunt, he leaned in close to me, snorted up something deep from his throat and spit it directly in my face.

I flinched and he laughed loudly in my face – "*fucking puta*" – before walking away.

"Have you learned your lesson yet, Luisa?" Esteban

asked and then he appeared in front of me. His shaggy, highlighted hair fell across his face, making him look younger, something I hated. I hated that a monster could walk around in this disguise, pretending to be human when he was anything but.

I didn't say anything. I could barely breathe from the pain.

Esteban reached over and wiped the spit from my face. He took the spit, looked at it dripping down his hands, then put it between my legs, roughly pushing his fingers inside me.

"You're still not wet," he said, his mouth close to mine, eyes watching me like I was his to eat, to destroy. "I thought a whore was always ready."

I turned my face away.

"You think I'm disgusting now, don't you?" he went on, voice amused but with an edge, like he would snap at any moment. "You didn't before. All those times we fucked but I guess I was just fucking you. You are such a fucking cunt, you know that. A god damn stupid little twat who thought she could cheat on her husband and get away with it. Did you actually trust me? Could you actually have been that dumb?"

Suddenly he grabbed me by the crown of my hair and shoved my head back into the pillar, my skull nearly splitting. "Are you that fucking stupid!?" he screamed in my face. He thrust his fingers further inside me, but the pain from my head was still washing over me like thick, hot sauce. "I was such a waste of your time! You thought I actually liked you. You thought I was actually attracted to you! You're nothing but this, a fucking cunt!" He curled his fingers inside me and with great force, dragged them out of me, his fingernails scraping down my inner walls until I screamed.

I screamed and screamed and screamed until he head-butted me and then unconsciousness came for me like a dark, welcome blanket. Esteban ordered the next guy to take me but by the time the man came up, his dick in one hand, a belt wrapped around his other, I went under, to a place I hoped I would never arise from again.

CHAPTER FIFTEEN

Esteban

E ven though the *federales* had help upholding their end of the bargain and had let Esteban (and Luisa, begrudgingly) walk free, Esteban still couldn't help but feel uneasy the moment he left their institution in Culiacan. He didn't trust them, obviously he trusted no one but himself, so he wouldn't have been surprised if they suddenly showed up at his door, wanting his arrest.

They hadn't though, not so far. Esteban wasn't really sure if they knew where Javier's compound was. They hadn't asked for any of that information the whole time he'd been in contact with them. He was sure they did know, but all they seemed to focus on was the capture and arrest (or, maybe the body, depending on how much "justice" they felt needed to be served) of Javier Bernal. He was all they ever wanted, all they ever needed.

In fact, it annoyed Esteban a little that they weren't at all concerned about what he did. *They should be following me, watching me,* Esteban said to himself as he stood in his new office, staring out the window and unconsciously imitating his old boss. *They should fear me.*

But they gave him something akin to a slap on the wrist and he and Luisa were let go. Of course, Esteban was already annoyed that the raid didn't exactly go as planned. They were supposed to show up in the early hours of the morning instead of at night. He had planned for them to get Javier when he was sleeping and vulnerable. Instead it all happened when Javier was on his A-game, ensuring he had a chance to try and escape.

What Esteban had really hoped for was for them to kill Javier, accidental or not, and really take him out of the picture. Instead they botched it. He knew he should have been somewhat grateful that they interrupted Javier when they did, otherwise he would be less one appendage, his weapon of choice and the symbol of everything he was, but at the moment he couldn't quite muster any gratefulness up.

There was one plus to having Javier alive and in prison though. Instead of doing away with Luisa like he had originally planned, he had reason now to keep her alive. Not just alive, but alive and ruined and ravaged. She'd become his new punching bag instead of Juanito and he made sure that every brutal thing he was doing to her would eventually get back to Javier and Sinaloa people. He wanted them all to know that he was the one with the power now, he had the control, and Javier had nothing. Javier couldn't even protect his own wife.

He hoped the message was getting across. His team was still small, though they were fiercely loyal. He had been building them up in secret for a year now, which was easier said than done. Most *narcos* wanted to serve Javier, not him, so he had to prey on ones just like Juanito – the weak-minded, the hopeless, the poor and desperate. Perhaps they weren't the most intelligent or quick soldiers, but at least they didn't possess any morals whatsoever and they would do whatever Esteban asked of them.

Esteban had made sure of that last part. Taking a page from the initiation tactics of the Zetas or the Juarez cartel, when he rounded up his troops, one by one, he'd made them do a slew of horrid things, from slaughtering live animals and working their way up to slaughtering live people. The last initiation that you had to pass through to make it into Esteban's good graces was to pick up an elderly couple off the street and decapitate one of them in front of the other, before burning the other alive in a barrel. Very few were able to do it – those who chickened out were decapitated by the others who did make it through the last test.

Those who passed though, they became part of Esteban's team. The moment that Javier was captured, they quickly infiltrated his compound and killed everyone loyal to Javier, even those who said they weren't, that they would be willing to switch.

Esteban had taken no chances. By the time he and Luisa arrived back, it all belonged to him. And so did she.

Now, Luisa was locked in her room and given no freedom. She was tended to by Juanito because Esteban couldn't stand to look at her beautiful face half the time, bothered by her strength and still apparent devotion to Javier. Juanito was a good choice anyway. He was starting to come into his own and he seemed to enjoy exacting the same pain on Luisa that Esteban had acted on him. Funny how the cycle always worked. So damn predictable.

And Luisa herself would cycle into a new life of horror and depravity. There would be no Javier now to rescue her, and even if there was, Esteban knew he wouldn't want her cheating, double-crossing ass anyway.

The circle will go on.

Esteban smiled at that thought and then looked around Javier's office. He sat down at Javier's chair, took a deep slug from his bottle of tequila and put his dirty bare feet up on the desk.

Now, he was home.

CHAPTER SIXTEEN

Javier

"They're going to eat you alive in there, *patron*," one of the prison guards said to me as I was led down the darkened hall. The guards always had that look to them, like their acne-scarred faces and missing teeth were part of the starchy uniform. Of course, most of the guards were no less criminal than the prisoners, it's just that they knew how to suck all the right dicks.

I mean, prisoners did too, but that was just to survive, not get ahead in some shitty job so they could continue living their shitty lives.

I nodded at the guard with a tense smile, making a mental note to take his head off at the first chance I got. I was counting on having more than a few chances and I was sure I'd have more than a few people I wouldn't mind decapitating before my time here was served.

But that would all wait. Puente Grande was no joke. The biggest and baddest prison in Mexico, it held the worst of the worst. I wasn't even the only kingpin in the joint – Almorez Fuente, who used to head up the Juarez Cartel before I had his local police force – *La Linea* – corrupted, was serving a long sentence somewhere in the building. I made another mental note not to be near him anytime in the future. He'd be out for revenge, though I knew a lot about that by now.

I was making a lot of mental notes. The minute the helicopter lifted away from my burning *finca*, I made the mental note of tracking down Este and Luisa and killing the both of them for what they had done to me. More mental notes followed after that. It's the only way I knew how to compartmentalize what exactly had just happened to me. It was the only way to know what to do next.

One was to be extra nice to the two prison guards who were leading me down the hall and past the assholes. They had done such a good job explaining to the other guards what exactly was going to go down. That I was going to be placed in a cell in the worst block of the prison, after being in solitary confinement for a few days. That I was going to have to shit in front of people and possibly eat it. That I was going to be fed oats mixed with rat droppings and rotten milk. That my tight little ass was going to be brutalized every hour, on the hour, until I was shitting out blood.

Not exactly the most politically correct talk from the guards, but it was enough to get all the prison workers to feel sorry for me.

Well, not all of them. Not the one guiding me on the left, Hiberto, with his tall, lean build and shaved head, and not the one on the right, Emilio, with his crooked smile and beer gut. They didn't feel sorry for me. They loved me, just as the warden did, just as the sniper on the roof, the cook in the kitchen, the administrator and about ten of the forty guards working here.

They loved me because I was a wonderful boss.

Hiberto and Emilio continued to lead me until we entered the middle of the prison block and then it became more of a parade and I was on display. The whole place, this dank, cold, cement, piss-scented hellhole, erupted into a volcano of lewd language. Some of the inmates, the more crazed ones, were yelling things at me that I think could have been complimentary. It was hard to tell since half of them didn't seem to know how to speak. The other half, the quieter ones with the bitter eyes, hissed shit at me. One actually threw legitimate shit, but I dodged that one quick.

I was a man who either made them a lot of money at one point or I was a man who ruined their lives and I was in the middle of them all, wearing an orange jumpsuit. I was now one of them.

Javier Bernal, captured at last.

But we didn't stop in that block. This was more for show, so that the prisoners, that everyone, knew I was here and this was my new home.

They led me up to the third level to the building and down another long hall with the occasional metal door here and there. I knew inside those doors there was nothing but a bucket in the corner and blanket. There were no windows. No furniture. Nothing.

That's where I had been ordered to be placed. That was to be my home for the next fifty years, or until I croaked, whatever came first. A cement cell that would drive any man to madness.

But instead, I was placed in the cell at the end of the hall. The door looked the same. Thick steel with a tiny sliding window in the middle, operable only from the outside.

Inside, though, was a whole other situation.

It was about three times the size of a normal cell. There was a toilet in the corner with a slight partition around it. A large, clean queen bed was in the middle, as was a small table and two chairs, a bookshelf filled with books, an MP3 player with earphones and speaker. There was a large window you could open and though there were bars on it, it had a nice view of a dried up river and the rolling brown hills in the distance. If you squinted past the parking lot of the prison, you could pretend you were in the middle of the country on vacation.

But this wasn't a vacation. I didn't take vacations, even if I was in prison. I had work to do. A lot of it. I had an empire I had to hold on to. It was all I had left.

"I hope this is comfortable," Hiberto said as they ushered me in. I stuck my hands in front of me and he quickly undid the handcuffs.

I looked around and shrugged. "It will do. Do I at least get my suits?"

He gave me an apologetic smile. "Sorry, *patron*. You must wear the jumpsuit, just in case someone shows up."

Someone that wasn't on my payroll.

I nodded, understanding. Orange flattered me anyway.

They removed the cuffs and headed back to the door. Emilio said over his shoulder, "We'll be by soon to bring you dinner. What type of wine would you like with it?"

"No wine," I told him with a shake of my wrist. "Espresso afterward will do." I needed to stay sharp.

After they left, I walked to the window and stared out at the horizon, blue sky melting into the haze of earth. I took in a deep breath through my nose and tried to pretend that everything was okay.

Everything wasn't okay, of course. Everything was absolutely horrible. But at least Este and Luisa's betrayal, though a surprise, didn't leave me ruined. Not on the outside, what they wanted.

The thing was, I wasn't stupid. I never completely trusted Esteban. He was good for some things, lousy for others, but I never in a million years thought he was loyal. After all, I could pick up on that bitterness, that desperation that swam behind his eyes and laced his every word. He wanted everything I had, he was always that way. When you combined that with the fact that I had been screwed by my partners and co-workers before in this business, I knew I always had to keep Este at arm's length.

I always knew he would try and fuck me over.

So, like any good king, I had a back-up plan. You had to prepare for the worst if you wanted to stay at the top. You had to expect it and in some ways, welcome it.

I knew that if I were ever captured by the *federales*, I would be put into Puente Grande. That was just the way it was. Of course if I were captured by the Americans that would be different, but I had good lawyers and I always had a chip to bargain with. Plus American prisons weren't as bad as shitholes like this, where prisoners died every damn day, beaten to death in their cells over nothing and no one batted an eye.

Knowing my eventual fate, for the last year I'd had my men round up the best men in the prison system. They were all paid an extra salary from me, $75,000 for the guards, $100,000 for the warden and director. There were twenty of them in total that called me their boss and would do whatever they could to not only ensure I had a pleasant stay here and that I would be fully protected, but they would let me escape as well.

Of course, the government and other officials couldn't know of this. They blindly thought their workers couldn't be corrupted but I was oh so good at corruption.

I owned them now and it was just a matter of time before I would be smuggled out of here, unbeknownst to the world. By the time that anyone of importance would catch on that I wasn't in prison anymore, I would be long gone. I would be reclaiming my throne.

That was the main problem now. That while prison couldn't hold me, I worried I couldn't hold on to my cartel. It was one thing to be captured. Most kingpins ran their business behind bars. But it was another thing to be captured, set up by a man who aimed to take everything you had, wife included. He would try and ruin everything I had worked so hard for. All that blood shed over the years and the sacrifices I'd made, just for him to take the reins.

Luckily, I had prepared for that too. I had a good amount of men from different cities and plazas that Esteban hardly knew about. They hadn't been at the compound with me for that very reason, but they were also very big, very bad, and very dangerous. My reach stretched farther than Esteban's ever could. So while I knew he was probably settling down in my old house, with my old wife, with his own crew of whatever fucking delinquents he could have mustered up, he wouldn't stay that way.

Problem was though, that he was going to try. I didn't

have TV in my room but I was sure I'd get the newspaper. I knew that Esteban would make an announcement soon and it would reach my ears, news to the people of Mexico that now he was in charge.

I would lose face a little from that, at least to the public. I hated losing face.

I took in another deep breath, feeling the rage begin to boil. I needed to keep thinking analytically, without emotion. I needed to put my plan in motion to get out of here and then put an end to Esteban, to get my revenge.

The minute my anger took over, the minute I thought about what I really lost, then I would lose focus. I would become a slave to feelings and that was a very dangerous thing for a person in my position.

I wanted to talk to Diego, so when Emilio brought me dinner – filet mignon in a mushroom cabernet sauce prepared by a private chef – I asked for him to get to me as soon as possible. I wasn't even sure if the man was alive.

They promised me they would pass the word on and after flipping through a worn copy of *Moby Dick*, I lay down in my bed to sleep.

But sleep wouldn't come. Though the mattress was soft and the sheets were smooth, I kept seeing images flash behind my eyes.

They were of Luisa.

Her with Esteban. The guilt on her face. Her body as Esteban fucked her. In and out. Him with her. My woman, defiled.

Looking back, I don't even know how I got through that. I supposed that was one of the benefits of being so angry, you go blind to everything. But now it was seeping back in, invading my addled mind. Her lips around his cock, how small and vulnerable she looked beneath him, his hands moving up and down her body like she was an afterthought, because he knew it so damn well.

As I lay there, my mind volleyed between being ashamed for making her go through with it all, to feeling righteous because she deserved it. I hated her and I still loved her. And if I dwelled on it anymore it was going to tear me apart. But maybe I needed to be torn apart, just for a minute, because I deserved shit just as much as she did.

I failed as a husband because of my own damn grief. And I failed at grief because I hated her so. And I hated her so because I loved her more than anything.

And that's how everything was going to end. In a big fucking mess. Because we were terrible people who did terrible things to each other. We were slaves to hate because hate was strong and we sacrificed love to fuel it.

The next day when Emilio brought me my breakfast, I was informed that while Diego was alive and well, he was a slippery snake to get a hold of. I'd say I taught him well but sometimes I thought Diego knew far more than I did.

Needless to say, that didn't put me at ease. And when Hiberto brought me newspaper, I cringed when I saw the headline "I'm the new boss" and a story about Esteban taking over the cartel. In fact, judging by the childish writing and his god damn spelling errors, I was pretty sure that Esteban wrote the whole article himself and passed it on to a journalist who had no choice but to publish it.

So, that didn't help. I spent the rest of the day stewing, trying to get in contact with Morales or Borrero. No luck there. They were both dead. Finally I was able to get a message to "Bandito" Bardem, a *narco* in Juarez, who promised to come and fill me in on what was going on.

Three days passed by before he showed up and by then I was ready to bite his fucking head off.

I hadn't seen Bandito in months. Short and stocky, he had a face like a piece of ham and a mustache that always seemed dipped in some kind of oil. Probably bacon grease. His shirts, though expensive, always had sweat-stains, and he was a slave to that *narco* look that the boys in Juarez all had, cowboy boots, lariat necklaces and giant hats. I thought he looked like Speedy Gonzalez from the cartoons I watched growing up.

But despite his god awful taste in clothes and mustache wax, he was a good man. A mean man. To be mean was usually good and Bandito could be as vicious as a viper. When he wasn't eating, of course. Which he was doing when he walked in the door, salsa verde dripping through his hands and onto the floor.

I raised my brow and breathed in deep, knowing if I blew up at him now there was nothing to stop him from walking out. I needed intel and I needed it from someone like him, who had power and who knew what he was doing, even if he looked like a piece of pork with boots attached.

"Javier," he said through a mumble of food. "Nice outfit."

"Same to you," I said as I sat down at the chair, motioning for him to take the other one.

He grinned at me and took his seat, finishing off the rest of the taco and wiping his face with his hands. I shuddered but he didn't seem to notice.

"Where is Diego?" I asked him.

He shrugged. "I don't know. He's alive."

"I know that," I snapped. "I need him here. There is unfinished business I need to attend to with him."

"Does this involve taking down Esteban?"

"Of course it does."

He nodded. "Yes. Well, I can help you with that. It can't be easy for a man like you to be made a fool of. And to know what's happening to your own wife."

I froze. I swallowed slowly. "What?" My voice was quiet but my heart thumped around loudly.

He frowned. "You don't know much, do you? Don't they keep you informed in here? Shit, this cell is nicer than my house."

That wasn't true, since he lived in a McMansion in El Paso, but still. "No," I said. "Nothing to do with Luisa."

"Oh." He wiped his lips again, nervous now. "Well, I don't know how to tell you this or even if you care but your wife . . . she's not doing well."

Everything inside me flinched. "What do you mean?" I asked, even though I didn't want to know. I wanted to pretend that I didn't care, to save face again, but I knew that was impossible.

"Well, she's with Esteban now, so what do you think?"

"I think she wanted to be with Este," I told him.

"If that was true then, it can't be true now. He's a sick fuck, did you know that too?"

I had my suspicions. Then again, how could he be any worse than me? Suddenly images of what I had done, the barbed wire, the machete, came at me and I realized if I had the power and nerve and rage to do that to them, he had the same ammo to do it to my wife.

"Is she alive?" I was barely audible.

"I said she wasn't doing well. If she was dead, she would be doing better, my friend. Esteban is trying to prove how tough he is and, well, unfortunately he's using her to do it. There are pictures . . . on the internet. He leaked them or someone from the cartel – well, his followers – did. I wouldn't look if I were you."

"I won't," I said. I didn't want to. I couldn't bear it. Just knowing what was happening, the humiliation, the retaliation was enough to cloud my judgement. I cleared my throat, trying to shake it all away. I needed a drink, badly. "Listen," I said. "I need Diego."

"I see that. I'll see what I can do for you. And you better hurry too or there won't be much left of her."

"She's pretty much dead to me as it is," I said. "She wasn't faithful. She brought this on herself."

"I know," he said and leaned forward to look me square in the eye. "But would you rather inflict your own revenge on her or let Esteban do it for you?"

I let his words sink in. There's no way I would let Esteban take away what was still mine.

CHAPTER SEVENTEEN

Javier

A week passed in the prison without word from the outside world and for the first time since I was brought in there, I was starting to fear that I may never get out. I was still treated like a king, but even though Hiberto, Emilio and the warden were all on my payroll and under my control, they weren't really part of the cartel. That wasn't their trade. They helped me the best they could but getting intelligence in and out was harder than it seemed. It was akin to sending a flea-ridden passenger pigeon into the sky and hoping for the best.

I had no doubts, of course, that they would help me escape but I also knew it had to be planned just so and I didn't want to leave the safety of the prison before I knew the plan that was in place. Everything had to be just right this time.

Finally though, on a hot humid night that sent moths to my window, just before I fell asleep, there was a knock at my door. I shuffled over to it in the dark and opened it.

Out in the hallway was Diego, backlit by a dim light. Behind him was Emilio who gave me a quick nod and then shuffled back down the hall.

"Javier," Diego said, his voice gruff. "I came as soon as I was able to."

"I have a hard time believing that. Did you expect me to shit where I sleep forever?"

His expression didn't change. He wasn't in a humorous mood, but then again when was he?

I gestured him inside the room and flicked on the lights. He looked around, nodding at the set-up.

"It's not half bad."

I closed the door behind us. "For an ape, perhaps. Now, what the fuck happened to you?"

He shook his head and sat down on the bed. "It's a long story," he said, almost sighing. "I managed to escape when the *federales* came."

"What about Evaristo?"

"He went with them," he said hesitantly.

"And then?"

"And then when I was headed over here, I was apprehended."

"By whom?"

"Evaristo."

Fuck. So then what the hell did this mean? Diego had been compromised? I mean, he was here wasn't he.

"You wearing a wire?" I asked him. "Because I'm already in prison, I have no problems in slicing your clothes open and finding out. If I hit an artery, it will be an accident."

He glared at me. "Calm down. What kind of idiot do you think I take you for?"

I shrugged. "Everyone seems to think I'm an idiot lately. Take off your clothes."

The expression on his face was almost comical. "You want me to what?"

"I'm not stupid and I have to make sure, so take them off. I won't stare too long, I promise."

Diego grunted and got up, shucking off his denim shirt. "I don't know what fucking games you were playing in your bedroom when this all went to shit, but you better not have anything kinky in mind."

"I was only playing mind games, the best kind."

Reluctantly Diego got down to his tighty whities and when I was satisfied that there was no wire on him, he redressed.

"All right then, get me up to speed and then get me out of here," I said impatiently.

He slowly belted his pants and gave me a dry look. "You really are the love them and leave them type, aren't you?"

"So now you're trying to be funny, after all this time?"

Diego sat back down on the bed, lips pursed, hands folded in front of him. "Here is the thing. Evaristo is with us."

"*With us?*"

"Yes," he said with a nod. "With us. He switched."

"You don't just switch."

"In this land, in this work, you do. You know that. Este switched."

I curled my fists together, trying to breathe out my annoyance. "Este never switched. He was always planning on doing this. We both knew he would try something."

"But he still switched. He turned on you."

"Well, so did a lot of people."

"Not Luisa," he said.

I raised my hand. "I don't even want you to mention her name," I snapped. "She has nothing to do with this anymore. She can't. This is about revenge Diego, that's all I want. I want everything back to the way it was and I want dead bodies at my feet, do you understand that? And I don't want no fucking *federale* agent standing in my way, regardless if he switched or not."

"He won't. He's here to help us, to be part of us."

"He's lying. We can't trust him."

"I think we can. And we need someone like him. Young and bright and determined. You know his story of how he grew up, he was never meant to be part of the *federales* and those damn politicians; they turned on him right away, demoted him. You were right about that, they were too afraid he snitched."

"He did snitch," I said. "He gave us the info. Just too fucking bad that has to take the backseat until I'm out of here and done with Esteban."

"He'll help us," he said imploringly. "And you'll want his help."

"Why?"

"Because he made a bargain with Esteban. He's got surveillance on him."

"So do we," I said.

"But not like the *federales* do. And yes, we know he's at the compound, but we have to make sure. And if we don't get Este there, we have to be able to track him. We have no idea what he's been doing on the side all this time."

I shook my head and sat down. "I don't like this. Adding people in, it's too complicated."

"I know, *patron*. But he's here, now, downstairs, and setting something up that will get you out of here immediately."

I looked at him sharply. "What? I don't need help getting out. I paid for this."

"He's going to make a statement after, saying you are still in your cell and unharmed. It will let us do everything we need to without anyone thinking you're loose, that you're a threat. Este will be caught off-guard."

"Wait," I said, my mind struggling to catch up. "Make a statement after? After what?"

"You need your own brand of crazy to fight his crazies," Diego said, standing up.

Suddenly an alarm went off from somewhere in the building.

"What the fuck is going on?" I asked. Outside the window, red lights flashed, spotlights were searching the hills.

"Prison riot," Diego said. "They're all being let out of their cages and whoever is left standing is coming with us."

"Well, that's a bit unnecessary," I said. "Not to mention morbid. A fight to the death, the winners join us? Who are we, savages?"

"You have no idea what's going on with Este, do you?" he asked and I saw a glimmer of something sorry in his eyes. It made my palms sweat. "After I tell you, you're going to want to create as much fucking mayhem as possible."

"It's Luisa," I said. "I heard."

He gave me a terse smile. "It's not just Luisa. Javier, it's about your sister. Alana."

Even with the flashing lights, the god awful siren blaring in my ears, everything in the room seemed to still.

Alana.

I could barely speak. "What about her? She's dead."

"I know." He breathed out deeply. "But it was Esteban who killed her."

Funny how some words could render you immobile. I could only blink at Diego, trying to comprehend what he was saying.

"Excuse me?" I finally said, my hands balling up into fists again, nails digging into my palm. I absently noted I needed a manicure, as if that was something normal and safe that I could focus on.

"Perhaps you should sit down," Diego said, carefully laying his hand on my shoulder.

I shrugged him off. "Esteban killed Alana?" I repeated slowly.

"It was printed today in one of the papers," he said. "I am guessing you didn't see."

I shook my head once, my mouth open, fumbling for words, for anything.

Sympathy looked strange on Diego's rough face. "I'm sorry. He announced to the world that it was he who stole the boat, who kidnapped your sister and then blew it to hell with her on it on the way to Cabo San Lucas. He even went on to say that he'd hired an American *sicario* to do the job, and when he couldn't, he killed him too."

An American assassin. Somewhere in the back of my fading mind I knew he was talking about Derek Conway, a man who used to work for me and then disappeared. Fragments of the last conversation I had with Alana came floating back, like a puzzle rebuilding itself in my head, piece by piece.

The only thing I could say was, "Why?" But even then I knew it was a stupid question. The only answer was because.

Because she was my sister.

One of the last of my family left.

Because he knew personally how much family meant to me, even if my own family didn't know it themselves.

He killed her to send me into a tailspin.

My beautiful, darling young sister.

Then he moved onto Luisa. Seduced her when she was lost and vulnerable and I was taking out my rage on the rest of the world, purposefully pushing her away, wanting her out of my life, wanting to drown in grief and violence and madness.

He took advantage of every part of me.

Now I was in jail, and he wasn't going to stop until my cartel was in his hands, until he'd wrung every last drop of blood from my body.

It takes a monster to know a monster.

He was the worst of us all.

And I was going to rip him from limb to limb, tear him from ass to mouth, skin him alive and piss on his broken bones until I lost all traces of whatever humanity I had left.

I was living, breathing wrath and I was never going to stop.

I don't really remember what happened next. Everything went black, but it could have been my rage or it could have been the prison's power system failing.

The door to my cell opened and Diego and I walked out, into a land of screams and anguish. I would fit in here just fine.

Hiberto, Emilio and the tall, rangy warden were there, armed to the teeth with guns, knives and batons. If they were nervous or excited, I couldn't tell.

One of them handed me a machete and "thank you" was the last thing I'd said until the slaughter was over.

I don't know how many people I'd killed. It didn't matter. At some point Diego had to stop me from chopping up an inmate into even smaller bits. I had let the hate and anger fuel me until I was some sort of machine.

Naturally, my first stop was the ugly guard who had first teased me when I walked in. I did as I told myself I would. Only, before I slowly ground the machete across his throat and took off his head, I hacked off his hands and feet, then shoved his foot in his mouth. I thought it would be ironic. Maybe it was barbaric.

After that I just went crazy, adding to the mayhem, while the two guards, warden and Diego stood by my side for protection, even taking part. I wasn't going to walk around here without them. They kept the fuckers out for blood at bay while I was able to let my lucid fire unleash.

By the end of it, the whole prison block, filled with the worst of the worst, was filled with dead bodies, and there was more blood underfoot than floor. There were only about twelve of them that remained. They looked like the walking dead, chains and steel bars and knives in their hands.

But they knew who I was and they fought well and they were willing to walk free, out of this place with me, while I exacted my revenge. Esteban might have been building an army of depravity, but now I had mine and then some. I had everything except my boot on his throat and I was going to get that next.

I marched out of the prison with blood on my hands, under a dark and empty sky. I was a free man. While the prisoners were taken into waiting SUVs, Diego walked me out to Evaristo, who was standing in an ill-fitting suit that could have only been a product of a government agency.

"Congratulations," he said to me, holding out his hand. He didn't seem the slightest bit disturbed that when I half-heartedly shook his hand, it left his palm sticky with blood. "You made it out alive."

"That was always the plan," I said wryly while I eyed Diego for support, just in case. Diego only nodded, giving me his okay once again that Evaristo was to be trusted. I couldn't be sure about that, even though, so far, he let me walk out of prison, the very prison that his company had put me into. Not to mention that he just let a slew of other inmates go. And the other half were brutally murdered.

"And I know I'm a new addition to your plan," he said with a quick smile. Though the torture happened weeks earlier, his face was still puffy in places. It made him look older, more respectable. "But I can help you."

"And what do you want in return?" I asked. There was always a catch. In the distance I could hear choppers and some of the men looked to the distance in fear.

"To have opportunity," he simply said. "To have respect. A chance to go further than I ever thought possible." He nodded at a man who had been standing silently next to him. "Get them wherever they need to go. I'll take care of this. As far as the country will know, a prison riot broke out, decimating all of the most heinous criminals. Javier Bernal remains in his cell, unharmed, and Puente Grande remains the unescapable prison that the world thinks it is." He looked to me again with a smirk. "They're all yours, every one of them. You'll be taken to a safe house and I'll be in touch later tonight."

At that he strode off toward the building, the sirens still going, the choppers coming closer. If we didn't move now, we'd be on national news.

We quickly hurried off into the waiting SUV and were taken into the night.

I didn't know where the safe house was, somewhere between Guadalajara and Mexico City, but it was remote and more secure than I could have imagined. It was pretty much a bunker cut into a swath of jungle. Even if it were daylight there was no way you'd see it until you were literally right on top.

It was also surprisingly spacious inside the bunker. The whole underground structure must have been the size of a mansion, simply decorated but still more than just a hole in the ground. There was a kitchen, bathrooms, dining and living rooms, plus various bedrooms with bunks and offices. Many of the doors were closed and locked. The crazy escapees, who I guessed were "mine" as Evaristo had put it, were led down the hall to the bunks. I didn't know how any of them could sleep next to each other after that.

There was something entirely unnerving about being underground, trapped like a misdirected gopher. I kept expecting for someone to point a gun in my face and demand my return to Puente Grande, or, at the very least, kill me.

But that didn't happen and as the night wore on, the more I realized I needed places just like this. Yes, mansions and spacious grounds and all the beautiful things I cultivated were something I wanted in my daily life, but I also needed to feel safe. After everything that had happened, I knew being safe and feeling safe were two different things.

I didn't sleep that night. The adrenaline from the slaughter, from the escape, was still coursing through my veins. I changed into a spare set of clothes that Evaristo's man had brought out for me – black pants and a linen dress shirt – and stayed up in the living area with Diego, drinking the few beers we found in the safe house's fridge, trying to calm down. For all my impatience, I knew we had to wait here for Evaristo before we did anything else. If I acted just on instinct, I would have stolen an SUV and driven right up to the compound near Culiacan, ambushed the house and hoped Esteban was home.

I still didn't know what to do about Luisa. The more I thought about her, the more disquieted I felt.

After I had lapsed into silence for a long time, Diego nudged my beer with his. In the dead air of the bunker, the sound fell flat.

"What are you going to do about Luisa?" Diego asked, reading me so well.

I exhaled out my nose, then shook my head and leaned back in my seat. "I don't know."

"Will you kill her?"

I closed my eyes and tried to find the truth. The truth could hurt me but at least it was real.

"I want to kill her," I said and then corrected myself as I imagined her dead in my hands. "I need to kill her. For what she has done to me."

"Javier, I don't mean to play Devil's Advocate here, but I don't think Luisa had anything to do with putting you in jail."

My throat felt thick, closing in. I looked at my hands, the blood still in my cuticles. "She was fucking Esteban. Isn't that enough?"

"That's up to you, my friend. But if you want revenge on her, you will have to wait your turn. Esteban comes first. He must be dealt with."

"I'll deal with him," I said, my eyes hard as I stared at him. "I'm more than ready to."

"I know. I just don't want things to go to shit when we find him."

"If anyone is to find him, they aren't to kill him. They are to bring him to me."

"That I think everyone knows. The whole country is

awaiting your revenge, you know. Esteban has set himself up to be the villain here, not you. In some ways, you've got more of your people's respect. Being in prison while he walks free with your wife, the same woman he publicly tortures, has made you out to be a martyr. And when you finally do get your revenge, they'll revere you more for it. Without meaning to, Esteban has led a whole new victory into your hands."

"But at what cost?" I asked quietly.

He'd killed my sister. He'd stolen my wife. Those were things that could never be made up for, no matter how much the country believed in me or set me up to be a demi-god, like so many *narcos* before me.

Diego nodded grimly. "You tell me what to do and I'll do it. If you decide to kill Luisa, I'll look away but I won't help you. But if you tell me to protect Luisa and save her from him, I will. I have your back, Javier."

I gave him a wry look. "She has a way of worming into your heart, doesn't she?"

His smile was grave and I knew how much he actually respected my wife. I had wondered if Diego had ever fallen in love, ever married, ever had children. He never talked about his past like that, but so many people wiped their past clean when they became a *narco* or *sicarrio*. They couldn't hold onto memories because memories were just fire and would burn in their hands. You couldn't hold a gun if your hands were scarred.

Mine were only bloody.

It was almost morning when Evaristo appeared in the bunker, coming down the narrow staircase from the world up top.

"Didn't get any sleep?" he asked, peering down at Diego and me as we sat on the couches, tapping our fingers and feet from boredom and anticipation. It was odd to see him now with that authoritative slant, after everything I'd done to him.

"We've been waiting for you," I said, suddenly exhausted. "Like little bitches."

He smiled and shoved his hands in his pant pockets. "You know, I'm the one who should have the problem with you."

"Is that right?" I asked carefully, sliding my tongue over my teeth.

"I'm the one who is still missing a toe."

I shrugged. "And I had to wear the same orange jumpsuit for a few weeks, all while you made a deal with the actual devil."

He sighed and sat on the arm of the opposite couch, rubbing his hand on the back of his neck. "Normally I would argue that. Javier, I know a lot more about you than you can even imagine. About your rise within the ranks of Travis Raines, the *gringo*, all the way to your takeover. About your little scuffle with the Americans in California, which then had you thrown into a US prison, then your release and the kidnapping of Luisa Reyes. The fall of Salvador. The Sinaloa cartel that you took." He paused. "But despite all you've done, I know you're not Esteban Mendoza. That there is a line between ambition and lunacy, between, well, evil and pure evil, if you want to be dramatic."

"Are you sure you don't want to be on the more dramatic side?" I asked.

He shook his head. "You know, I had a brief talk with your wife." I stiffened. "When you sent her to look after me. She's a good, kind woman you know. But full of spikes, as my grandmother would say. She told me you would go far, all the way to the top, and you would not fail. And I believed her. I wanted in on that. Esteban is just a rabid dog. He's dangerous and deranged and getting more psychotic as this goes on, as the power is finally passed on to him. I haven't just been studying you, I've been studying him. But he doesn't have your intelligence, your charm, or your connections. He is the losing side. You are not. You will take it all back and for once, I will be on the side that wins."

After a moment I said, "That's a nice speech. But you probably should have arrested Esteban while you had the chance."

"There was no chance with the *federales*. Contrary to your belief, they do things by the book. And that's why they always lose and will continue to lose in the end. Being good and just doesn't guarantee success. If anything, it can mean your failure."

I exchanged a glance with Diego. "A pessimist," he remarked.

"A realist," Evaristo countered.

"And so young at that," I added.

"It's in our blood, what can I say." He got up off the couch. "Unless you have any objections, tomorrow we strike your residence near Culiacan."

"My objection is that I'd rather strike it right now. While they are both there and are both alive."

"And you're too smart to know that we aren't about to

rush into anything. Try and get some rest," he said, undoing his tie and walking into the kitchen.

Sleep would be unlikely. But I found myself drifting away on that couch for a few hours, despite my own objections.

CHAPTER EIGHTEEN

Luisa

J avier always used to tell me he didn't think he had a
soul, and if he did, he was sure it was a dirty one. I
was more inclined to believe he did, despite the ways
he ruled his life. I believed that everyone had a soul,
somewhere deep in their body, and it was up to them to
let their real spirit free. Even those deemed bad, corrupt,
immoral, had light shining through them from time to
time. In Javier's case, I likened his soul to a dirty window.
The glow was muddled and what did come through was
in little cracks and smudges.

But those little cracks held the brightest light, piercing
through the darkness and shining a spotlight in some of the
blackest places of the heart. Javier had those cracks, that
sharp light, and it was blinding sometimes. I felt I was
special just to witness it.

That was just a memory now. I'd met men that had
no soul, men like Salvador, who proved my theory wrong.
And now I was with Esteban, a man who was far, far
worse than my ex-husband and abuser. Salvador was
rough and wicked but for all the bad that he was, it
wasn't unusual. Men like him thrived in the cartels, they
were born to be *narcos*. You knew who he was from the

start. He made no apologies, he wanted to frighten the world.

But Esteban Mendoza was pure evil. He wasn't even human, I knew that. If you believed in absolute evil, he was evil absolute. He hid under the persona of being a young, dumb, careless man and even though he certainly wasn't smart, his capacity for inflicting pain and suffering was beyond my understanding.

And what I couldn't understand, I had no choice but to fear. This was a man beyond reasoning and help and what hurt most of all, what made me feel like I was too stupid to live, that I almost deserved his cruelty, was that I had never seen it coming. I fell for him. Not the real thing, but at least a tempered version of that. I fell for the illusion of someone that was bad, but not *that* bad. I was lured in by a man who said all the right things and was there when my husband wasn't and made me feel like I was someone worth loving, if not liking. If not respecting.

I never dreamed that beneath the easy smile and jealous tendencies, the devil incarnate was lurking.

He was a living nightmare.

And I couldn't wake up.

Esteban kept me locked in my room most of the time. The irony was that it used to be the very room that Javier had held me captive in, the one with the windows that didn't open, couldn't break. Looking back, I would have given anything to have been under Javier's wrath instead of this. I held strong with Javier during that time because somehow, somewhere, I knew that I could get through to him.

Instead, Javier had gotten through to me.

But now, now it was different. It wasn't even a place. It was this black, nebulous hole of pain and humiliation. Sometimes it was Esteban who had his way with me, other times it was Juanito. At least he was someone I could appeal to. My tears seemed to keep his violence at bay, because Juanito's violence was only taught through Esteban. It wasn't in his nature, like it wasn't in so many people's nature. He wasn't born this way, it was thrust upon him and he was molded by the bad and the wicked. We were a nation of people under this heavy hand.

But Esteban's nature was evil from the moment he came out of the womb, disguising it from day one from the rest of the world, fooling us all. The minute his plan went into effect was the moment that he let it blossom, flourish, transforming himself into someone bad, into someone straight from Hell. And when he dealt with me, I could feel it.

It was all I could feel. Nothing but evil. I was sleeping in my own feces and urine, forced to drink water from the same water they let the hogs drink out of. Sometimes live chickens would be placed in my room, chickens who were angry and starved and they would peck at me over and over again until I had no choice but to kill them. I was given no food at all and when I asked for some Esteban shoved their rotting carcasses in my face, telling me that was my food.

By day five, I stripped the chickens of their feathers and was forced to eat them raw. It was either do that or starve and I needed every ounce of strength I could get.

Because despite everything that was happening to me

and the brutality that I kept witnessing, that kept branding me, I needed to fight back. It didn't matter if the room was covered in feathers and I was cowering in the corner naked, bruised and beaten, with matted hair, tearing into a putrid chicken with blood-stained teeth. I had plans to get out of here.

Or I was going to die trying.

And if I was going to die, I was going to try and inflict as much pain and bloodshed as I could as I went out.

Maybe then I'd die with a smile on my face.

I may have underestimated Esteban.

But I would make sure he underestimated me.

The days and nights passed slowly in the house. I had no way of keeping track because sleep rarely came for me and I kept the curtains closed all the time. I lived in darkness and in that darkness, I grew something sharp and ragged in my heart. It was strength and it was vengeance and it was enough to keep beating, to keep me alive.

It must have been the night because the room was dense black, more dead than usual. I was sitting, back against the wall, trailing a chicken feather up and down my bare body, trying to pretend I was somewhere else. That the feather was a soft caress, skin on skin, a lover's touch. Something nice, something sweet, something hopeful. Even though Javier could be rough with me at times and I liked it, he could also be gentle, tender and passionate too. I wanted to pretend the feather was him, his lips, his forgiveness for all my sins.

I sat there, just letting myself believe each stroke was full of hope, the tickle on my scratched arms, a balm on my cuts and wounds.

The door opened abruptly, light from the hall cutting abrasively into the room, and Esteban strode inside, his shadow menacing and seeming to hold more depth than it should have. In his hands was a toolbox, which he carefully placed on the floor before locking the door behind him.

We were engulfed in blackness again. I told myself to not be afraid, that he couldn't do anything worse to me, that I was strong enough to get through this but I couldn't help but suck in my breath, holding it in like it was too precious to spare in the same room as him.

"Sitting in the dark," his voice said, always so jovial. It made everything that much more wrong. "It's not healthy for you."

I heard him open the box and start to fish around for something. Metal clinked against glass. Things that sounded sharp. I suppressed a shiver and wondered if now was the time to act. If this would be my chance.

As he searched for something, I slowly, quietly, got to my feet, staying hunched over, and walked sideways along the wall. I knew the room inside out by now, knew where the bed was and the small armchair, the beside table. If I could get to the door without him noticing, then I could attack, as long as he didn't attack me first.

I didn't have much in the way of weapons. But I did have chicken bones that I'd broken apart until I found the sharpest, hardest shards. I'd then wrapped them all together into a short spear, with torn strips of my old nightgown.

It wasn't much, but I also had rage and the basic human need for survival.

He wasn't human, so he couldn't have that. And I wouldn't let him take it from me.

"Quiet these days, aren't we?" Esteban asked. The sound of the box slammed shut. I paused near the bed, my hands guiding me along it. I could almost hear him fiddling with something in his hands, though I had no idea what it could be. A knife but . . . more complicated than that.

There wasn't much else to my plan other than fighting my way out by either killing or maiming him and then hoping I could have an easy escape. It was just as likely that I'd die out there, by the hands of his crew that enjoyed torturing me and defiling me just as much as he did. But on the chance that I could get out alive, I didn't know where my feet would carry me.

The truth was, after everything was said and done, I would do what I could to get back to Javier. I would go to Puente Grande and beg to see him, just for a moment, knowing full well he would hate me. Possibly even kill me. But even though I was sure he wouldn't believe me when I told him I never wanted any of this, I at least had to let him know. He was still everything I had and I never did any of the horrible things I did because I stopped loving him.

How fucking pathetic was I? I was hiding in the dark from a psychotic torturer, plotting my escape, and my heart kept clinging to love.

Javier would have been so disappointed in me.

"You know, Luisa," Esteban went on, slowly. Though his tone was edgier now, his voice was still aimed at the spot I used to be. He thought I was still sitting there in the dark. I wondered how long it would take for his eyes to adjust or if he'd mistaken the dark shadows for me. "Everything good must come to an end. You must think of yourself as a good thing, don't you? After all you were the beauty queen of San Jose del Cabo. That must have done wonders for your self-esteem, for your impression of your own life. Didn't it?"

I kept my breathing as quiet as possible and started along the bed again. It was agonizing going so slow but I knew I couldn't mess it up by being impatient.

"Such a beauty they must have called you," he said. I heard his footsteps, now right across from me but heading toward the wall. "That's how you caught the eye of Salvador Reyes, isn't it? You were so damn fucking pretty that he had to make you his wife." His voice became lower, almost a conspiratorial whisper. "Don't you know that if you didn't have your beauty, you wouldn't be worth anything to anyone at all? Do you think Javier would have been so enraptured by you if you were fat and ugly, if your body at all reflected the kind of person you really are? No, of course not. But you got another free pass in your life's ride, while everyone else in this country suffers."

He was baiting me, getting me to snap back, to say something that would give him an excuse to beat me, even though he could find an excuse in anything. I had to literally bite my tongue, thick and swollen from lack of water, to prevent myself from saying what I really wanted to. Esteban must have grown up so damn jealous of everyone around him that it didn't matter what sex you were, he wanted what you had and he felt entitled to take it.

"It's not fair, Luisa," he said and now his voice was cracking with anger. "It's not fair that you got to have everything you did. And loving parents too? How fucking dare you!" He paused then took in a deep breath. When he spoke again, he was calmer. Ice. "I took Javier away from you. I took your cartel, your purpose. I'll take your parents soon, too. But now, tonight, I'm taking away something you never deserved to have. Your beauty."

My eyes widened as I heard the sharp scrape of rusty scissors being yanked open.

"Now are you going to be a good little girl or what?" he asked as he ran blindly forward, his footsteps echoing loudly.

I moved as quickly and quietly as I could, willing myself not to panic, to make noise, but it was hard when he yelled, "Where are you, you little bitch!?" and began to run around the edge of the room.

I heard him bump into the bed, swearing and grunting angrily, too close now for comfort. I had to run for it.

I started for the door, guided by the light underneath it and went for the lock. My hands groped for it, my heart on fire and nerves alight as panic threatened to consume me. I clumsily found the handle, then tried to place where the lock would be but by the time my fingers closed over it, it was too late.

Esteban was behind me and stabbed the scissors down into my shoulder, slicing through flesh, muscle, bone. An image of the chicken I ate flashed in my eyes, the way their bones could break, but it also reminded me of what I had in my hands.

Instead of screaming, I took that energy in and whirled

around stabbing wildly with my spear, hoping to get him in the face. The end of it went into a soft spot of skin, maybe the lower throat and he let out an enraged yelp as it stuck in.

Before I could do any more damage, he decked me in the face until I flew back against the wall, my face exploding in stars of pain.

I wouldn't let it keep me down. I scrambled to all fours, staying low and went at him, going for where his legs should be. One knee grazed my chin but I was able to wrap my hands around the other one, my nails turning into makeshift claws and I dug them into his skin as deep as possible. He screamed and tried to shake me off but not before I jerked my head down and bit into the back of his calf, tearing my teeth in, wanting to take out a chunk.

I had become a feral, wild beast.

I had to do everything to survive.

I felt the blood run down my chin, tasted his tainted flesh. I was holding on tight, digging my incisors in, more, more, more, but then his hand was in my hair and he was yanking me back away from him until I was on my back on the floor.

Everything spun but I knew I couldn't let it stop me. I tried to get back up but then his elbow was driving down into my collarbone, trying to break it and his other hand was repeatedly banging my head into the floor.

"You fucking bitch, you fucking bitch!" he kept muttering over and over again like a man possessed, until finally he stopped. I couldn't even move. I felt completely paralyzed from the head down, a sitting fucking duck who was about to have her own feathers plucked.

He briefly crawled off of me, heading across the room, and that's when I knew I had to run again, I could try again to escape, and if I got to the door, it was unlocked and I would make it out.

I was so close.

But I couldn't. I didn't know what he had done to me but I just couldn't move a muscle, no matter how hard I fought past the haze, no matter how hard I concentrated, willing my body to respond.

It felt as dead as the rest of me.

I'd never been more frightened, more helpless, more alone, in all my sorry life.

I hadn't wanted to cry at all with Esteban, I told myself I wouldn't shed one tear in front of him. I wouldn't give him the pleasure of what he was doing to me.

But now, now the fear was so real as I lay there, naked and broken in the darkness, bleeding, paralyzed. It came for me at once and the tears fell from my eyes, sliding down the sides of my face to the floor.

I was so sad. So damn sad.

This was how I was going to die and I was going to suffer for a long time before I did.

At least I tried.

I tried.

I fucking tried to live, I tried my damn hardest.

I made a million and one mistakes but I still tried.

God, I wished I didn't have to die alone and in pain.

I wished Javier was here with me.

I tried to bring the image of him in my vision. Like the feather against my skin, I hoped it would trick me enough to bring me strength to die with dignity, to

endure what horror was to come. I hoped it would erase
the fear. The sorrow that filled me up, a well of seeping
black drops.

Then a light went on in my face, my eyes squeezed
shut in response and Esteban chuckled.

"You're crying?" Esteban said mockingly as he came
back over to me. "The little girl is crying? You fucking
pathetic little cunt, I haven't even given you anything to
cry about yet."

I heard the scissors being picked up in his hand and
he kneeled beside me. He grabbed my hair and began
slicing through my strands. His movements were rough,
the scissors dull even though they razed my skull in places
and I felt the blood spill down my face and neck.

"You won't look pretty after this," he said, going around
my head until he was apparently satisfied. My head felt
lighter, colder, without all my hair which now lay on the
ground around me. I felt like I should have lost a part of
myself, if only I hadn't lost myself already.

Please move, move! I yelled at myself, at my body.
Please, please, please. Try!

"Hmmm," Esteban mused. I didn't have to open my
eyes to know he was looking over me. "You're not as ugly
as you should be. Hair can grow back, can't it? I should
know, mine comes in quite fast. I have to get it trimmed
every few months."

His blasé words floated over me, having no bearing. I
was lost inside my head, in a life or death battle for control
of my body.

Almost, almost, almost. I willed every muscle to react.
I tried to imagine every nerve coming alive. I couldn't

be paralyzed, I had to be stunned. But my body was stubborn. It didn't seem to understand what was happening, it wasn't connecting with the adrenaline that could save me.

Esteban took the scissors and trailed them from my collarbone, down the scar his men had left last week when they gang raped me, over to my breast.

"I could cut this off," he said softly and he scraped the blade over my nipple.

Move, move, move.

"No man would want you after that," he said, bringing the blade back over again until I could feel it cut. It was shallow but it was a warning of what was to come.

Please, please, move.

"Or I could take a chunk out myself with my own teeth. Chew up your fat. Spit it back out at you."

He was more than depraved now. He'd officially gone mad with his own brutality. He'd gone insane.

He continued. "It's only fair. You got my leg pretty good. Luckily I'm used to scars. But you don't have enough. Just the one on your back."

The one that said Javier.

Javier.

Javier would be so angry at me for giving up like this, for letting Esteban win.

"But men would have to get you naked in order to be repulsed. You could live your life a beauty as long as that didn't happen, as long as you stayed an untouchable queen. And I can't let that happen. We've come so far and what sort of *patron* would I be if I didn't do my worst? What kind of message would that send to everyone else?"

I felt him lift away from me slightly, taking the scissors with him. I didn't dare breathe out in relief. There would be no relief here.

I opened my eyes and looked at him, lit up in a cold glow by the screen of his phone which lay on the floor. He was reaching beside him and bringing up a metal jar with a peeling label.

Acid.

Sulfuric acid.

No, no, no.

But his eyes said yes and he quickly unscrewed the jar, holding it out above my stomach. He tipped it slightly and the liquid fell out in a single splash.

For a moment it was like I didn't feel anything, for a moment I thought I was free, but that's only because the pain was too much for my senses to bear.

Then it hit like a freight train of fire.

I screamed until my throat felt like it was being ripped raw as the acid ate away at my skin, a small but deadly puddle on my stomach.

"I'm sorry," Esteban said loudly, trying to be heard above my anguished cries. "But you know you deserve this. Luisa, you really do."

He moved the jar up to my face. "And this is where it's really going to hurt. Your beauty, your lazy power, gone. Forever."

I watched in horror at his cold green eyes. I watched at the small smile on his lips. I watched as his hand moved slightly and the jar tipped, the acid running to the edge of the rim.

I turned my head, pinching my eyes shut in time for

the acid to hit my left cheekbone, crying out again as my whole head felt as if it erupted in flames. It was as if the acid was burning a black hole into my head, into my heart, into my soul.

And somewhere deep inside me, deeper than the acid could go, my mind and body connected. The adrenaline pumped through me in one hard burst, kicking in like a jump-start.

I moved before I could even think. I reached out, knocking the acid out of his hands and then with strength I didn't even know existed in me, I leaped on top of him, pressing his head back into the acid on the ground. He yelped as the acid made contact, burning through his hair and I knew I had nothing more than a split second before he threw me off of him.

I swiped up the scissors from the ground beside me, making a fist around the handle, and plunged them straight down into his left eyeball.

It didn't even make me squeamish, not even as the eyeball bulged around the blades as they pierced through it. I just yelled, a crazed battle cry, in his face as I stabbed him.

Unfortunately I didn't have enough strength or time to push it all the way into his skull and brain.

My time had run out.

Esteban screamed in horrific agony and pushed me off of him. I did what I could to crawl away, my face and body burning as the acid ate at the nerves, looking for something else to use in defense. Over by the box of tools he struggled to get to his feet, knocking it all over, and in the glow of the phone I saw him place both his hands over the scissor handle and pull it out with one quick tug.

His eye came out with it, stuck on the scissors' end.

The scream to follow was animalistic, the sound of a creature dying, filling the room, yet it was quickly buried by the sound of gunfire outside the window. Esteban howled and staggered over to the door, flinging it open and running out into the hallway which was filled with gunfire and people shouting.

He took the scissors, and his eye, with him.

I was left behind.

To die or to live.

Mustering what strength I could, I started to crawl across the floor. My shoulder and breast gashed and bleeding, my hair shorn, my collarbone smashed in, my face and stomach burning away. I had to survive, after all this, I had to live.

I almost made it to the door before the last of the adrenaline was depleted from my veins. Then I stopped, collapsing on the floor, and the last tear fell from my eyes.

I had tried.

CHAPTER NINETEEN

Javier

We left just before dusk, three SUVs filled with some of Mexico's most wanted. Me, Evaristo and Diego were in the middle car, with one of Evaristo's men at the wheel. He didn't talk much, which I appreciated.

In fact, not many of us did as we rolled along the highways and backroads, heading up toward the capitol of Sinaloa and my home.

My home. It had started to sound foreign ever since I was put away. It was as if I had believed Esteban and his attempts to take over.

I wouldn't believe that anymore. It was my home and I was going back and I was taking back everything that was rightfully mine. I had no choice now but to rise like a phoenix from the ashes and rule again once more.

Around a kilometer away from the compound, we took a sharp left down an even rougher dirt road, one that used to lead to a poppy farm once upon a time, before the DEA hazed it down all those years ago. We rolled up and down potholes that would have swallowed a smaller car until we came to a small clearing among the leafy ceiba trees.

We parked and Evaristo turned around from the front seat to face Diego and me.

"Isn't this where your tunnel leads?"

Shit. He was good, he was able to lead us right here without me saying anything. The tunnel – built by the previous *narco* owner – lead from the house to an area beyond the hog's barn, then had another entrance point here, the old poppy field far beyond the rugged brush that surrounded the compound.

I studied Evaristo for a moment. "All this intel you had on me and you couldn't make a move. Why?"

He shrugged. "Same reason why we didn't go after Hernandez when we had him. We've been trying to borrow the book from the North Americans and give warrant and reason to our arrests. A waste of time, as you know. We had you. Have you. We have everyone, almost, except the ones who are really on the run, as you may have to be if and when word gets out. But we are not allowed to make a move until all the boxes have been checked. I think it has a lot to do with the North Americans meddling in our jobs, even though the *federales* would never admit it. There has been far too much money put into our force."

"I guess they're hoping you won't be so corrupt this time around."

He smiled. "And you can see they were wrong about that."

We got out of the cars and gathered around while Evaristo and some of his men opened the trunk and started handing out ammo. They had been briefed over and over again during the day over what was going to take place and, unsurprisingly, there were no objections. The whole lot of them were primed for more bloodshed, you could practically see them salivating at the mouth.

It didn't help that when morning came around, one of the men was found strangled to death. Apparently he had been a child molester and that's why he had been behind bars. Even the country's worst criminals had a limit to what they would tolerate.

Me, Diego and one of Evaristo's men were to go in through the tunnel – this was my decision of course. It was my home and I should be the first one to step foot in it and reclaim my property. I knew the tunnel would bring us up to a space behind the pantry in the kitchen. I had no idea if our entry was going to be quiet and undetected but the kitchen was as good of a place as any. We were also armed to the teeth, which helped. I alone had a grenade, two pistols and a hunter's knife, while Diego was armed with an AK and who knows what else up his sleeves.

While we were coming up from the inside, Evaristo would be leading the other men to come at the house from three different sides. Everyone inside would scramble and I would catch Este, hopefully while he was heading toward the very tunnel I had just come out of.

Now that we knew for sure that he was inside – Evaristo had been monitoring the site through government satellite images in the morning – I could feel the same anger from earlier simmering deep inside me.

I was going to take him down. I was going to make him pay.

Evaristo gave us the go ahead.

Diego and I hoisted up the flat board that had been covered in giant waxy leaves and peered down into the tunnel. We pulled down the agency-issued night vision glasses Evaristo had given us and proceeded to climb down the metal ladder and onto the dirt floor below. The tunnel had no lights and was far cruder than the one at the *finca*, but at least this way we could see without drawing attention to ourselves. Our communication between each other was kept to a minimum as well – we had all had earpieces but weren't allowed to use them until the time was right, just in case Esteban and all his high-tech glory was having the place monitored for frequencies.

Diego and I stared up at Evaristo through the tunnel hole, back lit by a vibrant night sky. He held up his phone. "I'm tracking you. When I see you get into the house, we will ambush. After that, you're free to use your radio transmitters."

I didn't care how efficient he was being, I didn't like being bossed around.

"Remember, I want Esteban alive," I told him.

He saluted me. "Yes, *patron*."

At least he still knew his place.

He turned back to my new army, an army of depravity, and Diego and I started jogging down the long tunnel. It wasn't a quick journey but luckily I'd been keeping in shape during the Puente Grande stint. The only reason the 1.5 km run felt longer was because with each second that passed by, I was gearing myself up to unleash utter destruction.

With every breath I took I thought of Alana.

With every footfall I thought of Luisa.

Back and forth, the two of them, until there was nothing but ugliness inside me.

It was the perfect insurance to ensure that I wouldn't hold back tonight.

Finally the tunnel started to slope upward and curve sharply to the right and I knew that we were under the house now. We paused before the ladder and listened. There was nothing but dead air and the sound of our own breath.

I jerked my chin at him to say, *You first this time.*

He nodded and climbed up, his hefty weight making the ladder wobble slightly, shaking loose dirt from the tunnel wall. This was where we had nothing but a hope and prayer that there wasn't anything stacked on top of the cover.

Diego pressed his hands along it and slowly began to push up. I held my breath as he struggled for a moment, so sure that something was going to immediately crash in the pantry.

But he kept pushing and he was able to slowly slide the cover over, fresh air smelling of flour and tin wafting down toward us. There was a slight clank as it knocked into something solid but other than that we were as quiet as possible.

Diego eased himself up the ladder and looked around once he was fully out. I quickly came up after him and together we were squeezed in the narrow space. If I hadn't been so strung out, I would have made a joke about his breath but as it was, nothing was funny at the moment.

My gun began to feel heavy in my hands. I needed to use it and soon.

Light was seeping in underneath the door, so I pushed my goggles up on my head and slowly pushed the door open.

The kitchen was empty. The only light came from above the stove. The fridge hummed and the house was silent except for muffled laughter coming down the hall.

A terrible scream splintered the room.

A man's scream.

Had the ambush already begun?

I exchanged a worried glance with Diego as we heard doors further down the hall being flung open. Footsteps.

People ran past the kitchen heading up the stairs toward the scream, not bothering to look our way.

All of them except for Juanito, that was.

He stopped dead in his tracks at the archway, staring at us like we were ghosts. I couldn't help but grin.

He snapped out of it, reaching for his gun, but mine was already aimed at him. I shot him in the kneecaps, both of them, just as his gun fired, bullets cracking the ceiling.

Then, as if on cue, all of the outside erupted in gunfire. The sound shook the walls and through the wavering windows bursts of light filled the sky. My army was here.

I ran over to Juanito who was screaming in pain and picked him up by the collar, shaking him.

"Alright you little fuckface," I sneered at him, trying to fight the urge to strangle the fucking life out of him. "Tell me where Esteban is and I'll make your death painless. Don't tell me and I'll break your bones with a hammer. Which one is it?"

His screaming wouldn't stop. I shook him again. "You can't protect him now, you'll never fucking walk again and he sure as hell won't give two fucks about a pathetic piece of garbage like you. So talk."

But before he could, Diego was calling out my name and I let go of Juanito, rolling over him just in time as the air above me burned with bullets. Diego fired back at the assailants and I kept rolling until I was behind the kitchen island. I quickly reached for the grenade which I knew could take out enough of them without damaging the structural integrity of the house, and tossed it out of the kitchen. It rolled down the hallway.

They yelled to move but it was too late and I pressed my hands over my ears as the blast went off.

"Jesus, Javi," Diego swore as pieces of plaster rained down on him. "You haven't even moved back in yet."

I didn't care if it was sloppier than my usual methods – it was efficient. I scrambled to my feet and stared at the wreckage. There was a ragged hole in the wall, smoke and flames licking the edge.

I shrugged. "I wanted to open up that room anyway."

Miraculously, or something of that nature, Juanito was still alive, holding onto his bleeding and blasted knees as he writhed on the floor.

He was missing half his face though, so it's not like he escaped the explosion unscathed. He was *very* scathed and crawling for freedom.

I covered my nose and mouth with the crook of my elbow and walked into the smoke, letting it wash over me. Juanito looked up at me with what was left of him, begging for mercy with an outstretched hand.

I stepped on his hand instead, crunching the bones beneath my boot.

"That was for my sister," I seethed. "I know you intercepted her call when she was calling me, for help."

"Javier, we have to go," Diego said, coughing and coming over to stop me. A war was raging around me but none of it mattered. All that mattered was an eye for an eye.

This time I stomped on Juanito's arm, driving it in with all my might, like I was squashing a cockroach, until I felt it break beneath me.

He screamed.

I smiled.

But I was the furthest thing from happy.

And Juanito couldn't even speak at this point. His mouth was a flap of burning skin, covering a gaping hole. He was useless.

I slid the hunter's knife out of its sheath and with one swift motion, stabbed it downward into the top of his skull.

The screaming stopped.

"Javier," Diego warned again, pulling at me. "That had been Esteban's scream, he's upstairs."

I nodded, trying to keep focus, and yanked the knife back out, wiping the brain and blood on my pants. They weren't my pants anyway.

Diego led the way into the smoldering hallway, stepping over the dead bodies of Esteban's fuckheads. Some of them were missing body parts, a foot here, a torso there, others were just a splash of guts on what was left of the wall.

We made our way up the stairs, firing at anyone who came at us and using the cover of smoke to our advantage. We kicked open doors, checked the rooms, searching for Esteban.

It wasn't until we came to the last room, what had once been Luisa's prison, that I realized what I was going to find.

Of course this would be her prison again.

Of course she would be in there.

With my heart already in a vice, I paused before looking in the room.

The door was already open and with what little light was left in the hallway, blurred by smoke and flickering from waning power, it illuminated Luisa lying on the floor.

I didn't recognize her at first.

She was nothing more than a pile of blood-splashed limbs, a corpse.

Her hair was all gone, shorn off in clumps around her. She was bleeding and cut, mangled and bruised.

Naked and burned.

I immediately lost my breath, like someone had thrown a brick at my gut and I grabbed onto the doorframe to steady myself. I couldn't feel my knees.

My angel.

My queen.

Ravaged.

Ruined.

I'd never wipe the sight of her from my mind, never forget the horror.

A sob choked in my throat but I didn't know if I was going to vomit right here or cry.

Diego dropped to his knees beside her, his hands hovering above her but he couldn't bring himself to touch her, as if touching her would break her into a million pieces.

"Javier," he said without looking at me. He didn't say anything else. I could only hold on as if that doorframe was the only thing keeping me from descending into complete madness.

She was so beaten, so broken, by life, by everything.

My queen.

My queen.

"Javier," Diego said again, clearing his throat. He finally lay his finger underneath her purple and black chin. "She's alive. Barely. But she is alive."

He looked to me and I saw my own hate reflected in them. "I'll take care of her," he said. "You get Esteban. He's the one who did this."

He didn't have to tell me that. I already knew. He'd done this and who knows what else to my wife, showing off for the world to see. Now, he'd discarded her here, alone in the dark, to die.

I wasn't put away in Puente Grande just so that he could try and take over the cartel. I was put there so I couldn't protect the one thing that mattered to me. I was put there so I and the whole world would see just how far he would go.

And he succeeded.

I couldn't protect her.

I failed.

But I would do what I could now, while I could.

I gathered up strength, burying my sorrow and shock

in some cold, hard place inside me. I knew Diego would keep his word.

I turned and ran back down the hall, slamming on my earpiece as I went.

"Where are you?" I yelled into it, shooting at someone just as they had come out from the burning hallway at the bottom of the stairs. The man fell with a yell and I ran past, heading for the back of the house.

I heard Evaristo's voice crackle in my ear. "Front lawn. Be careful, your own men are around the corner and they shoot first, ask questions later."

I'd forgotten he was tracking me. I shoved the back door open and ran across the grass, heading toward the koi pond and staying low so that neither friend nor foe could get a shot. "I found Luisa," I said, surprised that I could say her name without my voice cracking. "Diego is with her. I want Este."

"I want him too," Evaristo said. "But he's not here."

"That's not fucking good enough!" I yelled just as someone took a shot at me from the roof, the bullet missing me by a few feet and going into the pond.

What a terrible shot, I thought as I turned to look.

And there he fucking was.

Esteban was standing on the roof, alone, gun in one hand, his body lit by the lights below.

His other hand over his eye.

No wonder he missed, the fuck could barely see.

I didn't have to tell myself to shoot back, I was already pulling the trigger but a deafening roar filled my ears and I was shoved to the grass by a gust of whirring wind that whipped my shirttails.

I rolled onto my back, gun raised in time to see a Lama helicopter slowly rising from the other side of the pond, hidden by a clump of trees that I knew Luisa used to hide behind.

Luisa.

The image of her was burned in my brain.

The vicious ugly burn on her delicate skin.

I bellowed in anger and tried to get to my feet, to get a clear shot of Esteban but he was already running to the edge of the roof, ready to hitch a ride, while the chopper was now fully warmed-up and flying toward me, the guns of the men on board taking fire.

"He's on the roof!" I managed to yell to Evaristo before I rolled away. I went right into the pond, swimming deep into the reeds and lily pads that would provide cover. Bullets plunged alongside me.

My leg exploded in a bright explosion of pain and that's when I knew I'd been hit, but I still had to stay under. I stared up through the murky water at the lights of the chopper as it continued on its way, stirring the pond into waves, heading now for the house.

I burst up through the water, gasping for breath, and wasted no time in climbing out of the pond. Esteban was so close to getting on the helicopter. I ran as fast as I could with my damaged leg, trying to get a shot but they only hit the rotors.

Esteban leaped, making it on board and the chopper quickly pulled away into the night.

"Motherfucker!" I screamed.

I tapped my ear piece but the water had ruined it. I tossed it away in anger and then limped around to the front of the house, cautiously approaching as I was sure the war was still going on.

Thankfully, the battle had been in our favor and while many of our men were dead, we were still the last ones standing. The gunfire and mayhem was over.

"I saw him get away," Evaristo said gruffly as he saw me staggering around the corner. "We had a rocket launcher ready but it stuffed fucking up at the last minute. Piece of fucking shit."

He was mad. Really mad. And that's when I knew he was legit. He wanted Esteban as much as the rest of us did. It must have been eating at him all this time to know that it was his own government assholes that made the deal with him.

I shook my head. "It doesn't matter, we're getting him. Now. Every day after this. For the rest of my life, we are getting him. I want his head on a fucking plate."

Evaristo exhaled angrily and then eyed my leg. "You're shot."

"It happens," I said, not willing to dwell on it, not now. With the adrenaline still running through me, I could ignore the pain. "We need to deal with Luisa first."

He snapped his fingers and his main man, Paolo, came over. "Get this place cleaned up," Evaristo ordered him. "Find a place to burn all the bodies."

"We usually just feed them to the pigs," I pointed out. "But who knows what they've been eating lately."

Paolo went and gathered up the rest of the men for the dirty work while Evaristo and I went back inside the house, hurrying now to get to Luisa.

"We'll get you both taken care of as much as I can,"

he said as we made our way upstairs and to the room. "There are a lot of clinics I know, even out of the country where no one can watch you."

I nodded absently, unable to ignore the uneasiness in my chest. Diego was at the end of the hall, holding Luisa in his arms like some sort of action hero. He'd taken off his jacket and wrapped her in it, her head was back, arm swinging limply beneath her.

But he didn't need to be a hero right now. I did. Even though I was the opposite of one. An anti-hero was still a hero in the end but I would never be more than a villain.

"Shit," Evaristo swore under his breath as we got closer. "You're sure she's alive?"

I couldn't take my eyes off of her. Even when smoke billowed down the hall, enveloping us, I could see her through the haze, clear as day. Her beautiful skin, broken down like a bruised peach.

"She's barely holding on," Diego said and the tremor of worry in his voice told me we didn't have much time. I also could have hugged the damn man for taking care of her like that.

"Give her to me," I said, reaching for her.

"Your leg, Javier," Evaristo reminded me.

"Fuck my leg," I snapped as Diego handed her over, placing my wife in my arms. She was lighter than usual and beneath the blood I could see her ribs jutting out. She'd been starved on top of that, but I should have never expected anything less from Esteban.

The more I stared down at her in my arms, the more that empty space inside of me increased, spinning outward, invading every corner of which I was alive. She'd undone me many times in the past but I wasn't sure I could piece myself together again. Not now. I was ruined over what she'd done to me and I was ruined over what had been done to her.

Our marriage had been obliterated and this was all that was left.

I was going to hold on to that until my fingers were raw.

"We have to go," Diego said to me and I managed to say something back, I don't know what, but somehow I put one bad leg in front of the other. We walked down that hallway of what used to be our house, of what used to be a pretty good life, and I could almost hear her bubbly laughter, her intoxicating grin, from memories past. Fire and smoke filled the air, the stench of burning bodies, while my wife's bird-like body, her fragile life, was in my hands. I could have given into that thick rage that had gotten me here, I could have killed her – put her out of her misery, even – and had my revenge on her. It would have been so easy and the others would have looked away.

I just couldn't.

Maybe that made me weak. Maybe it made me strong. I didn't know and I didn't really care.

All of my vengeance was for Esteban now. He took everything away from me and made my loved ones suffer. Luisa never took anything from me. Instead, in her devastation here, she gave me something instead, and as I held her, I knew it was a piece of myself back, a part that I had lost along the way, a part I never thought I'd find again.

It didn't make me whole. I didn't think anything ever could. Some people weren't meant to be whole, to have soul.

But it was something.

I would not harm my wife. Not anymore and not in any way. I didn't know if she would pull through and if we could ever have what we once had, no matter how fleeting it had been, but I knew I'd have to learn to let go of that suffocating hate and start all over again. Learning to forgive her would be the toughest thing I'd ever have to do.

If she pulls through, I thought.

I had a hard time believing I wasn't carrying a dead woman in my arms.

CHAPTER TWENTY

Luisa

When I was a young girl, maybe eight or so, my father once took me to the dry bluffs above the ocean to see if we could catch a glimpse of the migratory humpback whales. Even though they were common during the winter months, I'd never seen them, so Papa took me to the best viewing area he could find.

Unfortunately it happened to be part of one of the fancier resorts that plied the beaches between San Jose del Cabo and Cabo San Lucas. He told me to dress up in my Sunday best, a white cotton dress with red embroidered flowers that I thought made me look like a princess, and he donned his straw fedora.

He drove us there in the afternoon, parking in the guest parking lot, and then we walked in through the hotel like we belonged there. I'd felt so special, so much like royalty, walking across that white marble floor of the lobby, so shiny I could see my own reflection. I remembered the sound of my Mary-Janes hitting the floor, tap-tap-tap, and hoping that no one would see my shoes, for they held a layer of dust on them. They'd know we were imposters for sure.

Once we made it outside though, Papa led me along the pool area as I tried not to gawk at the vacationing gringos, impossibly pretty people, reading, laughing, splashing without any cares in the world. We stopped at the bluffs, leaned over the fence, and watched for the whales.

I remembered how bright it was, that sun shimmering off the water. There were other people there too, guests, watching for them and talking excitedly in English. I wanted nothing more than to see these beautiful mammals break the ocean surface. The whales had always been a symbol of everything graceful and wild and free.

Everything I wanted to be.

We were watching for only a few minutes though, scanning the waves, hoping beyond hope to see them, before a woman in a white pant suit approached us. Her name tag said Gloria. She was Mexican too but at that moment she pretended she wasn't.

She didn't even ask if we were staying there – I guessed it was too obvious that we weren't. She just told us we had to leave.

My papa nodded, not wanting to cause a scene, but I stomped my foot and held onto that railing.

"I want to see the whales. The whales are for everyone to see."

"Not from here, they aren't," Gloria said snidely. "You must leave."

"But why? We are not harming anyone. We just want to watch."

"This hotel is for guests only, you are not a guest."

"Let's go, Luisa." Papa grabbed my arm and I saw so much sadness and disappointment in his eyes that it only made me madder. Here he was, trying to do something nice for me, something free, which we could afford, and we weren't even allowed to lay our eyes on the ocean that belonged to all of us equally.

"I will have to call security," Gloria said.

"So you can throw us in jail?" I cried out and now other guests were looking at us.

Then some older gentleman, white skinned with a crippling sunburn on his nose, approached us and said to Gloria, "It's okay, they can stay on account of me. They can be my guests."

I could have hugged that man, a vacationer with a good soul, but Gloria was having none of it. "They have to leave, sir," she said to him, blowing him off. "They don't belong here."

And though I'd grown up knowing how unfair life was, that was the first time I felt the pinch. Mexicans like Gloria and rich white people had rights that we did not. They had access to land and sights that should have been for everyone. They were privileged. They had power. They were the true royalty of the country.

I would realize, later, that they weren't even at the top of our food chain. The *narcos* were the true royalty, more than them, more than the government.

If you wanted to be queen, that's where you had to be.

I finally saw the whales one day when I was nineteen and driving to my waitressing job in Cabo San Lucas. But by then, the magic and everything they had meant to me, had long since disappeared.

And now, as I lay here in some bed, in a clinical, silent room somewhere, tethered between life and death, I saw the whales behind my eyes. Swimming, singing. They gave me comfort and kept me cool. They beckoned me to go under, to feel that silk water slide past my skin, to feel free and wild. They dove deeper and deeper but as they disappeared into the cobalt depths, I knew I couldn't follow them. Not now. Not yet.

I raised my palm in the water to say goodbye, watching their flukes dissolve into the great blue and then slowly I made my way to the surface.

Evaristo was standing over me, observing me closely.

"Luisa," he said. "Welcome back."

I tried to speak, to ask where I was, what happened.

If Evaristo was here, then it meant the *federales* had me.

A landslide of horrors came flooding back.

Esteban.

The look in his atrocious eyes.

The torture.

The endless pain.

My mind shut down. I was pulled under again after that, back to that deep, deep blue.

I don't know how much time passed before I felt myself coming out of it again. I blinked slowly, expecting to see ocean but only saw a white ceiling above me. The flecks on the ceiling came in and out of focus. It reminded me of when I was young and in school, staring at the cheaply-made walls to pass the time. I tried to feel my body from the inside out, working on moving my toes, my fingers, carefully. Everything felt tight, like a rubber band, especially my face and stomach where I knew I had been badly burned.

Horribly disfigured and scarred for life.

I closed my eyes and took in a deep breath, letting the air fill me, bring me life and strength. I had been ruined but I would survive. I would learn to live again, anew.

I heard someone shift beside me. I remembered seeing Evaristo. He must have rescued me from the house, perhaps the agency went back on their word and took Esteban down. Maybe he was in prison.

Maybe he was dead, killed in a gruesome, painful death.

I could only hope.

"Who is there?" I asked weakly, too afraid to turn my head, that the pain would be too much.

The person stood up, casting a shadow in the corner of my eye. My hand was held and I knew the grip better than I knew myself.

Javier's face came into my view, peering down at me with those golden eyes that seemed almost soulful. "You don't need to talk," he told me, voice soothing me like that feather on my skin.

It was too much. Tears welled up in my eyes.

"Don't you dare cry on me," he said sternly, gripping my hand harder. "Don't." He swallowed hard.

I sucked in my breath, trying to steady my emotions which were flying all over the place.

"Where am I?" I asked.

"In a private clinic. San Salvador."

"We're in El Salvador?" My mind raced. "Are you really here?"

He nodded, smiling only slightly. He looked older somehow, more grey at his temples, his features strained. It made me realize how horrible I must have looked, the burns, my face, my hair chopped off.

I closed my eyes and turned my head even though pain ripped through me in nauseating spasms. "I don't want you to see me like this," I said, voice choked in my throat, even though I realized how petty it sounded.

"I want to see you like this," he said.

"Because I deserve it."

"Because you're *alive*. When we first found you, I was certain you were anything but." He paused and I felt soft fingers on my scalp. "No one deserves this, not you."

But I did. I did. And I didn't deserve to have him by my side right now, being actually tender with me. I needed his wrath again, his punishment, his torture. I couldn't have been anything more than trash to him, after all the terrible things I had done.

My heart wept for a million bad choices.

And then I started to weep myself.

"Luisa," Javier said, leaning over further. "Look at me."

I opened my eyes and the tears spilled down the sides of my cheeks. I expected the burn to sting but I felt nothing at all. All the nerves had been burned away.

His gaze was deep, intense, until I felt it in my bones. "You're going to be okay."

I could barely shake my head.

"Yes," he said angrily. "You will be. You're my wife, my queen, and this is something you'll get over. We both will."

"How?" I cried out. "How can I get over this? Look at

me! Look at me, I'm destroyed, I'm barely even a woman anymore, barely even a human being. I'm mangled garbage. Look at us! How could you ever, ever forgive me? How could I ever get back the husband, the marriage I had? Why would I even be allowed that?"

His jaw tensed. He closed his eyes briefly, breathing out slowly through his nose. "I don't know," he said. When his eyes opened, they were lost. "I don't know how we can move past this, if I can forgive you, if we even deserve a fresh start. All I know is that I'll try. We'll try."

It wouldn't be enough. I knew that. We had hurt each other too much.

"I want Esteban dead," I told him, surprised at the strength in my voice. "I want him to pay."

The corner of Javier's mouth curled up now, his eyes glinting wickedly, like a million amber knives. "He will pay. I will make sure of that. He will pay over and over again, I promise you."

"No," I said. "I want to be the one that makes him suffer."

He shook his head. "You're far too hurt for that."

"I don't care."

"Luisa, your collarbone is broken. You're burned . . ."

"I. Will. Make. Him. Pay," I ground out, squeezing Javier's hand back with the same kind of ferocity.

He studied me for a moment, almost amused. "You really are the woman for me, aren't you? Have I ever told you that there's nothing sexier than seeing bloodlust in your eyes?"

"Javier . . ." I pleaded.

He sighed impatiently. "Look. We've tracked him as far as El Salvador. Evaristo is using the agency's satellites to get readings on known safe houses, I'm using my men across Central America to spot him, we –"

"Evaristo?"

He smirked. "Right, you didn't know. I escaped from prison with his help. He switched teams."

I frowned.

"He's not gay," Javier added. "Not that I'd blame him with a hot piece of ass like me around. He's just one of us now."

"You corrupted a fed."

"He corrupted himself. He just wanted to be on the winning side for once. His intel got us to you, we knew Esteban had you and was in the compound when we ambushed it. Unfortunately, that fuck got away."

"How did he look?" I asked, remembering our tooth and nail battle.

He cocked his head. "Not good. Somewhat blind. Why? Please tell me you fucked him up."

I could only manage a small, tight smile. "He cut off my hair. I put the scissors in his eye."

Javier broke into a wide grin and leaned down to kiss my forehead. "That's my woman," he said proudly and I tried not to wince at the feeling of his lips on my skin.

"I think the acid burned away some of his hair too," I added. "But that's not enough. I want more. I want to rip his head off with my own fucking teeth."

He raised his brows at me. "My god, if you weren't so damn injured, you wouldn't be able to keep me off of you right now."

At the thought of that, my heart sank and the smile fell from my face.

"What?" he asked quickly.

I turned my head away, staring at the wall, feeling everything. The shame. The knowledge that nothing would be the same. "How could you want me after everything?"

"Because," he said, sounding confused. "You're you."

"I'm not." I let out a small, sad little sob. "I don't know what I am now. A monster."

His eyes narrowed into slits. "We both know who the real monster is here," he said sharply.

"Please, you know it . . . I'm ugly. I'll never be the same. Even if I can get your forgiveness, I won't look the same to you again."

"Luisa, stop talking like an idiot. Give me time. Give us time."

"My looks won't change with time."

"Your looks?" He trailed his fingers down my arm. "What about your looks?"

"My hair, my scars, my burns." I could almost feel the same acid eating away at my soul.

"Hey now," Javier said, putting his hand under my chin and gently tipping my face toward him. He appraised my face, taking me all in coolly. Finally he nodded and said, "You're better now."

"What?"

He shrugged casually. "What can I say? I think you look better. With your hair short like that, you can see more of your gorgeous face. And the burns only make you look stronger. Like a warrior. Like the queen that you are. Like nothing will hurt you ever again, because you've lived through it already. What could be more beautiful than that?" He leaned over and kissed me gently on the lips. "You know now that you could never be ugly to me," he murmured.

My heart wanted to swell with his words, so terribly honest that it took my breath away. When Javier was cruel he was brutal, but when he was tender, it was almost more disarming.

Yet, at the same time I knew he wouldn't be quick to forgive me and that we had so much distance between us we needed to gap. He might have implied that he was still physically attracted to me, a fact that brought with it a whole mess of other issues, but I didn't know when he would let me in again.

"Sorry to disturb you," Evaristo said, opening the door to the room while lightly knocking on it at the same time.

Javier glared at him. "She finally comes to and there you are. Can't even give us a damn minute."

He smiled at me brightly, looking so different in a suit and not the tortured man in the basement. "Luisa, I'm glad you're awake. You've been out of it for the last few days."

"How long have I been here?"

"A week," he said.

"And you still haven't found Esteban?" I asked.

"Actually," Evaristo said quickly, coming over to me. He turned to Javier excitedly. "We have. We just spotted him on the satellite footage, in a village in the mountains, southeast Guatemala."

"Well, fuck," Javier said, gesturing wildly, his eyes wide

and bright, "what the hell are you doing waltzing in here like this? Let's go!"

"I want to go," I said quickly.

Both men looked at me as if I were insane. I probably was. But I couldn't rest here, not without finding Esteban with them and taking out his other eye.

"You're in no shape to move," Evaristo said. "Stay here, we will have people taking good care of you. You'll be protected around the clock."

"Leave Diego here," Javier said, which surprised me. "He can guard her."

It seemed to surprise Evaristo too. "You sure? We might need him."

He shook his head. "I'm not leaving her in the hands of someone I don't know and trust."

"Forget trust," I told them. "I'm not afraid, I just want him dead." I tried to get up but the pain was so great, spreading like fire. I cried out and Javier gently pushed me back onto the bed.

"No, Luisa," he told me. "We will get Esteban alive. And I will bring him back here for you. You can do whatever you want with him. I promise."

"Please."

"I promise," he repeated. He jerked his chin at Evaristo. "Come on. Let's find Diego and get going."

The two of them stalked off. For a moment I thought perhaps, if I just tried hard enough I could move, but my whole upper body failed on me. The agony was just too great. I lay back, breathing hard, wishing my anger could fool myself into thinking I was okay. But all it did was tire me.

My last thoughts before I fell asleep were of all the terrible things I would do if Javier brought Esteban back here.

For the first time in a long time, I smiled.

CHAPTER TWENTY-ONE

Javier

I t wasn't easy leaving Luisa behind in her condition but there was no fucking way I was going to let this go. My mind was on a single track and that track led to blood and bone.

It also wasn't easy leaving Diego behind either but it had to be done. I didn't trust anyone but him at this point. He understood too, vowing to watch over her as he had before, though I read it on his face that he wanted to join in on the massacre.

True to my word though, if we did manage to capture Esteban alive, I would take him back to Luisa and Diego and we could all fucking take turns doing whatever it was that our hearts desired.

I'd never seen such thirst for blood and violence in Luisa before.

I had to say it unnerved me in the best possible way. I saw in her what I saw in myself, something dark and frightening and unstoppable. The fact that she actually drove a pair of scissors through Esteban's eye stirred up something deeper inside me than just my cock.

It was wrong of me to want to encourage that bloodlust but I couldn't help it. They say a marriage only works if it's an equal partnership and this would establish her as a real cartel queen. Not just having a say in the business and giving her opinions but actually getting her hands dirty. Bloody. That said *narco* royalty like nothing else did.

"Remember we want him alive," I said to Evaristo, raising my voice to be heard above the churning rotors.

We were en route to Las Aguas, a tiny village outside the town of Nueva Santa Rosa, the two of us in one chopper with some of the best backup men I had. There were another two choppers carrying in the derelicts of my new army, the ones who fought the hardest and craziest at the compound. Even I was a little afraid of them. Nothing was more dangerous than a meathead with a machete, but at least they got the job done.

"No promises," Evaristo said. "If it's a choice of killing him or letting him get away, you can guess which one I'll be taking."

We didn't fly directly to the village. That would have been too risky. Instead the choppers landed in the next valley over and then we piled into SUVs I had arranged earlier. They took us high into the mountains, climbing the steep road at night so we could remain unseen. The next morning, when the haze cleared, you could see we were settled on a ridge that looked down over the tiny village of stucco houses nestled along a narrow river.

The village couldn't have more than a hundred people in it, with Evaristo putting his estimate at fifty. The only reason we had an inkling that Este was here was because one of the Guatemalan ops had a visual ID on Este in Santa Rosa. Some digging around later not only confirmed that it was him, but that he was headed over the mountains. Using the *federales'* fancy tracking system, they were able to intercept a phone call made from someone called "Fez" who was asking about my own whereabouts. Voice recognition placed the caller as Esteban and triangulated the signal to somewhere in this valley.

Besides, I could feel him close by. I could barely sleep, not because I was on a sleeping bag on the cold ground, but because I could taste the blood already.

"He's there," Evaristo said that morning, handing me a cup of instant coffee. It wasn't much better than gas station runoff, but it would have to do. I never understood why roughing it had to be "rough." Even a French press and some good local beans would go a long way out here.

"You know for sure?"

He nodded. "Just got off the phone with the agency. The satellite images are being printed on the computer right now but I already got a look at them. There's only one structure down there big enough, nice enough, for Esteban and his men. A barn and neighboring house."

"Makes sense," I said, my palms itching to go as I took another sip of the god awful brew. "They are animals after all."

"I'm not sure ours are much different," he noted, nodding at one criminal who was busy taking a piss onto a sleeping man's head.

I rolled my eyes. When this was all said and done, I'd be a lot better off if I could just kill them all. They might have been good for getting this job done but they were far too stupid, not to mention uncouth, to be associated with the name Javier Bernal.

I leaned in closer to Evaristo. In the harsh light of dawn I was aware of how young this kid really was. "Let me ask you, how long do you think you'll play the loyal *federale* for?"

He grinned at me sheepishly. "For as long as they think you're still in prison. As good as those guards and the warden are, the cover-up only lasts for so long. Even with the prison director under your thumb, the truth will come out. And when it does, all fingers will point to me."

"You'll be on the run then," I told him. "You'll have to change your name. Your appearance."

"That's if I live that long, *patron*." He shrugged. "I will use them while I can, while they have used me. And they have used me. You know, they prey on the weak, that's the difference between you and them. You, Javier, you prey on the strong. The government preys on the weak, the ones without much choice. The ones like me. Then they mold you to be their little toy soldier. You live your short life fighting their battles without really knowing what you're fighting for." His eyes scanned the distant peaks as the mist lifted off. "The cartels have caused so much violence in this country but that's nothing new. Mexico is a country built on violence and corruption. You know how Cortes founded the country?"

I nodded. I didn't remember much from school. I dropped out when I was young, after my father died, having to work in his business and take care of my mother and sisters. But that didn't stop me from seeking knowledge on my own and the inception of Mexico was something larger than life.

"Well," Evaristo went on, "then you know that barbaric

violence and a shitty class system has been our way from the very start. Those at the top feed off of each other. Those at the bottom suffer endlessly. The cartels rule because the government allows them to. Because it benefits them both."

"And thank god for that," I added.

"Yes, thank god. Or the devil. Whichever one you choose."

Paolo came over to Evaristo. "Sir, we have confirmation that Esteban Mendoza is there right now."

I knew one hell of a wicked grin was spreading across my face. I'm pretty sure it stayed on the whole time as we quickly loaded into the SUVs and were taken down the rocky, steep road that was nothing more than a deer trail all the way down into the valley. It was still so early that we hoped we wouldn't be detected.

We eventually reached the bottom in one piece and raced down the one dirt road through the middle of the village.

The few villagers that were up saw us and started yelling but we zoomed past them, heading all the way to the house and the barn. We piled out, weapons in our hands as the dust rose above us. The bigger men went in through the front door, kicking it down with their heavy boots and breaking windows.

Evaristo and I went around the back, .45 pistols drawn, ready to shoot. I had to remind myself over and over again that I wasn't shooting to kill, just to maim. From the way I was gripping my gun, I was afraid that I might just kill him on the spot.

Suddenly the promise I made to Luisa was gone and

all I could think about was just putting the bullets through his head repeatedly. It would take away the fun but it would feel oh so fucking good. Just to see him caught. See the fear of death. I wanted to smell it off of him.

At the last minute I shoved Evaristo out of the way and entered the back of the house first, not giving a damn if he was the one properly trained for this or not. I'd done okay so far.

The house was empty though. There was no one there and not a single sign of them being there at all. Floorboards were ripped up, looking for tunnels that were never found, and the place was swept for leftover communication, anything to point to Esteban, but there was nothing.

Nothing, but still, I knew he had been here. I knew we had been close.

Too close.

I turned to Evaristo. "Burn the place down," I said.

"The house?"

"The village. They know he was here. They know he left. Interrogate them all. If they can't give us answers, then we burn it."

Evaristo frowned, hesitating. The good and evil he was just discussing was now battling in his head. "This isn't even Mexico, Javier."

"So," I said simply. "Word will still get back to him. Burn it all."

He put his hand on my shoulder. "Listen, there is a fine line between revenge and lunacy. Concentrate on him, not on those he may or may not have involved."

"Burn it to the fucking ground!" I screamed in his face,

my skin growing red hot, spittle flying out of my mouth and onto his cheek.

He slowly wiped it away but nodded. "Yes, *patron.*"

Evaristo still gave the frightened villagers a chance to live. They walked into the mountains, staring back at their homes as they burned and burned, the smoke rising high above the valley floor.

I felt absolutely nothing as I watched it all disappear behind us, the SUV climbing into the hills. I thought the destruction, the flames, would at least burn off some of the debilitating frustration I felt at having lost him once again, but it didn't.

It just made things worse.

And with the way things were, I wasn't sure how much worse it would get before it finally got better.

CHAPTER TWENTY-TWO

Luisa

I t took five days for Javier to return back to San Salvador. Diego hadn't had much contact with him and the last we had heard before it went to radio silence was that he was in the mountains without a signal except from the satellite phones. The two of us waited day in and out, anxiously trying to pass the time.

Not that Diego would ever show any anxiety. The big beast of a man was as cool as a cucumber, reminiscent of how Javier could be on his good days. Or maybe those were his bad days. It was hard to tell when both fire and ice could burn you.

By day four, I was doing a lot better. I was in a sling now and could walk around, though moving my shoulder hurt like hell, even with low doses of morphine. Sometimes it felt like there was a grinder inside me, working to the bone.

The morphine was more for the burns anyway. Thankfully the one on my face was healing faster and didn't need a bandage, even though I wanted it covered up more than anything. The one on my stomach was trickier and sometimes the pain got so bad I would break down and cry.

Diego wanted the nurses to give me more drugs but I was adamant against it. I wanted to be as clear-headed as possible these days, even if it hurt me to do so. I played one-handed cards with him instead, determined to pull through and save face.

When Javier walked into the room on the fifth day, I knew it was bad news. Not just because he didn't have Esteban with him but because I was certain he would have notified us along the way if he had been successful. No one likes to broadcast their failures.

Needless to say, I was glad to see him. Even though I felt like an absolute wreck with my beaten looks and pain that half-straddled the morphine cloud, the sight of him, defeated or not, warmed my bitter heart.

"No good, huh?" Diego asked him while Javier strode across the room and collapsed into one of the stiff metal chairs by the wall.

Javier leaned forward, pinching between his brows, but didn't say a word.

Diego looked at me. "Perhaps I should leave you two alone." When Javier didn't move nor utter his protest, Diego got up and left, closing the door behind him.

I leaned back against the wall and started gathering up the cards, leftovers from our simple game of *Burro Castigado*. "Do you want to talk about it?"

Javier shook his head, his eyes still closed.

"That's fine," I said. "I'm doing better, by the way. I can leave here tomorrow they said."

Finally he looked at me. "Good." He sighed heavily. "Sorry, I didn't mean to . . . you look a lot better."

I smiled softly. "I thought you said I already looked better." I gently touched the burn on my face for emphasis. It had stopped being numb, a good sign even though the outer damage wouldn't go away.

"I meant it," he said. But he still didn't get up. I was acutely aware that whatever exchanges we shared when he first saw me here weren't about to happen again, not now.

"Do I dare ask what happened?" I said cautiously, worried that the question would press all the wrong buttons. He was tense, stressed, and if he hadn't unleashed his fury on Esteban there was always the chance he would unleash it on me.

But he didn't. He sighed and leaned far back in his chair, legs stretched out in front of him. His dark jeans were coated with a layer of dust and it was only then that I noted how uncharacteristically messy he was. Even his longish hair was out of place.

It actually made him look a bit boyish. Not quite vulnerable because Javier was anything but, but still . . . younger. Perhaps more real.

"He was there, Luisa." He wiped his hand over his face and stared out the window. "He was there. We were so close. We missed him by a matter of ten minutes I'm guessing. If we had known that to begin with, we could have got him. We wasted too much time in his house . . . we've wasted too much time already."

"But," I said, running my hand over the cards and flipping them up one by one, "there is no time limit on revenge. Don't they say it's a dish best served cold?"

"The Americans say that," Javier said, eyes hard. "The longer he's out there, the longer that he's allowed to think he's won. He's *not* won."

"No," I said. "I'm still alive. And you're here with me." I swallowed hard, afraid to go on. But I had to. "Aren't you?"

He looked at me sharply. "Of course I am."

"And so he knows that. He knows we're coming for him. That's why it's best to wait a while. Wait for him to relax. Let his guard down."

He got out of his chair and stormed over to me, eyes blazing. "You're telling me," he said, waving his hand over my body, "that you're okay with just letting him get away with this, with what he did to you? Can you honestly say that you can wait to catch him one day when he's not expecting it? Is that what you can do? Fuck." He turned around, back to me and shook his head. "Well I can't do that. I can't live my life knowing he's out there and that he's ruined us."

My heart grew heavy. "Don't forget I had my hand in that too."

He whirled around. "Oh, I haven't forgotten," he snapped. He closed his eyes and ran his hand through his hair, trying to compose himself. When he opened them again, his gaze was directed at the floor. "The sooner he's dead, the better it is for us. The sooner we can move on and pick up the pieces."

And what makes you think we can do that anyway, I wanted to ask but I didn't dare. I was too afraid of the truth. The truth that, despite everything, my forgiveness was the last thing on his mind.

My body would heal before we ever did.

I flipped over the last card. Queen of Spades.

Unlucky.

The next day I was able to leave the clinic as promised. I said goodbye to the nurses and doctors who took care of me but to them I was just another anonymous person coming in from the endless violence. Diego and I had theorized that they didn't just work for the agencies in the area but for whatever cartels were willing to pay the highest price. With that in mind, I was glad that Diego was there to guard me. Any doctor would have sold me out to someone willing to pay for it.

I went with Evaristo, his second-in-command Paolo, Diego, and Javier in a small convoy of cars out toward the western coast of El Salvador. There was one humble safe house on a golden beach, another a few yards away, nestled in the jungle.

Javier and I commandeered the beach house with Diego, while Evaristo and Paolo watched over Javier's army in the other.

It was strange being in such a small space with just the three of us. Javier and I had one bedroom to ourselves overlooking the ocean, while Diego's was stationed near the front. Though we couldn't see them, there were other guards patrolling the grounds, making sure we were safe. It was hot here so close to the equator and there was never a moment where you weren't coated in a thin sheen of sweat.

The whole set-up reminded me of when I first married

Salvador and in more ways than one. Our honeymoon had been at a similar place, with similar protection. And I had been similarly nervous.

The thing was, despite everything that had changed between Javier and I, what had done the most damage had nothing to do with him or me.

It was Esteban.

Because of him and his men, I'd grown averse to Javier's touch. Anyone's touch, really, but especially his.

That night when we arrived at the house, we settled into our new room. It was clean and comfortable. Nothing fancy. Teak frames on the mirrors and doors, a ceiling fan, terracotta-tiled floors. The kind of place vacationers would rent for a taste of Latin America.

There was one queen-sized bed in the middle. The sight of it made my heart jump.

I carefully got ready for bed, taking my time to change into my nightgown in the washroom. Everything took longer with my shoulder incapacitated. Javier had offered to help me a few times but there was no way now that I'd let him see me naked.

I didn't want him to be repulsed.

And I feared what would happen if he were turned on.

When I finally emerged, he was in bed, the sheet pulled up to his abdomen. I knew he was naked underneath.

He wasn't smiling though. He was reading me, almost desperately, as I stepped out of the bathroom. I was a bit unsteady on my feet, a side effect of the massive amounts of codeine I'd been prescribed for the pain, even though it hadn't done much for it so far.

Javier made a move to help me and I tried to shoo

him away but he was adamant. And naked. And had a formidable erection as he led me over to my side of the bed.

"You're still in pain," he noted, lowering me down.

"I'm fine."

He gave me a half-smile. "You know my dear, we do own most of the drugs in the world. I'm sure I can give you something stronger than fucking codeine."

"It's fine," I said again. Javier didn't get high on his own supply and neither did I.

He came around to his side of the bed and turned on his side, facing me. I had no choice but to sleep on my back, my shoulder wouldn't allow anything else.

The tension between us was hard to ignore. It was physical, like you could see it hanging in the air. Even the creaking ceiling fan couldn't blow it away. So many things left unsaid. So many things that begged to be said again.

And I was caught between a rock and a hard place.

The need to feel beautiful.

The need to never feel beautiful.

"Luisa," Javier said quietly. His gaze held me even when I wanted to look away. "You know I don't care."

I anxiously rubbed my lips together before saying, "About what?"

"What you're worried about."

He reached out and ran the tip of his finger along the scar that one of Esteban's men had left on my chest, the one that led all the way to my stomach. The scar he left before he raped me. Before they all did.

I could still see them, could still smell them, even

when I didn't close my eyes. They were always there. They had permeated my soul.

I shuddered and Javier abruptly took his hand away. A few heavy beats passed between us.

He swallowed. "We can get past this," he said thickly.

I couldn't answer because I didn't know what he meant. There was so fucking much to get past now, how could we ever get ahead.

"It's just skin," he added.

"No." I stared up at the ceiling fan. "It's not just skin. It's a memory. My skin remembers."

He breathed in sharply. "Does it remember me at all?"

I turned my head to look at him, taken aback by the rawness in his voice.

"I hope it will," I said.

I hope that more than anything, I thought.

He held my gaze and I could see that frustration and impatience mount. He was thinking that Esteban was out there still and all the damage was in here.

❧

"Here you are," Javier's voice rose above the crashing waves.

I turned my head, hugging my shawl close to me as he walked out onto the beach barefoot, in linen pants and a dress shirt. He was holding two glasses of red wine. It was hard to get the good stuff in El Salvador, let alone the reserves that we owned back in Mexico, but it would do for now.

At the moment, it seemed like everything would do for now.

We'd been at the safe house on the beach for just over two weeks. Everyone was well-fed, well taken care of, but tensions were high.

With no action at all, the criminals needed an outlet and one was found wandering around the bedroom while I was trying to take a shower. Needless to say, Javier showed up and shot him on the spot. Diego was berated for letting his guard down for one second, though I wouldn't and couldn't blame the man. He'd done so much for me, for all of us, already.

Me, I felt myself spin the other way, toward fear, sucked in a big black hole I couldn't quite crawl out of. I shut down and closed myself off from everyone, including my husband. It just wasn't worth the risk.

Meanwhile word had gotten out that Javier was no longer in Puente Grande. The prison director was sacked, the warden was found beheaded in a ditch and a handful of guards went missing.

As predicted, Evaristo was on the chopping block for that fiasco. He promptly disappeared from the agency, having already put a new life in place. Javier found it grossly amusing that Evaristo had taken on the identity of a priest, Father Armando, but desperate times seemed to call for desperate measures. At the house he was still Evaristo but when he went out into the nearest towns for supplies or recon, he was Father Armando, complete with the whole black-robed garments.

No one here seemed to be living anymore. We were just existing. Waiting. It's funny how far revenge can drive you, you're willing to give up so much for just one sweet taste.

I still wanted mine. It's all I ever thought about. The more Javier, Evaristo and Diego scanned networks and emails and plotted and mapped, searching for him, the more despondent they got. But me, all I could think about was murdering the man who put us all here. After a while even my guilt seemed to abate, just long enough for me to believe I had the right to kill him as I saw fit. After that was done, then I would deal with everything else I had shoved aside.

Including my husband. Now Javier had handed me the glass of wine, reaching out to me when I'd been anything but receptive.

I took the glass from him, thanking him quietly.

He eased himself down on the log beside me.

"How is your shoulder?" he asked. Normally I'd say he was making conversation but I'd barely seen him lately. Most of the time I slept. Dreamed of blood.

I pressed the small bump on my collarbone where it had broken. I didn't need a sling anymore, which was good. "It's fine. I can't lift my arm over my head or far out to the sides but at least I can use it now."

He nodded and brought his attention out to the waves. They pounded against the shore, sending ocean spray into the air that only seemed to add to the heat. "It's been dead-end after dead-end." He sighed angrily. "I know you said revenge is a dish best served cold but the longer this takes . . . the more I fear we'll never get him."

That doesn't sound like you, I wanted to tell him. Javier's determination usually knew no bounds. Strangely enough he was an eternal optimist in such a negative business, always believing he would get his way in the end.

Then again, I didn't feel like myself either. I don't know who I felt like. Everything was different. Our location, our team, our relationship. Even the face that looked back at me in the mirror wasn't of Luisa Bernal. She was no queen. She was a scarred, broken woman.

"Talk to me," Javier said imploringly.

I slowly met his gaze. "I don't know what to say."

He studied me for a moment. "Did Esteban ever say anything to you about his plans, about safe houses, about where he might go in an emergency?"

I shook my head. "I don't know."

"Think!" He smacked his hand against his thigh.

I balked, gripping the stem of the wine glass. "You seriously think I want to remember? Do you want me to pull up the memories of what happened there? I'm trying to block it out, Javier! Don't you know what he did to me?"

"Of course I know what he did to you," he said sharply. "You won't even let me touch you. I'm your fucking husband."

"You're also a fucking liar and a cheat!" I yelled, overwhelmed by the anger blanketing me. I got to my feet, the wine splashing around the glass.

Javier got to his feet too, eyes blazed, nostrils flaring. "You were the one fucking him to begin with!"

"Only because you did it first, only because you pushed me away. You treated me like garbage. I thought our marriage was over and he was the only one who showed any interest in me. And yeah, I regret it a million times over and over and over because I was an idiot who slept with the devil and invited him in to fuck up her life, our life. I was so, so, so *stupid* and this all happened because of me. But I can't forget . . ." I sucked in my breath, trying to calm down. This was the first outburst I'd had since being in the clinic.

He reached out and put his hand behind my neck, holding me. "I am sorry."

I looked away but he squeezed me harder. "I am sorry," he repeated. "I'm not going to make excuses because I was just looking for excuses to hurt you, hurt myself and I don't know why. But it happened and there is nothing I can do about it."

I stared at him with sadness. "You'll do it again."

"No," he said adamantly, shaking his head. "I will not."

"You will. Because when you touch me, I remember them. I can't be with you like that . . . and I know there's only so much you can take. You'll go elsewhere. It will happen again and I'll have no choice but to watch."

"You will not remember them," he said, pulling me to him, wine spilling everywhere. "I will make you forget."

"It doesn't work that way," I protested.

He kissed me anyway. I froze but his lips were persistent, drawing out a deep, hard kiss. His tongue was wet, warm, feverish against mine, desperate to unleash something in me. I wanted to give in right there, I wanted to succumb to the lust, to the love, to his wildness. He moaned into me which only shot vibrations right into my core, making me swell with need and want.

I had to have my husband back.

He threw the wine glass to the sand while I barely held onto mine. He put one hand on my head, where if I had long hair he would have made a fist, his other hand to my waist, pulling me close to him. He pressed me into him, his dick hard and straining against me, while he slid his fingers down over my ass, taking a hefty squeeze that normally would have sent me into overdrive.

But I couldn't do it.

"No," I mumbled against him, pushing him away.

"No?" he repeated, breathing hard, trying to come closer again but I shoved him off as much as I could with my arm.

"I can't do it," I cried out softly. "I can't do it, I'm sorry." It hadn't been his hand on my ass, it had been Esteban's and it hadn't been his cock vying for me, it had been one of my rapists. That vile look, the sour breath, the humiliation, the pain. I closed my eyes and opened them again, hoping Javier's face would set me right.

The man was hurt. Angry. Frustrated. He stared at me so intently I thought he might be able to see all the ugliness inside, the traces they left behind. Maybe he did see that, because he stepped back and turned away from me, running his hands through his hair, breathing out hard through his nose.

"I'm sorry," I called out softly. "When you touch me, it's not you."

He stopped a few feet away, his hands balling at his sides. He leaned his head back, seeming to ask the fading sky of something. Finally he turned around to face me.

"Don't you think I need this too?" he asked, voice breaking. "That I need to do this? This isn't about fucking you Luisa. This is about erasing him."

There was a bitter taste in my mouth. As hard of a

time I was having with this, Javier was too. He was a possessive man through and through and he needed to own me both body and soul.

Esteban was a tar-black cloud, hanging over every inch of us, never letting go.

"I know," I told him, suddenly just so empty and weak with everything. "I'm sorry."

We stood there on the beach for a moment, the wind picking up and brushing his hair across his face, and stared at each other. So much space between us now, a space I didn't know if we'd ever bridge.

"I'm sorry too," he eventually said. He opened his mouth to add something else but then closed it and walked off toward the house, leaving me to the early stars and dark waves.

Later that night, I dreamed of Esteban.

This wasn't new, I had nightmares nearly every night. He would douse me with acid again and again or tie me to the bed and let the chickens peck me to death.

But this dream wasn't frightening. I was in it like an apparition, floating past him and Juanito as they planned at the kitchen table. Discussing a map. A place that Esteban wanted to go, a place he'd been before.

The dream ended.

But it was enough to jog my memory.

I woke up in the middle of the night and reached over for Javier, shaking him.

"What is it?" he asked, immediately awake. I could see his eyes shining in the dark as he sat up beside me.

I put my hand over his and squeezed it.

"I know where Esteban is."

CHAPTER TWENTY-THREE

Esteban

"Are we there yet?"

Esteban wasn't sure which one of his idiots had asked that question. Though there weren't many of them left, they were all starting to look and act the same, like monkeys who'd been given Kool-Aid and AK-47s. Esteban had thought he was being smart by recruiting such derelict soldiers, but that was just another thing that wasn't going his way at the moment.

Now they were hiking through the jungle outside of Catacamas in the Honduras. His lone helicopter ate shit weeks ago, just before the PFM raid in Guatemala, and he'd been on the run ever since with no time to bring up new supplies.

Yeah, things really weren't going as planned.

Javier had become a thorn in his side once again. The prick had escaped from prison without anyone noticing and the next thing Esteban knew, his compound was under attack from him and that bootlicking fed, Evaristo Sanchez, who was obviously no longer working for the *federales* and had cut some sort of deal with Javier.

Esteban hated the fact that he didn't see that one coming. If only he'd used his brain he could have brought

Evaristo over to his side before this all happened. He'd been too cocky and that was his downfall, as usual.

But Esteban wasn't really using his brain anymore. He was dipping into the cocaine a bit much, which, even though it made him feel smart and invincible, it was really doing the opposite. In the past, Este would take it to just get through the day, even though it had a tendency to make him more violent. The more coke that Este did, the more his logic was derailed, the more that he made stupid mistakes.

He was on the brink of insanity, if not far over it. He was doing things that even he thought he'd never do and had reached a new point of depravity. Unfortunately it was costing him. If he had thought a little clearer, perhaps Luisa wouldn't have been able to drive those scissors into his eye.

He didn't even miss his eye. Sure it fucked up his depth perception and he was pretty much useless with a weapon of any kind, but he thought it made him look cool. He refused to wear an eye-patch too, preferring for others to stare into the ugly, gaping hole in his face that complemented his facial scar so well. "Eyeless Este," his men had started to call him.

He liked the nickname. It was better than "Erectionless Este," which some *puta* had called him back when he was a teenager. It was because of her that he discovered he could get an erection after all, but it was only when violence or the thought of violence was involved. He never killed the little bitch but he sure did make her scream. After that, she never uttered anything towards him again. None of the girls did.

What he didn't like about his whole situation though, is that half his hair at the back of his head had fallen out in clumps because of the acid. He'd started to wear a baseball cap after that, cursing Luisa for being such a crazy cunt.

So with Evaristo and Javier now working together, Esteban had to work hard to stay one step ahead. There had been too many casualties though and now that it was common knowledge that Javier Bernal was alive and well, whomever Esteban had tried to coax over to his side was going back to Javier.

That was a hard pill to swallow. To know that after all he'd done, Javier was still on top and still calling the shots. It didn't even bring him any pleasure anymore to know that he'd made his beauty queen less of a beauty. She was still with him, still his queen, her crown tarnished but wearable.

The drugs made things better. They always did. It's too bad his crew were starting to dip into it as well, making them even more apelike than normal.

But Esteban had one last card up his sleeve, one last place to go.

A place he'd discussed at length before with Juanito, poor naïve Juanito, just in case something were to have happened.

At least he was smart enough to have had a back-up plan.

They would journey up the thick, unyielding jungle to the compound in the trees. He at least knew from the last time it was used that there were more guns, ammo and even a helicopter there, if they were lucky. In that fortress where so much blood had once been spilled, so much drama had taken place, Esteban would recoup. He would re-plan. Then he would do whatever it took to rule again.

There were hostages he could take – Javier still had a sister in New York, did he not? Luisa had her parents in San Diego – and there were enemies of Javier's he could convince to join his side. Hell, the *federales* might even want to strike another deal. If Javier was put away again, there was no way he'd be walking out of there alive.

Esteban smiled at all the possibilities. He just needed to get to his new castle and wait.

CHAPTER TWENTY-FOUR

Javier

I stared at Luisa for a moment, trying to see her features in the dark. She squeezed my hand, a simple gesture that shot fire up my arm.

"You know where Esteban is?" I asked, trying not to get my hopes up even though my pulse had already kicked up a few notches.

She nodded. "Yes. I had a dream just now. But it wasn't a dream, I was remembering something I'd heard. Him and Juanito discussing the *fincas* and safe houses that they knew of. Esteban said there was one in the Honduras, inside a national park. He said you'd never go back because of what happened there. I think that's where he is, where he thinks you'll never go."

All at once I knew she was right. The place she was talking about could only be the former compound of the former Travis Raines. It was a place where a lot of shit went down a few years ago, even though it felt like another lifetime. It *had* been another lifetime, back when Raines was still alive and I was caught up with enemies and ex-lovers. I left that place the leader of Raines' cartel, even though I'd lost something, someone else, in the process.

I never did well with humiliation. Esteban knew that.

"It's not easy to get to," I told her, even though I knew I'd go through hell and high water to take that man's life.

"I don't care," she said. "And I'm going with you."

I knew she'd say that. "Am I a bad husband if I don't object?"

She shook her head vigorously. "I wouldn't expect anything less from you."

Honestly, I didn't like the idea of her coming along. I wasn't kidding when I said it wouldn't be easy to get to. To attack Este undetected meant we could only drive to a certain point and then hike the rest of the way. We couldn't bring helicopters, they'd give him too much warning. The journey would take at least a day and a half and I wasn't sure if she could handle it in her condition, even if she was healing up nicely. And I sure as hell didn't know if she could handle the actual ambush. It was risky to have her there.

But I also knew it was riskier to leave her behind. I needed Diego for this one. Besides, I owed it to her. I promised her she could get her hands dirty. I wanted to see what she'd do to Esteban if she had half the chance. So even though I was purposely putting my wife in harm's way by letting her come along, it was still the right thing to do.

Only in our fucked up little world would *that* be the right thing to do.

I couldn't sleep after that. Neither could she. We decided to wait until morning to wake up Diego and Evaristo and fill them in, so the two of us went into the kitchen, brewed a giant pot of coffee, *good* coffee, and sat at the kitchen table, going over maps and Google Earth images. It was all we could do now that we didn't have access to the *federales* information, but it helped.

I had to admit, it was kind of romantic. Her and I drinking coffee, the waves crashing outside, the world dark and sleeping, while we planned the murder and torture of Esteban Mendoza. I might have been falling in love with her all over again. Something about that relentless fire in her eyes.

Of course the more we talked, the more I stared at her and fell for her, the more I needed to be inside her again to claim her as mine once more. I understood why she couldn't stand for me to touch her in such a way and it crippled me to the bones. Because she was mine. Just mine. Always mine.

I hadn't been denied much in my life but Esteban was still denying her from fully belonging to me. But I had no choice but to suck up that rage, let it fester bitterly inside, and unleash it on him later. Our plans got more and more in-depth as the night slinked off into morning.

When Diego stirred and Evaristo came by for his morning debrief, the both of us were pumped up with bloodlust. Our bags were packed, knives were sharp and we were ready to go fuck shit up.

It didn't take long before we got the army up to speed. They were like a bunch of caged animals, nearly foaming at the mouth once they realized they finally had the chance to run free again. After seeing them in action before, I had no doubt that they were going to lose their minds during the ambush, but my only rule again and again was that no one was to touch Esteban except for me or Luisa.

The drive to the park took seven hours, our convoys crossing the border into Honduras with no problems. With a fake priest – Father fucking Armando – in the car and our false passports, we were undetected. I did a lot of business in Honduras but with me on the most wanted list all over again, you never knew where the *federales* or even the DEA were or who was on what payroll.

"Did you know there's a town called San Esteban near where we're going?" Luisa asked from beside me, studying a map.

"Must be fate," I remarked, adjusting my bullet-proof vest. I'd made sure we all had them on. It saved my life last time I was there.

We didn't end up going as far as San Esteban, but we did drive into a rural town bordered by steep terrain laced with thick vegetation. Just on the outskirts was an abandoned barn that I had used once before to hide our vehicles. The field around also made for a great helicopter landing sight, if we were lucky enough to return that way. If we didn't, then it would be a long hike back, though at least we'd be heading downhill.

After we parked the SUVs in the barn, I gave everyone a run down about the trail and the property and what to expect. We were a motley crew but at least we all had blood and vengeance on our minds. While the dust motes danced around in the barn, lit up by the setting sun, I had flashbacks to the last time I was there, when I had another motley crew of my own, bound by another form of revenge. Funny how life could come full circle like that.

Thank god I didn't have to deal with any *gringos* this time around. They were only good for ruining things and maybe a good fuck.

When we were ready, armed with packs and ammo, we set off down the long dirt road until we approached the outskirts of the Sierra de Agalta national park. I led them into the forest, Diego behind me, then Luisa and Evaristo, Paolo at the end and all the crazy fuckers in between.

It was a long, laborious climb into the night, with only small flashlights shining the way. Even without the sun, it was hot as fuck, the thick canopy seeming to keep in the heat. Sweat poured down my face that I didn't bother to wipe away. Every so often I would ask if Luisa was okay and she always said she was. She wouldn't let me think for a second that she was tired or needed a rest.

Still, I knew she was stubborn and made sure we stopped often enough, even though it made everyone more restless and anxious, including me.

Finally at around one am, we came across a small clearing beneath a few banyan trees and decided we should rest for the night. Just a few hours – none of us would be able to perform our best if we didn't have some sleep.

There was only one sleeping bag between Luisa and I and even though I had so much anticipation thrumming through my veins and needed to get off something fierce, I knew it was best if I didn't share it with her. She would balk at my touch and I wouldn't be able to stop touching her once I started.

"Take it," I told her, leaning up right against the tree while she spread it out on the leaf-covered forest floor.

She didn't argue. "Are you sure you're all right sleeping like that?"

I nodded. "I probably won't sleep anyway. I'll be watching over you."

She gave me a small smile and crawled into the bag. True to my word I did stay up most of the night, sharpening my knives and stabbing any large bugs or reptiles that came our way. It was satisfying to pin the snakes to the ground, even more so when I pretended they were Este.

We set out again just before dawn, walking faster and faster the closer we came. Finally the jungle seemed to glow, the trees opened up, and the outer wall of the compound appeared, spotlights shining from the top of the wall.

"You must rack up quite the power bill out here," Luisa said but I immediately put my finger to my mouth to shush her. This was the last chance we had to go over everything before we were too close to the house and within earshot. I didn't know who was here, let alone if Esteban was here at all, but we couldn't be too careful, not now.

I quickly went over the plan again. Similar to the raid on the compound in Sinaloa, we would all split up, with Diego, Luisa and I going in from the back while the rest flushed Esteban out. There were no tunnels here, so there was no place for him to go but the jungle, with the easiest route heading back from the pool and pool house.

That's where we would be waiting.

"Good luck," Evaristo said, shaking my hand.

I grinned at him. "Thanks, *father*."

He rolled his eyes and then took off with the rest of them along the wall, heading north. Luisa, Diego and I turned and ran along it to the south. Once we came along a tree that would be easy to climb, I swung myself up there until I dropped onto the wall, Diego and Luisa staying below.

Flattening myself, I brought out my binoculars and took it all in.

Travis's old complex was larger than I remembered. The pretentious asshole had it built in the same style as a French estate and had been terribly out of place at the time. Now, since the property had come under my possession and I hadn't been here in many years, it was looking more natural, like it belonged. The jungle had reclaimed it and vines had begun to grow up the sides of the sprawling house, resembling an ancient relic instead of the palace it once was.

The pool was black with stagnant water and leaves, the pool house was gone, collapsed under the weight of vines. A helicopter sat on the landing pad but I couldn't be sure if it would start or not. After I'd taken over Travis's cartel – albeit briefly, before his loyalists splintered off and formed a new version of the Zetas – I'd only stayed up here for a few months. I'd come and go into Mexico all the time but it was the only place I felt secure enough to start building a new empire.

Everything was pretty much as I had left it, which made me smile because if the outside looked this bad, the inside had to be pretty disgusting. I wondered how Esteban liked it, holing up inside a rotting palace filled with shit, mold and snakes.

Because, now I knew for sure he was there. In fact, I could see him right through my binoculars. He was in the kitchen, staring out the window at nothing, a cup of something, coffee maybe, in hand. For a moment he almost looked human, but I knew I shouldn't be fooled. That was the man who betrayed me. The man who killed my sister. The man who made my own wife flinch whenever I touched her.

That was the man I was finally going to kill.

I gripped the binoculars hard in my hands, trying to calm my heart and stop myself from just rolling off the wall and sprinting toward him, guns a blazing. But I was too far away and I knew one of his men would try and pick me off by then. I could already see two of them patrolling the outside, one with an AK in his hands, the other with what looked like a sledgehammer. I had no idea what he expected to do with that if someone approached (throw it?) but I knew if I could get my hands on it, I would have a lot of fun, especially if it were between me and Esteban.

I jumped back down the other side of the wall between Diego and Luisa. "He's there," I told them. "We need to keep moving and come up the back. He's got a patrol set-up."

Luisa's eyes flashed beautifully. "Did you really see him?"

I gave her a nod. "In the ugly flesh."

She gave me a vicious little grin but didn't say anything else. She didn't need to.

We ran along the wall until it curved to the west and then used another tree to get ourselves over the wall. Luisa was more difficult because of her shoulder but she managed to do it, grinding her teeth from the pain.

The back of the property provided the most coverage and was pretty much a tangled forest between the wall and the pool. We slid through it, going from tree to tree as we moved forward, making sure to stay as hidden as possible. We all had guns, which was a good and bad thing. Good because we'd be protected, bad because the sight of Luisa holding one always made my cock hard as concrete. She knew this too, which is probably why she was avoiding looking at me. It was as distracting as sin during a time I didn't need any distractions.

When we got to the last shrub that offered a bit of coverage between us and the house, I told Diego that as soon as we heard the ambush begin, he would run straight ahead and start picking off any of the patrollers. Meanwhile, Luisa and I would head for the helicopter.

"How do you know if it even works, it's a pile of rust," Luisa whispered as we all kept crouched down.

"It doesn't matter if it works or not. Esteban is a chickenshit. That's the first place he'll head. And that's where we'll be waiting."

Suddenly the air erupted into gunfire. It was bedlam at the house.

It was time to go.

Diego nodded at me then leaped out from around the bush and took off toward the mansion. I cautiously poked my head over the leaves and watched him go, shooting as he ran at a few of Esteban's soldiers who were spraying bullets into the air. Diego was one of the best marksmen and he took them down without missing a stride.

"Okay, now," I told Luisa, grabbing her by her good arm and hauling her up. We ran alongside the filthy pool, curving toward the helicopter, while the house lit up like sparklers, a cacophony of gunfire and screams. I knew Evaristo and my army were doing their job, I just hoped it would be enough to drive Esteban out of the house and to supposed safety.

Then Luisa tripped, fell, nearly taking me down with her as she landed on the grass. She cried out and I went back for her, bringing her to her feet.

Just in time to hear something land near us with a dull thump.

Roll toward us.

I whipped around to see a grenade at our feet.

No pin.

"Run!" I yelled at Luisa, covering her with my body and turning us away. We ran for the trees again but didn't get far enough.

The grenade went off, a blast that tore through my ears, filling my vision with fire and stars. It ripped Luisa out of my grip, sending me flying forward in the air until I landed in a heap at the base of the same bush we came from.

I lay there for a few moments, unsure if I was alive or dead. I couldn't hear. I tried to get up to my feet, wondering if I even had feet anymore. I did but they didn't work. I fell back down.

Luisa.

Luisa.

I managed to roll over and lift myself back onto my elbows.

The world spinned and I couldn't see her anywhere. There was smoke and flames licking the grass from where the grenade went off. My head felt like a million of them were still exploding inside.

Luisa!

But I couldn't scream. I staggered to my feet, weaving forward, until I saw her.

She was floating face down in the pool.

I didn't know where that grenade had come from, who threw it and if there were any more but I didn't care. I jumped right into the thick, black water and swam for her. Halfway across the pond, just out of arm's reach, my feet tangled in weeds and branches, trying to pull me down and my body, so tired, so nearly decimated by the blast, wanted me to just give up.

I couldn't protect her before but I would die trying to protect her now.

I started kicking, propelling myself forward until I was free. I reached Luisa, quickly turning her over and trying to clear leaves from her mouth.

"Luisa," I croaked quietly, my voice almost absent.

She didn't stir.

And bullets rained from above.

Son of a *bitch*.

I grabbed hold of her and swam her to the edge, hauling us out of the pool with what strength I had left. Every now and then I'd aim my gun and shoot at the dark figures in the distance, not caring anymore whose side they were on.

Once out of the pool, I threw her up over my shoulder, her body heavy from the water, and ran for the chopper. Inside, the helicopter body rusted and covered with weeds, I brought her to the backseats, placed her on them and started giving her CPR.

"Come on," I said to her, tapping her cheek quickly, listening for breath. "Come on my queen. Don't die on me now, not after all this. You're so close." I breathed into her again, then tore off her bullet proof vest and started pumping at her heart. "You're so close."

"Not close enough," a voice said.

I closed my eyes, trying to absorb the fucking fury of it all.

I slowly turned around to see Esteban pointing a gun at me.

"Jesus," I exclaimed, unable to help myself. "You look like fucking ass."

For one thing he had no eyeball. Luisa really fucked him up that way. It was just a bloody hole of pink and black tissue. His hair was falling out, with huge bald patches everywhere. He was the ugliest motherfucker I'd ever seen, inside and out.

Part of me wanted to laugh, but I wasn't about to provoke him, not with Luisa not breathing beside me. Also, there really was nothing funny about the situation whatsoever.

Still, he wasn't easy to look at.

"Put your hands up," he said, gesturing with the gun.

I frowned at him. "Put your hands up? You've been watching too many American cop shows, *puta*."

He stomped forward so the gun was just inches from

my face. I stared down the barrel and then raised my brow. He wasn't going to shoot me, not yet. He had a speech prepared, he wouldn't let me die without me hearing about all the different ways I was about to die. I knew this because I had planned on doing the same with him.

But I needed to get Luisa to start breathing again. Time was running out to a point where I wouldn't be able to bring her back.

Don't think about it, I told myself. *Get around the situation.*

But the situation said the two of us were fucked right up the ass, which was usually my favorite thing but not this time. No, definitely not this time.

I breathed in deep through my nose.

"So let's hear it then," I said. "Or can I at least save my wife so she can hear whatever bullshit it is you're about to spew."

"I don't have much to say, so let her stay dead," he said with a nasty smirk. He quickly rubbed underneath his nose and stared down at me with one bloodshot eye. "She was a feisty little cunt, I'll tell you that. But nowhere near the finest pussy I've ever had. Maybe even overrated. Gave it up a little too easily. A little too loose, to be honest. I hope you've been keeping that whore on a leash because there's no way your small dick could have stretched her out like that."

I swallowed the bile in my throat, every nerve inside me rattling like a beast in a cage, wanting to unleash. But the gun was pressed against my nose and even though I knew he'd lost some depth perception with that missing eye, he wouldn't miss blowing my brains out if he pulled the trigger.

"But no," he said, "other than that I don't have much to say. I don't believe in buying you anymore time. You got this far Javier, but you didn't get all the way to the end."

"You're not going to torture me at all?" I asked, my eyes boring into his. "That doesn't sound like you."

He shrugged. "I'm a busy man, hey. Seeing you finally fucking die will be good enough for me. Seeing your ugly *puta* already dead beside you is just icing on the cake." He sniffed hard through his nose. The guy was high as a kite. No wonder he just wanted to get this over with.

"So you're saying you don't want me to suck your dick?" I asked.

He blinked at me. "What?"

Suddenly Luisa wheezed loudly from beside me, taking in air, coming alive.

It was enough to startle Esteban.

It was enough for me to take advantage and knock his hand out of my face.

He pulled the trigger but it was too late for him, the bullet went whizzing into the side of the chopper and I leaped on him, forcing us both to the floor where we rolled toward the doors. For a moment he was on top, then I was on top, trying to hold him down and keep the gun from firing again. I was strong but he was on one hell of a cocaine high, which meant his adrenaline was on overdrive.

Then Luisa was above us both, gun in her hand, trained at Esteban's face.

"Do it!" I yelled at her, my arms straining to keep him down, sweat dripping off my face and on to his.

"We're doing it my way," she said, voice hoarse, then aimed the gun at his legs. "Get out of the way, Javi."

I briefly slid my legs off of him, enough for her to take the shot at his knee, blood splattering all over us.

Esteban screamed in agony, momentarily losing grip of his gun which I knocked free of his hand. Luisa quickly ran over to scoop it up, then immediately turned it around and shot a hole through his palm, close range.

Este bellowed like an animal, weakening beneath me and I raised my head to look at Luisa. She was grinning wildly, like she'd just received the best Christmas present ever.

"Hey," I said to her. "I told you we were going to share him. Don't hog all the fun."

She looked somewhat bashful. "Sorry."

I quickly got off him and flipped him over on his back, his blood spreading on the floor. I pulled out a pair of handcuffs I'd had on me and clipped him over the wrists, even though there wasn't much left of one hand.

"The seats," I told Luisa.

She ran over and straightened out all the seatbelts while I hauled Esteban over.

"Fuck you, fuck you," he kept saying, even though his body was starting to shake from the shock.

"No, I fucked you, remember," I reminded him, shoving him on the seat horizontally while Luisa quickly tied the belts around his legs and waist, keeping him in place. "You better not go into shock on me."

I looked to Luisa. "Do you have the vial or did we lose it in the blast?"

She reached down and patted her soaking cargo pant pockets. She undid the button on one and brought out a small wet box that contained a syringe full of adrenaline. I didn't want to give it to him yet, not until he was on the verge of unconsciousness, but I was glad we had it.

"How are you?" I asked her while Esteban moaned and thrashed on the seats.

"I feel like I drank a pool full of shit and my head won't stop pounding and everything sounds like it's coming from underwater. But other than that, I'm great." She smiled brightly. Well, as brightly as one could for being about to torture the living hell out of someone.

She looked fucking fantastic.

I wrapped the last of the belts across Este's chest, buckling them, then I straightened up, bearing over him.

"Este, Este, Este," I said to him.

"Fuck you!" he screamed. He sniffed deep then spit forcefully at my face. "You fucking shit!"

I rolled my eyes and wiped it away.

"Well, that's just rude," I chided him. I looked at Luisa. "Get your knife out. Cut out his tongue."

"No!" he screamed but I quickly drove my elbow into his mouth, shattering his teeth and jaw. It would help.

His head rolled to the side, his moaning never stopping, and spit out his teeth in a pile of blood. "That's for being a traitor," I told him. "For killing my sister. For hurting my wife. There's plenty more where that came from."

I reached down with my hands, forcing his broken jaw wide open. He gurgled on his teeth and blood, choked on his own screams. "You better hurry, my dear, I don't want him to die just yet."

Luisa came beside me and I moved my body out of the way so she could have easier access. "Take my knife from my boot," I told her, shaking my leg at her. "Stick that end of the knife through the tip of his tongue, otherwise you'll never get a good grip. Then use the other knife to saw it in half."

She didn't even grimace. "You seem to know your stuff."

I shrugged an ascent. "Normally I'd use clamps but we have to improvise here. At least he won't be able to talk anymore."

And so Luisa did as I suggested. It was easier to get Esteban's mouth wider without so many teeth, plus he wasn't able to move it to offer resistance, so there's that. She stabbed the tip of his tongue with the knife and as she held it in place, blood drowning the blade, she was able to saw it off.

The sounds coming from Este were inhuman but then again so was he. I didn't feel anything except the need to cause more suffering, to finally get even.

Even so, I quickly turned him over so that he'd bleed out of his mouth and not have his lungs fill up with the stuff.

I leaned in close to his ear, his gurgles sounding like music.

"You know what Este?" I said. "At one point, I actually liked you. You with your fucking flip flops and your Jennifer Aniston highlights. I really did. You were annoying as fuck and extremely stupid, but I thought there was something, I don't know, *endearing* about you. Then the more I got to know you, worked with you, the more I realized that you just had one big epic hard-on for me and my life. That you wanted to be me more than anything. You wanted to be me so much that it actually drove you insane. That's when I realized you were nothing more than a pathetic piece of shit, an ugly fucking dog that wouldn't stop following me around, sniffing the Alpha for scraps, licking my balls to win favors. And that's what you still are. Only now you've had a taste of what you could have become. And now you'll know what it's like to die a complete failure with the taste of my balls still in your mouth."

I looked at Luisa, who was staring down at him with a hatred I'd never seen before. "Hey," I said to her. "You do what you need to do. That will be enough for me."

She swallowed, taking in a deep breath, as if trying to compose herself. "Unzip his pants."

I smirked. I had a feeling it would come to this. I was sure that any woman who had been raped would only dream about doing the same thing.

Este now was too weak to fight back. I unzipped his pants, bringing them down to mid hip, until his dick flipped out.

I laughed. "Not so impressive, are you now." Este could only twitch in response.

I moved over and pressed down on his hips to hold him in place.

"You do the honors Luisa," I said but turned myself away so I wouldn't have to watch. I may have done far worse to others in my life but there were still some things that made me squeamish. I'd like to say it kept me humble.

"I never forgot what you did to me," Luisa said to Esteban, her voice hushed, strained, almost confessional. In some ways it felt like a private moment, like I shouldn't be there to listen. "I lived with it day after day. I'm sure I will live with it for many days more. But I've gone through it before and come out stronger and I will do the same after you. It will be even better because I know that after this, you won't be able to hurt me anymore. I know that you'll die suffering, just as I had suffered. Right now you are you, you are my old boss, you are Salvador and every other man who had their way with me or at least tried." She paused and I could feel her adjust beside me, poised to make the cut. "And me, well I'm every woman that you all ever hurt, ever touched, ever raped. I wish I could say I will take no pleasure in this, but if my husband has taught me anything, it's to be unapologetic. So, I'm not sorry. You deserve this. Then you deserve to die."

The air filled with sounds that even I hoped I would never hear again. Knife. Flesh. Blood. Esteban's guttural, wet cries of utmost agony.

By the time Luisa was done dismembering him, he was twitching uncontrollably and I knew he was close to going into shock. I avoided the bloodbath by his crotch and looked her dead in the eye. To my surprise, even though she was breathing hard, her eyes wide, she didn't look upset, or mad, or anything other than calm. Peaceful.

"Should I get the adrenaline?" she asked. "I think he's going into shock."

I shook my head, suddenly exhausted. "Let him go. I think we're done here."

She seemed to think that over, squeezing the knife handle, wondering what else she could do to him. She was impressing me more by each second.

I put my bloody hand on her shoulder, marveling at how much of Esteban's blood had spilled on us. I was going to suggest that we watch him die, then get back to find the others. The gunfire had stopped and I think I knew which side had won once more.

But she walked over to him and stood over his face.

His one good eye fixed on her.

It seemed to beg for mercy.

She held the knife above it.

In one swift motion, she plunged the knife into his eye, into his brain, right to the hilt.

Esteban Mendoza jerked once, twice, then finally stilled.

He was dead.

He was *very* dead.

I watched her carefully, not sure how she would react now that it was all over and the adrenaline would be sure to wear off. I may have been used to this, I had ways of separating the act from myself and I had ways of enjoying it too.

But she wasn't used to torture except for the torture done to her.

"Luisa," I said softly, coming up behind her. I placed my hand on her arm, slid it down over her grip on the knife and pried her fingers loose. I slowly pulled her back, leading her away from his disfigured corpse.

"Talk to me," I whispered, turning her around to face me. I placed my hands on both sides of her cheeks, leaving sticky red handprints underneath.

She closed her eyes for a moment and breathed in deep.

She opened her eyes. They burned for me. "I love you," she said.

My heart expanded, building with an internal fire.

"I love you too," I murmured. "My beautiful queen."

I kissed her sweetly, softly, not wanting to scare her off as I had before, unsure how she would take me.

But she kissed me back.

It might have been the best kiss I ever had.

CHAPTER TWENTY-FIVE

Luisa

I didn't know what I would feel when I finally got my revenge, when Esteban was finally dead at my own hands. I assumed I would feel guilt, maybe regret. The old lesson that revenge isn't always so sweet, that it can cause you to lose your very soul.

But the moment I sawed off his tongue, cut off his dick and stabbed that knife right into his degenerate brain, I didn't feel any of those things.

For one, instead of losing my soul in the process, I felt like I'd gained one. That whatever part of me I'd lost, the part he'd *stolen* from me, came right back to me.

I felt full, whole.

And I felt momentous relief. It was wave after wave of cool, freeing reprieve, soaking me to the bone, giving my tired spirit wings again.

No, I didn't regret a god damn thing.

Javier was there, for me, throughout it all. It was his sister that died, his friend that screwed him, screwed me, hurt me. But he let me do what I needed to do, even though I knew he was dying to do it himself.

But he gave me the knife and he set me free.

I couldn't thank him enough.

Or maybe I could.

He pulled me away from Esteban's dead, disgusting body and held my face in his bloody hands and I felt nothing but pure, complete love for him.

I'd been reborn. I'd never wanted him more.

So when he kissed me, so soft and sweet, I answered with all the passion that had been buried away for far too long.

He moaned into my mouth, his hands touching my sides, so careful, so cautious.

"I need you," I told him, breaking away as his lips went for my neck, a wet, warm caress. I placed my hands over his, pressing them into my body, no longer afraid of him, no longer afraid of anyone. "Now, I need you now. All of you. All of you, Javier."

He pulled back, searching my eyes. "Are you sure?"

I knew that he wasn't talking about the location.

I rubbed my red-stained hand down over his crotch, feeling his hardness, his life pulse beneath me. "Fuck yes."

Something ignited in his eyes, as if he were finally seeing me for *me* for the very first time. His lips crashed against mine again, mouth so hungry as if he needed to consume me to live and I gave it right back. This was a wild, unrestrained need and I thought I might die right there and then if I didn't get enough of him. The passion crackled between us, electric, a million fuses waiting to be blown.

I wanted to set them all off.

His hands were all over me, clawing and desperate and I clung to him like a crazed animal, our clothes half torn, while the causality of our depravity and sweet revenge was just a few feet away. But I couldn't see that, couldn't see anything but Javier, didn't need anything but him.

We were down on the floor, one way, then another, blood sticking beneath us. I got on my knees and grabbed hold of the back of the pilot's chair while he yanked down my pants and thong. His fingers, feather-soft, like ghosts, trailed up and down my legs, over my inner thighs, making my skin quiver. But I needed more than that, I needed to be taken and claimed, devoured whole.

"Stop torturing me," I cried out and he gave a wicked chuckle in response.

"Oh, but what beautiful torture this is," he murmured, licking a path down my spine, his fingers still teasing like angel wings. His head lowered, tongue snaking over my skin and I was desperate, straining for him, pressing myself back.

His tongue slid between my cheeks, dipping down, and I was greedy as hell, unable to stop the moans as they reverberated through my body.

"Fuck," Javier said, voice rough. "I've forgotten how good you taste. Nectar from the fucking gods. And mine, all mine."

Suddenly his grip on my thighs became hard, fingers digging in and I knew he was giving into his uncontrollable lust. He had patience in spades but not this time, not now, not after everything we'd just gone through. He pulled back and his pants unzipped and I began to whimper quietly with mounting anticipation. I needed him to fill me, I needed more sweet release.

The desire was so acute, it *hurt*.

The tip of his hard cock pressed into me, just enough to tease, to get wet, and he took a firm hold of my hips. For one moment there was stillness, silence, and I thought I'd never breathe again. I thought the want and need would splinter my body into a million pieces.

Then he pushed in, so fucking deep, so damn thorough, groaning with insatiable lust, the same lust that made my knees shake, that threatened to undo my grip on the chair. His hand slid up between my breasts, cupping them, flicking over my hardened nipples, causing my nerves to ricochet until my whole body was electric. I was feeling what I thought I would never feel again.

"You're mine," he said huskily as he thrust forward. His balls hit between my legs as he rhythmically pounded me from behind, in and out, so deep, so thick. "Tell me you're mine."

I groaned, nearly unable to speak. "I'm yours."

"All of you, all of you," he said. Breathless, desperate.

"I'm yours."

"Your pussy is mine, your soul is mine." He leaned forward, biting the side of my neck, voice ragged with lust. "Your heart is mine. You're all mine. Every part of you, Luisa, every part."

"I'm yours," I said louder, moaning again as his fingers swirled over my clit. I was swelling with desire, dripping wet, a hair trigger. I wouldn't be able to hold back for much longer, I couldn't.

We were uncontrollable animals, primal, basic and so fucking dirty and there wasn't anything we could do about that.

"You're my queen." His sweat dripped onto my back,

his breathing hard. Everything was slippery and we were barely holding on but he was tireless, wouldn't stop his frenzied thrusts. The whole helicopter started to shake.

"I'm your king."

"You're my king," I managed to say before my eyes rolled back and I was lost in the delirium, his delicious thickness, the way he filled me whole. I couldn't imagine life without him, couldn't belong to anyone but him.

My king, my king, my king.

I went over the edge.

In a rush of stars and colors and waves.

I was unbreakable now, unstoppable.

I was his.

I came so hard I thought my body might never stop, the spasms rocking through me like I was the epicenter of a violent quake. I was flooded, with dark, hidden parts of me rising to the surfacing and rushing away, leaving me raw, bare to the bone.

It was only him and it was only me. King and Queen. That's all that existed in this rusted, bloody space, between these two tortured, filthy souls.

Tears spilled down my cheeks, a deluge of emotion no longer under wraps. All the death and pain had bloomed into something wild and beautiful. Something real.

He held me close to him, my back pressed against his slick chest, his pumping slowing as he poured himself inside me. His moans were intoxicating, the sound of his pleasure that he was getting from me and only me. Then he was gasping for air, almost as if he was in disbelief that he had finally claimed me once more.

"Luisa," he whispered, kissing my neck. "Luisa." But

he didn't say anything else. He rested his head on my back and tried to regain his breath, his chest heaving against me.

We must have stayed like that for a few moments until I felt him slide out. When I managed to turn around, my limbs shaking from the strain of our love making, I realized what a massacre this had been.

We were both a wreck, covered in blood and sweat. Javier's hair was messed, damp, stuck to his forehead, his eyes glazed with peace and wonder. He held out his hand and helped me to my feet, holding on tight as I slid slightly on the wet floor.

He ran his fingers over my cheek and smiled. "Well, I've never done that before."

I raised my brow, pressing my hands on his chest. "You've never had sex next to a corpse? I have a hard time believing that."

"First time for everything, my dear," he said, kissing my forehead. He exhaled and looked around the helicopter, at the blood, guns, body parts, then shrugged. "I guess we should go and make sure Diego and Evaristo are still alive."

I could tell I wasn't the only one who had forgotten the war that had waged on out there. He held my hand, giving it a squeeze, and led me out the helicopter doors. We walked together across the overgrown lawn, my arm in his, past the dead bodies and the smoldering smoke. Diego, Evaristo and a few others were conversing by the house.

They looked at us in surprise and waved.

We waved back at them.

King and queen.

EPILOGUE

Javier

"I've decided on a name," I said, walking out to the balcony where I knew Luisa was relaxing.

She was lying down on the chaise, reading a spy thriller, which she then lay down on her chest and turned to face me. She peered over her large sunglasses expectantly.

"Oh?" she said, amused. We'd been doing this for a few weeks now and every time she had a name, I disagreed and every time I had one, she'd do the same. Normally a game like that would drive me insane with impatience, but this was actually somewhat fun.

"Yes," I said, coming over to the railing and leaning against it. The Pacific crashed just a few feet from the house, though the surf wasn't as angry today and all the surfers who bobbed in the distance were looking disappointed. I relished the fact that Esteban would have been rolling in his grave had he known Luisa and I would end up by all his favorite surf spots. I even considered taking up the sport out of spite, but the idea of all that salt water drying up my hair was too off-putting. Besides, Esteban was deader than dead and the two of us were very much alive.

Two, plus one on the way.

"Well, what is it?" she prodded, running her hands over her stomach. It was absolutely huge now. It made her look monstrous, which I'd found wildly attractive for some reason. Six weeks to go and our son would be born.

Son.

Some days I couldn't even fathom it. Couldn't even wrap my head around it. But it's what we needed, not just for us, for our marriage and our souls, but for the business. The moment I found out Luisa was pregnant with my child (and yes, I made sure it was in fact *my* child) I was over the moon with fear and relief, the two feelings in a constant battle. Fear that I would fuck things up as I had been known to do with every human being I'd ever come into contact with. Relief that finally I had an heir to take over the cartel. My blood. Someone I could truly trust, someone that I would raise to be just like me.

I mean, why not? Another version of myself couldn't hurt. He'd be wicked, intelligent, unapologetic, handsome, and if he were really lucky, taller than I was.

Up until now though, we couldn't decide on a damn name. If it had been a girl, I would have honored Alana by bestowing her with that name. But the sonogram proved it was a boy and for that I was grateful.

I was certain we'd have a brood of kids in the future regardless, and if we had a girl, she'd need an older brother not only to protect her, but to look up to. Sure there was risk in having a family. I knew that for a man in my position having loved ones increased the chances of loss and pain. But it didn't matter anymore. It would be worth it. It already was.

I came beside Luisa and put my hands on her stomach, gently tracing over the side where the acid burn still remained, albeit fading away. "He's Vincente," I told her. "Vincente Bernal."

"Vincente," she repeated. "Vincente Bernal." She smiled. "I like it. No, I love it. Does it mean anything to you?"

I shook my head. It didn't mean anything. It just came to me that morning. "It just means our son."

I leaned forward and kissed her, putting my hands into her hair, which was now chin length and glossy black. Her scars on her face were fading and barely visible when she covered them with makeup, but I still liked her bareskinned. She looked more like a warrior that way. She looked more like Mrs. Bernal.

"Ahem." I heard Diego's voice.

I pulled away from Luisa to see him standing by the French doors.

"You and your timing," I said to him.

He gave me a vaguely apologetic look. "Sorry, *patron*. Luisa. I just wanted to make sure that everything was on for tomorrow, for the meeting."

I nodded and waved him away with my hand. "It's fine. Go and enjoy the beach or something."

"Yes sir," he said, even though I knew he was going right back inside to guard our bedroom door.

Luisa tugged on my arm. "I wish you didn't have to go to Tijuana."

"It's just for the night," I told her. It had taken a while, but a few months ago we were finally able to kill Angel Hernandez, the leader of the Tijuana Cartel, and I'd promptly taken over the plaza.

Naturally, I couldn't have done it without torturing Evaristo to begin with, but that was now water under the bridge. He was living in the nearby town of Todos Santos, acting as a priest for a tiny Catholic church which was a bit of a riot in itself, since the man wasn't holy whatsoever. Considering the church was so small to begin with, we all thought it would be the perfect cover now that Evaristo Sanchez was a wanted man across the country. The *federales* really hated a snitch – after all they'd tried so hard to prove to the government and the DEA that there was at least one official organization that could not be corrupted by the cartels.

Well, that didn't go so well for them. It just proved that no one was above corruption in this country and if there had to be any changes made in Mexico, it had to start with the government. If they weren't paid so poorly they probably wouldn't have to take bribes from people like me anyway.

But in the end the way the country worked was better for us, although I'm not so sure about Evaristo. Though he'd become somewhat of a right-hand man to me, a lot of his time was taken up at the church. Father Armando, as he was known, was a handsome devil and after he took his place as priest, suddenly the congregation doubled. Mainly women who were fawning over him, though there were a few husbands dragged along.

Still, there was a lot of business to conduct in Tijuana as the plazas and power shifted and I was becoming something more of a business man again, constantly going back and forth. It was one of the reasons why we settled along the Baja Peninsula, so I could be closer to the new expansion and one of the busiest drug lines into America. It was worth it though – we were now more powerful than ever.

"Look," I told her, straightening up. "Next time I'm up there, you can come with me and we'll get you across the border. I'm sure your parents want to see you one more time before you give birth. It must be good luck or something."

"I don't think we need any more luck," she said, even though we both knew that wasn't true. We may be at the top, but that didn't mean we would stay there. There was no security in this business, just a survival of the fittest. Luck could go either way, but as long as you had your own moral code and were willing to fight to the death to protect what was yours, you would go far.

And I still felt I had farther to go.

"Oh," she said quickly, reaching down beside her and picking up a tote bag that carried a stack of magazines. "I found something weird today when I came back from town." She pulled out a postcard. "It was at our front door. I thought maybe they got the wrong house but . . . I don't know."

I took the postcard from her hands, staring at the glossy surface. It said "Utila, Honduras" on it and had a picture of a white-sand beach.

I immediately felt uneasy.

I quickly turned it over and read the back.

There was no return address and no address to us. How could there be when this house didn't even exist officially.

The postcard just had a simple sentence scrawled on

it, in familiar handwriting that knocked the wind out of me.

Pepito,
I'm doing okay.

Everything stilled around me, except for the postcard which began shaking from my tremoring hand.

Luisa raised her sunglasses on her head, staring up at me curiously. "Pepito," she said. "Alana called you that a few times."

I swallowed hard. "My nickname, when we were young." I stared at her, waving the card vigorously. "This is Alana!"

She smiled. "I was hoping it was."

She was alive. All this time, my sister was alive. And apparently living on the island of Utila, so close but so far.

So alive.

All the grief, guilt and sorrow that once pulled me under and made me sink to the greatest depths of violence and depression I had ever known all bubbled up at once, overtaking me.

I collapsed on my knees beside Luisa and cried.

I cried because I couldn't remember the last time I had cried. *If* I ever had.

She sank her fingers into my hair and held me as I got it all out, all the years of fucking up, all the terrible things I'd done to the people I'd loved. I would make no apologies for who I was but I would to the ones I cared about the most. I had been a terrible brother and for that

I was sorry. I didn't deserve to have Alana back in my life. But she more than deserved to live.

When I was done, I felt cleansed. Definitely not pure, just . . . refreshed. Somewhat similar to when I would go on a violent rampage, but at least my hands weren't dirty this time. It was bloodless. I was clean.

"How did she find me?" I asked her.

She shrugged. "She's a Bernal. She's resourceful."

"She must be with Derek," I said, remembering what Diego had told me. As a first-class assassin, Derek was infinitely resourceful but if he was keeping my sister alive, keeping her happy, then he could spy on me all he wanted. I owed him the world.

I took in a deep, steadying breath, composing myself. "What do I do next?"

Luisa kissed me softly on the forehead. "Javier, my love. Go to Tijuana. Do the right deals. Kill the right people. Then come back here and fuck me." She ran her hand down the side of my face, smiling wickedly. "This is your empire. Go build it."

And so I did.

Get ready for the Dirty Angels Trilogy...

Mexico is lawless. It's lethal. It's scorching-hot. It's dog eat dog in the world of the drug cartels.

But sometimes, forbidden love can blossom from poison.

And when it does, you've got to guard it with your life. You've got to watch your back.

Available now from

headline
ETERNAL

headline
ETERNAL

FIND YOUR HEART'S DESIRE...